TRIDENT FURY

THE KURGAN WAR – BOOK 3

BY
RICHARD TURNER

1

Captain Tarina Pheto stared down at her flight console and let out a sigh. She was bored and tired. They had been floating in space for nearly twenty-four hours, and so far, there had been absolutely nothing on her screen. Not even a comet or asteroid flying nearby to relieve the monotony. Behind her, her friend, Captain Wendy Sullivan, was fast sleep. She had dozed off a couple of hours ago, and Tarina didn't see the point in waking her up. She actually envied her friend's ability to relax. Tarina knew that there would be no rest for her until they were rescued. She tried stretching out inside the confines of her fighter's cockpit but found that her arms were too long when they touched the roof.

All of a sudden, the proximity alarm on Tarina's console light flashed on, scaring her. She checked her screen and saw that whatever was out there was located directly above them. Her heart began to race. It had to be a rescue ship. Tarina turned her head and looked out the window at the top of her cockpit and found what she was looking for. A vessel, the size of a cruiser, was slowly descending toward them. Fear instantly replaced euphoria. It wasn't a Terran vessel but a Kurgan one.

"Is something going on?" asked Wendy, waking from her slumber.

"I'm sorry, Wendy. It doesn't look like we're going to make it home," said Tarina. Her hand began to shake as she reached for the ship's self-destruct switch. She didn't want to die, but their orders were explicit. At no time could their jump fighter fall into the hands of the enemy. Every pilot in the First Special Warfare Squadron understood that they had to be prepared to sacrifice their lives if need be.

Wendy closed her eyes and awaited her death.

The enemy ship was soon right above them. Its cargo bay doors slid open. Tarina intended to wait until they were inside before she blew up their ship, hopefully taking the Kurgan vessel with them. Within seconds, they were floating inside the enemy ship. Through her cockpit glass, Tarina could see Chosen auxiliaries and Kurgan soldiers in survival suits waiting to take possession of their captured prize.

"Goodbye, Michael," said Tarina as she flipped up the red safety cover and placed her index finger on the self-destruct switch.

The doors beneath their craft began to close. There was no chance to escape now. Tarina looked over at the Kurgans as they ran toward her ship. It was time. She pushed down on the self-destruct device. However, nothing happened. She flipped it up and down a couple of times trying desperately to end her life before the Kurgans could get their hands on her and her ship.

"Tarina, what's wrong?" asked Wendy.

"The ship, it won't self-destruct." Out of the corner of her eye, Tarina could see a Chosen soldier reaching for the hatch to open the cockpit. "No!" she screamed at the top of her lungs.

In the dead of night, Tarina bolted straight up in bed. Her breathing sounded like she had just run a marathon. Her slender body was covered with sweat.

"Easy does it," said a soothing voice.

Tarina turned and saw Wendy sitting next to her. "You were dreaming again," explained her friend. "You were back in the fighter, weren't you?"

"Yes." Tarina pulled her legs up to her chest and wrapped her arms around them.

The room was dark. The silvery light from a nearby moon shone in through a window beside their bunk bed.

Wendy glanced down at her watch. "It's nearly dawn. I know you, you won't go back to sleep, not now. Would you like to go for a walk and clear your mind?"

Tarina nodded and climbed out of her bed. She slipped on her sandals and stood up. Like every woman in the camp, Tarina wore a loose-fitting gray shirt with matching pants. There was not much need for anything else as the temperature outside never dropped below thirty Celsius, even at night. Together the women quietly walked past the rows of beds filled with sleeping people until they came to the back door and stepped outside.

Since they had arrived at their re-education center after a week of questioning, both had been surprised by the lack of security. There were no fences, no guard towers; they weren't needed as the camp was on an island in the middle of nowhere. Above them in the night sky floated several dirigibles. They were brightly lit up with messages of peace and the hope for a better tomorrow under the Kurgan Empire. The steady stream of propaganda never stopped. All day and night the people in the camp were bombarded with images of a better life that awaited them all, but only after they had taken the Kurgan religion into their hearts. Tarina had noticed that the families with children were always the first to convert, followed by youths separated from their parents, and then the married couples. The elderly and prisoners of war almost never left the island.

"Come on," said Wendy, placing a hand on Tarina's shoulder. They walked in silence to the beach where they found a washed up log and sat down.

The rhythmic sound of the waves lapping the sandy shore helped calm Tarina's troubled mind. She had shaved off her snow-white hair the day after they arrived in the camp, leaving her brown skin smooth on the top of her head.

"Thanks," said Tarina. "You always know what it takes to look after me."

"Think nothing of it. You were there for me after Lloyd died back on Derra-5. I don't know how I would have gotten over his death without you by my side."

Tarina reached over and squeezed Wendy's hand. "What do you think today's lesson will be? The Holy Principles of Kurgan or the sacred tenets of a pure life under the lord?"

Wendy groaned. "Not more tenets. I can say those bloody things in my sleep, and there are over one hundred of them."

"Me, I'm hoping for a lesson on how to escape from this miserable rock."

Wendy chuckled. "That would be good, wouldn't it? However, we have no idea where we are. We could be just across the border on an old human colony, or we could be thousands of light-years inside Kurgan space. Even if we did somehow manage to steal a ship, we couldn't make a jump back home if we don't know where we are to start with. If we blindly jumped, we could end our flight inside the middle of a burning sun, and that would put an end to our dreams of making it back to the fleet in real short order."

"Wendy, you're the smartest navigator in the whole fleet. Don't tell me that you wouldn't take the chance to escape if it were given to you."

"You know I would. However, in case you hadn't noticed it, we're on a rock surrounded by water. Kurgan ships only come once a month and that's to take the converts to their new homes."

"I know, but I'm getting scared. There's a rumor floating around the camp that they intend to move all of the prisoners of war to another planet."

"Tarina, you of all people should know better. There are a dozen new rumors spread each day in the meal lines and not a one of them has come true."

"I hear you, but something in my gut tells me that something bad is being planned."

Wendy placed an arm around Tarina and squeezed her tight. "Well, if something is going to happen, at least we're together."

Tarina turned her head and looked into her friend's eyes. "Wendy, promise me that if you ever get the chance you'll try to escape."

"You know I'd never leave you."

Tarina's tone turned serious. "Promise me."

"Okay, I promise to make a run for it if I can. You're scaring me. I've never heard you talk like this."

"And I've never felt this scared in all my life." Tarina placed a hand over Wendy's. Somehow she knew their lives were about to change, and they were helpless to stop it. Her eyes teared up at the thought that she would probably never again see the man she loved. She looked up into the night sky and wondered where Michael Sheridan was and if he was still alive.

2

A bone-chilling wind whipped down the narrow street stirring up the snow. People turned their backs to the gust of air, trying to keep warm. The smoke from dozens of fires burning out in the open hung low in the air.

Michael Sheridan pulled his hood up and kept on walking. He wasn't wearing his usual combat uniform. Instead, he was bundled up from head to toe in old, worn civilian clothing. He stopped for a second and took refuge from the wind in the doorway of a building. He glanced over and saw his reflection in the glass. His dark green eyes looked as bright as ever. However, he barely recognized the face of the man in the glass. His face was dirty and his neck itched from the beard he had grown. Sheridan looked at his watch and saw that he had less than fifteen minutes to meet his contact. He gritted his teeth and stepped out into the blustery cold. He turned a sharp corner, almost hitting an old woman who was sitting on the ground with a cup at her feet. Sheridan dug out a couple of coins and tossed them into the cup before picking up his pace. After weeks of careful planning, he couldn't afford to be late.

He hadn't gone more than a block when the feeling of being followed returned. He fought the urge to turn about and see if there was someone behind him. As he passed a closed shop, he glanced out of the corner of his eye and saw the reflection of two men walking less than ten meters behind him. He had no idea who they were, nor did he care. He just knew that he had to lose them.

Up ahead, he saw an alleyway. He waited until the last second before turning on his heel and dashing down the rubbish-filled lane. Sheridan could hear the sound of feet running to catch up with him. He soon came to an abandoned junkyard and dove through a hole in the fence. Without looking back to see if his pursuers were still following him, Sheridan took cover behind a tall pile of old machinery.

He reached into his pocket and pulled out a small handheld Taser and turned it on. Although he was armed, he wanted to know who was after him and why.

A man's gravelly voice called out, "There's no use in hiding. You can't escape from here. Why don't you just walk out where we can see you? We mean you no harm. My boss would just like to ask you a few questions."

Sheridan felt like yelling 'screw you' but decided to keep quiet instead. He ducked down and edged his way deeper inside the maze of junk. He could hear the two men talking to one another as they searched for him. It did not take him long to reach the back of the yard. He could see an open gate that led out into another alley.

The sound of a foot stepping on broken glass made Sheridan whirl around and fire his Taser. A small shell containing a five-hundred-volt electrical charge flew straight into the chest of a man carrying a pistol. In the blink of an eye, the electricity shot through the man's body. He moaned and fell to the ground, writhing in agony. Sheridan dashed over and kicked his opponent in the head, knocking him out cold. He bent down and turned the man's face toward him. Sheridan shook his head when he realized that he didn't recognize the thug. He dug out a small patch from his coat pocket, peeled off the back, and applied it to the man's neck. Designed to help wounded soldiers on the battlefield, the patch contained enough drugs to put the man out for at least twelve to twenty-four hours.

From behind a nearby junk pile, the gravelly voiced man asked, "Yuri ... Yuri, did you get him?"

"Da," replied Sheridan trying his best to mask his voice.

A second later, a man with a thick beard and a long fur coat walked out in the open. His eyes widened when he saw Sheridan standing there with his Taser aimed right at him. He tried to bring up his weapon but was not fast enough. The Taser shell hit him, activated, and sent a crippling shock of electricity through his beefy frame. Light flashed before his eyes as his knees buckled and he fell face-first to the snow-covered ground.

Sheridan moved over and picked up the big man's pistol.

"My God, what was that?" asked the bearded man as he rolled over and sat up.

"I shot you with a five-hundred-volt cartridge," replied Sheridan, keeping his pistol aimed at his opponent's head.

"My body hurts everywhere."

"Then it worked. Now, who wants to talk to me and why?"

"Boss Abbas, that's who." Abbas was the reputed leader of the colony; he lived in a guarded compound on the outskirts of the city and was not known for his hospitality. It was rumored that like the gladiator matches of ancient Rome, Abbas liked to watch captured prisoners fight wild animals to the death.

"I asked, 'why.'"

"I don't know. He didn't tell me," replied the man, brushing the snow off his jacket. Hidden in the sleeves of his jacket were two porcelain knives.

"I'd stop that if I were you," warned Sheridan. "You're not that quick. Now put your hands on the ground beside you, or I'll shoot you."

The bearded man stopped what he was doing and did what he was told.

Sheridan knew he would get nothing more from the man. He tossed the man a med-patch. "Put that on your neck."

The large man stared down at the patch with suspicion. "If I refuse?"

"It's the med-patch or a bullet . . . your choice."

With an angry scowl on his face, the thug placed the patch on his neck and was out in less than three seconds.

Sheridan checked that the man was asleep before tossing his pistol away. He checked his watch and swore. He had to get a move on, or he was going to be late. A minute later, he stopped outside of a building and bent down to tie his bootlaces. It was an old ploy. While bent over, he checked behind him to make sure he hadn't been followed. Satisfied that he was alone, Sheridan stood up and opened the door to the tavern. The bar was packed. Right away, his nose was assaulted by the noxious smell of stale cigarettes and body odor. He pulled down his hood and ran a hand through his thick black hair and made his way to a corner booth where he took a seat.

"What will ya have?" asked a young woman.

Sheridan looked up and saw that the woman was a mere girl. He doubted she was more than sixteen years old. "Whiskey," he replied.

The girl smiled and left to fetch the drink.

Sheridan unzipped his jacket and put it down on the chair next to him. He slowly looked around trying to see if his contact was there. If he were in the room, Sheridan could not see him among the crowd. The server soon returned with his order. Sheridan paid the girl and tried his drink. It was the weakest whiskey he had ever drunk. It had been watered down to the point that it could barely be considered alcohol. That was fine with Sheridan as he had no need to get drunk; the next couple of hours he needed a clear head and a steady hand. He knew he'd been drinking a bit too much over the past few months and needed to cut back.

A fight broke out at the other end of the bar. People rushed over to watch the brawl. Sheridan turned his head to see what was going on. The momentary lapse in attention was all his contact needed to step out of the crowd and slide into the booth.

"Oy, you need a haircut and shave," said Master Sergeant Alan Cole. He was wearing a mix of civilian and military clothing. His gruff face had a five o'clock shadow on it. Cole's hair was as it always was—cut right down to the wood.

"I hope you didn't start that fight just to sneak over here with me."

"Who, me?" replied Cole, trying to act innocent, but Sheridan knew better.

He was happy to see his friend looking healthy. They had been inserted into the Port Royal colony a month ago to gather information about smugglers and pirates operating from the distant world. Far removed from the normal shipping and transit routes, a small but thriving lawless community had been established. If there hadn't been a war on, the military would never have paid them much attention. They had become such a nuisance, stealing from military depots and boarding supply ships destined for the fleets fighting the Kurgans, they were now being targeted for eradication.

"Any trouble getting here?" asked Cole.

"A couple of Abbas' goons tried to stop me."

"What happened?"

"I got to try out my Taser on them. Let's just say they won't be bothering anyone for quite some time."

"You and your toys. Glad you tried it out on them and not me. I guess all of our poking around has not gone unnoticed by Abbas' stooges."

"Yeah, I think you're right. What about you? Any luck finding us a way in?" Sheridan asked.

"I met a guy who can take us to Boss Abbas."

Sheridan glanced at his watch. "We had best get a move on, the Raider Task Force will be here in just over three hours, and we haven't found the missing air-defense weapons yet. I'd hate to think how things would go if the assault force tried to land into a storm of anti-ship missiles."

"It would be a bloody slaughter." Cole stood and looked at the exit. "Looks like the coast is clear. Come on, let's go."

Sheridan followed his friend outside. They walked down a side street until they came to an open-air market. Vendors stood by their stalls trying to out-shout the competition. Anything and everything was for sale. Sheridan spotted brand new Marine Corps weapons and uniforms as well as night-vision and communications gear. What surprised him the most was one disreputable-looking woman hocking a military-issue drone that appeared to be in perfect condition. What a smuggler would want with a drone was lost on him, but there was a man haggling with the vendor trying to get her to lower the price.

A couple of minutes later, Cole stopped outside of a slender two-story building and knocked on the front door. A man's voice from the other side of the door called out, "Who is it, and what do you want?"

"It's me, Alan, now open the bloody door. It's friggin cold out here."

The door opened slightly. A man peered out. "Who's that with you?"

"He's me mate. Mike. I told you about him. Now quit screwing around and let us in."

The door opened just enough to let the two men slide inside. Sheridan looked around and saw that they weren't alone.

Standing farther down the hallway was a woman with two small children at her feet. She looked at the two strangers with mistrust in her eyes.

"Pauline, take the kids and keep out of sight until I'm done," said the man.

The woman took her children by the hand, stepped back into the kitchen, and locked the door.

"Mike, I'd like you to meet Mister Smith," said Cole.

"Good day," said Sheridan, doubting that Smith was the man's real name. Their host was short and skinny with smudged, sliver-rimmed glasses perched on his hawk-like nose.

Smith turned to face Cole. "If I get you into Abbas' compound, I want to hear it from you that you can get my family and me off this planet with a full pardon for all my past crimes."

"That's why we're here," replied Cole.

"All right then. Come back in the morning and I'll get you in there."

"That won't do. We have to go there now," said Sheridan.

A worried look crept across Smith's face. "I can't do that. I usually don't go there this late in the day. Besides he's hosting some of the other smuggler clans' leaders at his home tonight. Security will be tight, very tight."

"I don't care. Get us in there or the deal is off."

Smith looked to Cole for support but never got it. "You heard the man. It's now or never, mate."

"If I do this I want to be paid for my services. Shall we say one million credits?"

"A pardon and a lift off this rock are all you're going to get from us," said Sheridan. "The clock is ticking. Take it or leave it."

Smith muttered something under his breath. He stepped back and raised his hands. "Okay, I'll do it, but let me speak to my wife first. She's scared already; this is only going to make things worse between us."

"You have two minutes and then we're leaving," stressed Cole.

Smith shuffled off to speak to his wife.

Sheridan looked at Cole. "He's the best you could find?"

"Beggars can't be choosers. It took me a week of negotiations just to get him to agree to this."

"Well, let's hope that the missiles are still here or this trip will have been for nothing."

The walk through the maze-like streets of the colony to Abbas' guarded compound took less than thirty minutes. Tall steel walls with guard towers every one hundred meters enclosed the sprawling complex. A drone hovered in the sky, keeping watch on all who approached Abbas' home.

Cole reached out and stopped Smith. "Before we go another step, I want to know what your plan is to get us in there."

"I do daily maintenance on the compound's heating system. I'm going to tell them I forgot to do something and want to make sure that it won't fail during the night."

"That explains you, what about us?"

"I'll say that you are looking for work and that I'm teaching you all about my job."

"Sounds pretty flimsy."

"It's the best I can think of. I'm not used to thinking on my feet."

Sheridan bit his lip. He would have preferred more time to concoct a better story, but time was in short supply. He knew it was now or never. He looked at Cole. "Let's go."

At the front gate stood two mercenaries dressed in full body armor. They were covered entirely with state-of-the-art armor designed to withstand any small-arms fire and most fragmentation devices. Sheridan knew that it was heavy to wear and impractical to fight in, but for standing guard, it was perfect.

As they got closer, Smith waved at the guards. One of the men stepped forward and raised a hand. "What do you want?" asked the guard, his voice sounded metallic through the helmet's speaker.

"I think I may have screwed up earlier," replied Smith. "I want to double-check my work on the heater before the sun goes down."

"What about them?"

"They are my apprentices. I can't do this forever. The sooner I train someone to replace me, the sooner I can spend more time with my young wife . . . if you get my meaning."

The guard motioned for Sheridan and Cole to step forward. He slung his assault rifle, grabbed a scanning device from his belt, and turned it on. He pointed at Cole. "You first."

Covered by his partner, the mercenary ran the scanner over Cole's body. When he saw that there were no weapons concealed under Cole's clothes, he made him stand by Smith. Sheridan was next. The guard was almost finished with his sweep when the device chimed by Sheridan's head.

Sheridan smiled. "It's only a hearing aide."

The guard ran his scanner back and forth. It only went off by Sheridan's right ear.

"Do you want to see it?" asked Sheridan. "It isn't much, but without it I'm as deaf as a post in my right ear. I bought it for a couple of credits in the bazaar last week."

The guard shook his head. "You can proceed."

Sheridan nodded and walked over to Cole's side. His heart was racing in his chest. They had no weapons on them. If the guards had opened fire, they would have been dead in seconds. Before leaving Smith's home, they had hidden all of their weapons in a cupboard, intending to pick them up when they were done.

The guard spoke into his communicator. A couple of seconds later, the front gates slid open. "Go on and be quick about it."

"Right you are," replied Smith, taking the lead.

As they stepped into the compound, Sheridan was stunned to see how large it really was. Even with an orbiting satellite, the fleet had no idea just how well defended Abbas' home really was. Blocked from view by an electronic field that obscured the complex from observation, it stretched out for four city blocks. Sheridan saw that there was at least a company of well-armed mercenaries spread throughout the compound, along with anti-tank and anti-personnel weapons that were mounted on several stolen military eight-wheeled fast-attack vehicles.

Cole nudged Sheridan in the ribs and indicated with his head at a row of tall objects covered by tarps. It was apparent from the shape and size that they had found the missing air-defense missiles.

Smith led them past the missiles and down to a set of stairs that led underground. They walked along for a couple of minutes before coming to the room that housed the compound's generator. Smith typed his passcode into a panel on the wall. The door slid open. He turned to face Cole. "Okay, I've lived up to my part of the bargain. I've gotten you inside and now I'm leaving before you get caught."

"Just a minute," replied Cole, grabbing Smith by the arm and pushing him into the room.

"I'm not getting anything," Sheridan said, tapping his hearing aide. Built into his earpiece was a powerful receiver-transmitter. Until a minute ago he had been able to hear comms chatter from the ships waiting on the far side of the planet to begin their assault.

"Perhaps all the metal down here is blocking your signal."

"No. I should be able to still hear the *Orleans*," he responded, mentioning their assault ship.

"You won't be able to receive or transmit anything inside the compound," Smith explained.

"Why?" Cole asked.

"Not only has Abbas installed a satellite scrambler, he also had a comms shield installed a year ago to prevent anyone from doing what you're trying to do. He's paranoid about his security. I'm sure you've heard that there have been several attempts on his life in the past. All of them failed, and the clans that tried to kill him were slaughtered. Not even the women and children were spared. He's an animal."

"We've found the missiles, but we haven't found where they are being controlled from," said Sheridan. "Until we know where that is, we're not leaving."

"What do you want to do?" Cole asked.

Sheridan looked around until he found a toolbox. He opened it up and took out most of the tools. "I'm going to go for a quick walk around the compound. If I get stopped, I'll simply say that I was sent to find more tools to fix the heater. You can keep an eye on Smith until I get back."

"Don't you think I should go?"

Sheridan smiled. Cole never changed. If there was a dangerous assignment, he was the first to volunteer. "It's okay, I'm supposed to be an on-the-job trainee. Not knowing one tool from another will come in handy."

"If you're not back in fifteen minutes, I'm coming after you."

"I hope to be long gone from here by that time."

Sheridan picked up the toolbox and made his way back outside. Snow had begun to fall from the cloud-covered sky. Sheridan pulled up his hood and walked back toward the missile battery. At the first launcher, he put his toolbox down and bent to tie his laces. As before, he checked that he wasn't being followed. He brought his head up and looked for an obvious spot to house the computer system that controlled the Skybolt missiles. It took him only a few seconds to eliminate all the nearest buildings except for one which was guarded by two men in full armor. He stood up and walked toward the mercenaries.

One of the guards saw him coming and pointed his assault rifle at Sheridan. "Stop where you are. What do you want?"

Sheridan stopped in his tracks and pointed to his toolbox. "My boss told me to go and look for something he called a sonic spanner. I thought there might be one in that building."

"You thought wrong. Now move along or I'll be forced to shoot you."

Sheridan stepped back. "Whoa, there. There's no need for that. I'm leaving." As he took another step, he saw the door to the building open and a man move outside to confer with the guards. In the brief moment, he saw military-grade computers stacked in their hardened cases sitting against the far wall.

"I said, move along," warned the mercenary, charging his weapon.

Sheridan spun about and began to walk quickly back the way he came. His mind was a whirl. He doubted that the assault force would spot the missiles before they were launched if Abbas were jamming everything around his compound. He and Cole had to find a way to either mark the command center for destruction or neutralize it themselves.

A young girl's voice cried out.

Sheridan turned his head and stopped walking when he saw a group of at least thirty young girls being forced into the back of a couple of transports. As the vehicles drove past him, Sheridan swore under his breath when he saw that the girls all looked to be no older than thirteen or fourteen years of age. His gut churned at the thought that the girls were most likely about to be moved off-world and sold into prostitution. He hurried back to Cole and passed on what he had discovered.

Sheridan asked Smith. "Those girls, do you know when they are scheduled to be flown out of here?"

The mechanic shook his head. "I have no idea. Abbas is hosting several other clans here tonight. Perhaps he intends to auction off the girls at that time?"

"Makes sense," said Cole. "Any idea where this might occur?"

"In Boss Abbas' home. He has several tunnels built under his mansion. I'd bet good money that the girls will be held there."

Sheridan checked his watch. Time was running out. "I need to get outside of the compound so I can tell the *Orleans* where the missiles are, and more importantly, where the command center is."

Cole grabbed Smith and pushed him toward the door. "Okay, mate, lead on and don't even think about trying anything foolish on the way out. I can snap your neck faster than you can call for help."

They walked back up onto the open ground. It did not take long for them to spot the front gate. Everyone picked up the pace. When they were less than fifty meters from the exit, a couple of armored vehicles came out of nowhere, sped past them, came to a screeching halt, and turned their weapons on the three men. The ten-wheeled metal beasts each had a turret with a cannon and four anti-tank launchers on it.

"Stop where you are and raise your hands over your heads," warned a voice from a nearby guard tower.

"You piece of crap. How much did they pay you to rat us out?" said Cole to Smith.

"A hell of a lot of credits. I've got debts to pay and a family to feed," replied Smith as he stepped to one side and waved up at the guard in the tower.

Sheridan and Cole looked at one another and then raised their hands in surrender.

The ramp at the back of one of the armored vehicles lowered. A squad of mercenaries ran out and rushed to take up positions around the two Marines. From behind them, another personnel carrier drove up and stopped. The ramp dropped and an obese man wearing a gold-colored suit and parka stepped out.

"You have done well," said the man to Smith.

"Thank you, Mister Abbas," replied Smith.

"Kill him," ordered Abbas.

"No!" pleaded Smith. A split second later, a shot rang out. Smith's head blew apart from the impact. His dead body tumbled to the ground.

Abbas walked over to the men guarding Cole and Sheridan. "Good afternoon, gentlemen. My name is Salih Abbas. There is no need for you to introduce yourselves; I know precisely who you are. Welcome to my home, Captain Michael Sheridan and Mater Sergeant Alan Cole of the Marine Corps."

19

"How long have you known who we are?" Sheridan asked.

"Oh, not very long. My late mechanic's wife called me and told me that you were on your way. When you arrived at the front gate, I had your faces scanned by my UAV and in less than a minute, I had copies of your service records on my computer."

"Sweet," said Cole. "I thought only the Kurgs had access to our files."

"Surprise," replied Abbas.

Sheridan looked over at the bloodied corpse lying on the ground. "Why did you kill Smith?"

"Smith?" said Abbas. "Oh, you mean Mister Phillips. He showed me that he could not be trusted, and loyalty is what I treasure above all else. His wife, on the other hand, has earned my undying trust and ten thousand credits for selling all of you out."

"Wonderful place you've got here," said Cole.

"Please lower your arms. You look foolish," said Abbas. "Now, gentlemen, if you will promise to behave, I won't have you shackled and dragged behind one of the APCs."

Both men dropped their arms.

"I can play ball," said Cole.

"I guess we don't have much choice now, do we?" added Sheridan.

"No, you don't," said Abbas.

Sheridan was led at gunpoint into the back of one of the armored vehicles and Cole the other. The ride to Abbas' home took only a couple of minutes. Once there, the two Marines were escorted up to the second floor of the palatial home. Everything inside was either made of gold or was made to look like it was. They were moved by a couple of guards out onto a balcony overlooking a large pit dug into the ground.

Sheridan looked down. Even through the blowing snow, he could see the ground. His stomach turned when he saw the remains of several people scattered about.

"There is so little entertainment out here," said Abbas, sounding bored. "Profits are always high, but I do miss the social circuit back on Earth."

"I guess the rumors are true," said Sheridan. "You do feed people to animals for fun."

Abbas smiled. "Yes, I like to use Arctotherium angustidens. Although it isn't native to this planet, I've always been fascinated with giant bears, so I had a couple brought here. As you can see by the remains, my pets are well fed."

"How big are these giant bears?" asked Cole, peering below

"These two are truly marvelous specimens. Both are over five meters long and weigh in excess of eighteen hundred kilograms."

"I don't get it, Abbas. Why are you bothering to explain any of this to us?" Sheridan asked.

"Two reasons. I enjoy theatrics; it's a throwback to my college days. And secondly, because, my dear captain, I know all about your pitiful force of Marines on the far side of the planet. I was able to buy your task force's order of battle and operational orders for less than I would have expected."

Abbas glanced down at his watch. "When your friends begin their assault in precisely fifteen minutes, they will do so straight into my air-defense missiles. Those that survive the initial barrage will be quickly rounded up by my people and brought here as entertainment for my guests. Now, if you'll excuse me, I have other business to attend to."

Sheridan and Cole were grabbed from behind and dragged back inside.

"Boss, what do you want us to do with these two?" asked a white-haired guard with a deep scar running down his grizzled face.

"Take them below and lock them up with the other prisoners," replied Abbas. "When their comrades begin to fall from the sky, throw them both into the pit with the bears. They can die knowing just how badly they and their pathetic friends have failed."

3

The first thing Sheridan and Cole smelled when the elevator opened was the musky odor of the bears pacing back and forth in their cages at the far end of the dimly lit hallway.

Sheridan was pushed from behind. "Walk or I'll shoot you in the leg," warned one of the guards. "It'll slow you down for the bears."

"Yeah, they won't have to work too hard for their supper meal for a change," added another mercenary.

Sheridan stood up straight and began to walk, with Cole keeping pace right beside him. As they walked past the first row of cells, a hand reached out and grabbed Cole's arm.

"Help us," pleaded a terrified girl.

Cole turned his head and smiled. He gently took the girl's hand off his arm. "Just hold tight, love. This will all soon be over."

"For you maybe," said the white-haired guard.

"You know, your face looks familiar," said Cole to the guard.

"As does yours. I take it you were in the First Division a few years back."

Cole snapped his fingers. "Yeah. Now I remember you. You were turfed out of the service for selling drugs."

"Parade square soldiering got to be too dull, so I branched out into more lucrative work."

Cole spat on the ground. "If you think working for someone like Abbas makes you better than me, you've lost your mind."

"Whatever, soldier boy. I'm not the one about to be fed to a bear."

Sheridan knew that Cole was trying to drag things out as long as possible. With four guards covering them, it was going to take split-second timing to overwhelm them before they could raise the alarm. Although they had been scanned by the guards at the front gate for concealed weapons, the scanner they used failed to detect the ceramic blades hidden in the folds of both men's clothes.

"Quit stalling and get moving," said the old mercenary.

Out of the corner of his eye, Sheridan saw Cole nod. It was time. With a practiced move, Sheridan pretended to trip over his own feet. His right hand reached for his belt and grabbed one of his concealed knives. He turned to his right and jammed his blade straight into the neck of the closest guard.

The startled mercenary saw the move but was too slow to block the knife. In the blink of an eye, it struck home. Blood shot out like a red fountain.

Before the dying guard's partner could react, Sheridan dove at him and tackled him to the ground. They rolled back and forth on the ground, desperate to get their hands around their opponent's neck.

Cole was equally fast. He pivoted on his heel and smashed his right fist into the neck of the white-haired man, crushing his windpipe. The man let go of his pistol and reached up for his throat. Cole grabbed the weapon out of the air, turned it on the last guard, and shot a hole straight through the man's forehead.

Sheridan felt a hand on his shoulder.

"Let him go," ordered Cole.

Sheridan released the guard and rolled away. Before the man could reach his weapon lying on the floor beside him, Cole stepped forward and fired his pistol, killing the man.

"Down here," called out a man's voice.

Sheridan scooped up the dead mercenary's rifle, flipped off the safety, and looked down the corridor.

"Help us, please," the voice pleaded.

Sheridan jogged down the hall until he came to another cell. Inside, he could see about a dozen men. All of them looked like they were crews from the ships Abbas' pirates had boarded.

"Step back," ordered Sheridan as he brought up his rifle and fired into the cell's lock, breaking it open.

A black man was the first out of the cell. He grabbed Sheridan by the hand. "Thank you, thank you. There used to be more than thirty of us jammed in there."

Sheridan did not need to be told where the other men had gone. His blood began to boil. Before the day was out, he was going to make Abbas pay.

"Are you with the armed forces?" asked the black man.

"Yes, but there are only two of us here right now. Follow me. Master Sergeant Cole will give you some weapons to fight with."

Cole had already blasted the lock off the cell holding the young girls. He turned to face his friend. "What do you want to do? We can't stay here, not with the task force on its way."

Sheridan looked over at the freed prisoners. "Who's the senior man here?"

"I am," replied a tired-looking man with a scraggly beard on his face.

"Okay, then you need to protect these girls. Sergeant Cole and I have to disable a missile battery or none of us is going anywhere."

"I can fight," said the black man.

"I know you can, but right now I need you and your comrades to look after these girls."

The man nodded and took the dead guard's weapon.

"Lead on, sir, Cole said, grinning.

At the elevator, Sheridan spotted a control panel on the wall. He reached over and flipped a switch. At the other end of the corridor, the doors holding in the bears slid open. The beasts lumbered out into the execution pit. "Abbas is expecting a show. No need to deprive him of one," Sheridan said to Cole.

On the first floor of Abbas' home, the elevator doors slid open. Sheridan and Cole stepped out with their pistols held out in front of them. No one noticed them. A couple of men guarding the front doors were looking out at the commotion going on outside. All through the compound pandemonium reigned. A loud warning siren blared, signaling the beginning of the attack on the colony. Mercenaries ran to their stations. The tarps were pulled from the missiles as Abbas' men made ready to bring down the approaching landing craft. Cole walked forward and raised his weapon, shooting both guards dead without hesitation.

"How long until the landing craft get here?" asked Cole.

"Two, maybe three minutes," replied Sheridan.

"Where did you say the missile control room is located?"

"Over there," Sheridan said, pointing to the heavily guarded building.

Cole reached down and dragged a guard's dead body away from the door. He opened the door and popped his head outside. "Come on," he said, tapping his friend on the arm.

Together they sprinted over to the nearest APC. "We'll never make it past the security in the control room. However, we really don't need to," Cole said as he pressed a button on the back of the vehicle. A second later, the ramp began to lower.

Both men brought up their weapons. They opened fire the instant they could see inside, dispatching two men who had taken cover in the armored vehicle.

Sheridan went to step inside only to be grabbed from behind.

Cole said, "Have you ever taken any training on the Puma APC's turret?"

"No. But I did familiarization training at the academy."

"Move aside," said Cole, pushing Sheridan out of the way. He ignored the dead bodies sprawled on the floor of the vehicle and crawled up into the turret. He knew about as much as Sheridan did on the turret's fire control systems but would never admit it to him. Cole took a seat and looked down at a small panel. He reached over and flipped on a red switch, which he hoped was the power to the turret. Lights all over the panel came to life. Cole grabbed the joystick and turned it to his left. The turret hummed as it swung over. He looked into a small screen at eye level, which showed him what the weapon's sight was aiming at.

Sheridan heard Cole call out, "Where did you say that building was again?"

He turned on a screen in the back of the vehicle that showed what the gun was looking at. "Swing left!"

Cole heard the order and began to move the turret over.

"Stop! You're going too fast. Back the turret up slowly."

Cole brought the turret back as slow as he could.

Sheridan tapped the screen in front of him when he saw their target appear. "Stop! That's it. Light it up."

Cole flipped off the safety on the joystick with his thumb, silently praying to himself that he had selected the right ammunition, and then pulled back on the trigger. The whole vehicle rocked as the APC's powerful forty-millimeter cannon opened fire.

Both Marines watched as the armor-piercing rounds tore through the walls of the building, shredding everything inside. Cole kept his finger on the trigger until he had nearly expended the entire belt of ammunition.

Below, Sheridan studied the picture on his screen. There wasn't a living soul anywhere near the destroyed control room. "Looks like you did it," he called out.

"Yeah, but the gig is up," replied Cole.

Sheridan moved the picture on his screen and saw two APC's turning their turrets in their direction. His blood turned cold. If they opened fire, they did not stand a chance. Sheridan yelled, "Shoot them!"

Cole hurried to line up his sight on the closest vehicle and pulled back on the trigger. The APC shook as he blasted the other vehicle. A red warning light flashed on the weapon control panel. Cole had fired off all their ammunition. His heart skipped a beat. He jumped down from the turret and grabbed Sheridan by the arm, hauling him out of his seat. They barely made it outside before the surviving mercenary APC opened fire, tearing off the turret Cole had been in mere seconds before.

They hurried to take cover behind a row of old wooden boxes. In the sky above them, they could hear the distinct sound of the landing craft's engines as they raced to their pre-arranged landing zones. Escort gunships, racing just ahead of the approaching Marines, fired off a volley of missiles at anything that looked hostile. The first to go were the guard towers surrounding the compound. Next were any armored vehicles and defensive positions protecting Abbas' fortified palace. Sheridan poked his head up and saw the APC that was hunting them vanish in a red fireball when it was struck by an incoming missile. The force of the impact sent him flying back against the wall, knocking the wind from his lungs.

"I think that's our cue to leave," Cole said, pointing back at Abbas's home.

Sheridan rolled on his side and tried to take a breath. Slowly, painfully, his lungs filled with oxygen. He felt Cole pick him up onto his feet. His head was spinning and his one good ear was ringing. He thought he heard Cole say, "No time for that; you can catch your breath when we're inside."

Sheridan staggered alongside Cole. The world behind them was on fire. In less than a minute, the gunships had swept away any opposition in their sights. The sound of the ships' miniguns firing depleted uranium rounds sounded like a buzz saw cutting through the air. A mercenary who tried to bring down one of the gunships with a shoulder-launched missile was turned into crimson mist when he was struck by a burst of automatic gunfire.

Cole kicked open the front doors and hauled Sheridan inside. "Are you okay?"

Sheridan nodded. "Yeah, just speak to me in my right ear. I can't hear a thing in my left."

The building shook as a missile struck the top floor, obliterating it. Dust and paint rained down from the roof.

"Come on, let's join the others in the tunnels; it'll be a lot safer down there than up here."

They ran for the stairs and took them two at a time as they rushed below ground. When they arrived at the floor where the prisoners were located, they slowed down to make sure that they weren't going to accidently bump into anyone lurking in the shadows.

Cole brought up his pistol and stepped into the long, dark corridor. He looked both ways before indicating with his head that it was safe.

"Let's check on the prisoners," said Sheridan.

Together they jogged down the corridor until they came to the cell that had held the girls. Cole pulled open the cell door. Everyone inside the dark room looked tense and scared. "It's okay; all that racket you hear is just our friends flattening Abbas' goons before coming to get us."

No one said a word.

A puzzled look crept across Cole's face.

"Move," said a threatening voice. Like the Red Sea, the people in the cell parted. Sheridan swore when he saw Abbas and one of his henchmen standing there with pistols pointed at the heads of a couple of terrified young women.

"Drop your weapons and step back," ordered Abbas.

Sheridan and Cole hesitated for a couple of seconds until Abbas twisted the barrel of his pistol on the side of his hostage's head. They set their weapons at their feet and moved away from the cell entrance.

Abbas, the mercenary, and their hostages stepped out of the cell. He brought his pistol around and aimed it at Sheridan's head. "If you think this means the end of my operation, you and your precious fleet have seriously misjudged me. I have a dozen places spread throughout this sector where I can begin again."

Sheridan stared down the barrel of the automatic pistol. His heart was jackhammering in his chest. If he was going to die, he wasn't going to let Abbas see him flinch. "You're never going to make it off this planet alive and you know it. Any ship attempting to flee will be stopped or blasted from the sky. Give yourself up."

Abbas chuckled. "Not likely, Captain." Before anyone could react, he pointed his weapon at Cole's chest and pulled the trigger. The sound of the pistol firing echoed down the long corridor.

"No," screamed Sheridan. In desperation, he turned and reached for his friend only to be grabbed from behind by Abbas' mercenary. Sheridan watched in horror as Cole's body crumpled to the floor. Cole writhed in agony for a couple of seconds before exhaling and lying deathly still.

"You're coming with us," said Abbas. "I think the military would pay handsomely for the safe return of the son of an admiral."

With hate burning in his eyes, Sheridan spun about and glared at Abbas. "That was a really dumb move, Abbas. If it's the last thing I do, I'm going to make you pay for that."

"I don't think so. Now, march!"

Sheridan did not move. He stood there staring at Abbas.

Abbas saw the defiance in his opponent's eyes, swung his pistol over, and shot one of the prisoners still inside the cell right between the eyes. "Start walking or I'll kill these two girls right in front of your eyes."

"Okay, you win," Sheridan said, turning about.

A minute later, they came out near the execution pit. Sheridan could hear the bears moving about, startled by all the noise coming from above.

"Head for that elevator," said Abbas, pointing over at the far wall. "It'll take us to my private shuttle craft."

Sheridan moved as slowly as he could. "Think about it, Abbas, you're not going to make it. Surrender is your only option."

"Captain, your people will never see me. My ship has the latest in stealth technology built into it. I'll be past their pathetic blockade and on my way to freedom long before anyone notices me missing."

Sheridan gritted his teeth. If anyone had access to the best in stolen military technology, it would be Abbas. He had to stop him before he got to his ship and vanished. When he was less than a couple of meters from the elevator, he remembered that he still had a ceramic knife hidden in his jacket. He slowed down and stepped to one side to allow Abbas' thug to press the button for the elevator. The moment the mercenary's arm was extended, Sheridan whipped out his blade and jammed it as hard as he could into the man's hand.

The mercenary screamed in pain and pulled his hand back.

In a flash, Sheridan smashed his right hand into the injured man's head, knocking him senseless. The man's pistol fell to the ground. Before Abbas could get a clear shot, Sheridan grabbed the mercenary by the neck and spun his body around, using it as a shield.

The two girls with them saw what was about to happen, screamed in panic, and pulled themselves free from Abbas' grip. He snarled at them but let them go; he wanted to kill Sheridan more than he wanted the girls. He could always get more girls. He did not care that one of his men was in the way. Without hesitating, Abbas opened fire.

Sheridan felt each bullet as they struck the guard's body. Luckily, the man was wearing some form of light body armor under his jacket or the rounds would have passed through and struck Sheridan as well. For what seemed like an eternity, Abbas fired his pistol until the slide remained back—he was out of rounds.

The odds were now even. Sheridan tossed the dead mercenary's body to one side and yelled at the top of his lungs before charging straight at Abbas. He struck the man hard in his stomach, bowling him over. Both men tumbled to the marble floor. Sheridan was the first to recover. He jumped up to his feet and looked around for a weapon. He spotted the dead guard's pistol lying by the elevator and dove for it.

Abbas may have been a portly man, but he was fit and fast on his feet. He saw the weapon at the same time and rushed to grab it as well.

Both men collided into one another and slid across the smooth marble floor. Sheridan rolled over and swung his right elbow at Abbas' face. He heard a crunch as the cartilage in his opponent's nose shattered. Blood ran like a river down Abbas' face. If Sheridan thought that was the end of it, he was sorely mistaken. Abbas wiped the blood to one side, got up on his knees, and pulled a curved blade from behind his back.

Sheridan saw the knife he had jammed into the dead guard's hand and grabbed a hold of it. He yanked it out and stood up.

Both men were breathing heavily.

Like a pair of weary prizefighters in the ring, Sheridan and Abbas circled one another looking for a weakness.

Abbas struck first. He swung his knife down aiming to cut his adversary's right arm wide open.

Sheridan saw the move and at the last moment tried to pull his arm back. Abbas' sharp blade still sliced through his jacket all the way down to his skin. A burning pain shot up Sheridan's arm making him wince. He jumped back, trying to put some space between him and his attacker.

Abbas twirled his knife around in the air. "Hurts, doesn't it?" he taunted.

"You'll find out soon enough."

"I doubt it. You don't rise to the top of the Clans by being nice. Now stand still and I'll promise to make this fast."

"Screw you!" snarled Sheridan, thrusting his blade at Abbas' face, forcing him to step back.

From the pit, a bear let out a deep roar, followed by its partner. "They're hungry," said Abbas. "You were supposed to be their supper."

"Sorry to disappoint them."

"It's not too late," replied Abbas as he flipped the knife in his hand up in the air until he took a hold of the tip of the blade. With a lightning-fast move, Abbas dropped to one knee and threw his knife straight at Sheridan's chest.

It all seemed to happen in slow motion to Sheridan. He saw the knife coming straight for him. He started to turn, but realized that he wasn't going to be fast enough. He lowered his left arm to block the blade. A split second later, the knife struck home, slicing through his jacket before lodging itself into Sheridan's forearm. He let out a gasp. It felt as if someone had just jammed a red-hot poker into his arm and was sadistically twisting it around.

"Time to die," said Abbas as he reached for another concealed knife.

Through the pain, Sheridan knew he had to do something or die in the next couple of seconds. He closed his mind to the pain, turned toward his adversary, and ran straight at him. Abbas had not expected an attack and was defenseless when Sheridan hit him head-on and thrust his knife deep into his fat stomach.

Abbas gasped. His eyes widened in surprise and fright. He reached over and grabbed the hilt of the bloody knife. On unsteady feet, he staggered back a few paces and turned to look over at Sheridan before collapsing to the floor. He knew his wound was mortal. Abbas lay there moaning, unable to stop his coming demise.

Sheridan felt his head grow woozy. His feet gave out underneath him. He tumbled to the ground, looking over at his dying opponent. From out of nowhere, an arm reached down and grabbed a hold of Abbas and started to drag him toward the open pit. A couple of seconds later, the man tossed Abbas into the pit. Sheridan heard the bears roar. They were followed right away by the sound of a man crying for his life. He struggled to sit. Through the haze in his mind, Sheridan saw a man walking toward him.

"You okay, Captain?" asked Cole, his face coming into view.

Sheridan reached out and touched his friend's arm. "You're dead. I saw you die."

"Not bloody likely," said Cole as he unbuttoned his shirt. He tapped on a spot that had hardened the instant it was struck. "Liquid armor did the trick. This is better stuff than the sets they issue us back in the Corps. I told you to buy some last week when we were at the bazaar."

"I got sidetracked."

"Typical officer. Listen to me next time," admonished Cole as he began to check out Sheridan's wounds. "Looks like you'll live. A shot for the pain and a couple of stitches and you'll be as right as rain."

"What happened to Abbas?"

Cole grinned. "It was feeding time at the zoo."

4

The morning began like any other. Tarina and Wendy woke up to the sound of a Kurgan prayer being read out over the camp's PA system. After washing, they joined the rest of the people from their building at the mess tent and waited in line to be fed their usual breakfast of fruit and grains. Overhead a dirigible showed the same video it had for months: a young human family finding peace among the Kurgan Empire.

"I'd pay good money for something new to watch," murmured Wendy so only her friend could hear. Negative comments about the re-education training were not taken lightly by the Kurgans and their Chosen helpers. Wendy pulled her long red hair back and tied it off. She had let it grow ever since they had been taken prisoner, reasoning that while they were light-years away from the fleet that she could do as she pleased—at least with her hair.

"Some news from back home would be nice," mused Tarina.

Both women chuckled and kept moving in the long line. Once they had their food, they sat down at their usual table and began to eat their meal. They were joined by Diane, a single mother with a boy, named Jerrod, who was barely more than a year old.

"So how are you today?" Tarina asked Jerrod, who saw her looking at him and smiled.

"I think he likes you," said Diane.

"He's the only thing that brightens up this awful place."

"Then I'm sorry to tell you that I spoke to our group leader and asked to be moved from the camp to a Kurgan colony. Growing up in a camp is no life for my child."

Tarina nodded her understanding. "I don't blame you. I haven't any children of my own, but if I did, I would have made the same decision."

"Thanks, that means a lot to me. I know that he'll grow up as a Kurgan citizen, but at least he'll live."

"Look after yourself," said Wendy.

"I will."

The PA system came to life. For the next two minutes, the names of several dozen camp inmates were read out. They were told to report to the camp's gymnasium right away. Tarina's and Wendy's names had been part of the list.

"I wonder what that's all about?" said Diane.

"I don't know," replied Wendy, looking around the tent as people began to rise from their seats.

"Oh, Lord, no," said Tarina.

"What's wrong?" asked Diane.

"Military, they've only called the names of people from the military."

Wendy turned to face Tarina; her eyes were filled with fear. "Do you think the rumors are true? Are we being moved?"

"I don't know, but I bet we're about to find out."

Ten minutes later, a Kurgan female walked into the gym accompanied by a Chosen translator. Tarina, Wendy, and all the other prisoners of war were formed up as if on parade. Unlike the male warriors who wore segmented body armor from the bottom of their feet all the way up to their necks, the females wore long white robes that covered everything from the neck down. The

Kurgan stopped in front of the assembled prisoners, looked everyone over, and then began to speak through her translator.

"Good morning, I am sorry to take you away from your studies; however, I have received a message that must be read to all of you without delay. As prisoners of war, you have been treated with the utmost respect by the Kurgan Empire. It was our deepest desire that you would see the path to peace through the Kurgan religion and join us as citizens of the Empire. This regrettably has not been the case. In this camp and others like it spread throughout the Empire, you have all proven to be stubborn and less than receptive to our teachings. I am to give you one last chance to join us. Any man or woman who feels that they can find peace in the Empire will move off to the far side of the gymnasium and wait for me there."

Tarina looked around. Not a single person moved.

The Kurgan female shook her leathery head. "This is your last chance. Join us or face the consequences."

Tarina's stomach began to churn with fear. *Were they going to be shot?*

"Very well, you have chosen your path. You will be in *Kyseth* before me."

Tarina held her breath. *Kyseth* was the Kurgan word for heaven. They were going to be killed.

A young soldier standing near Wendy heard the word and began to cry.

The Kurgan female stepped forward. "It is not too late." She held out a hand. "Come with me, my child, and I will save you."

The soldier took a step back, hurried to wipe the tears from her face, and tried to look as defiant as the others.

"Fools, you are all fools." With that, the Kurgan female turned and strode out of the room. As she was leaving, a platoon of well-armed Chosen warriors ran in and lowered their weapons at the prisoners.

Wendy reached for Tarina's hand and held onto it for dear life. Both women held their breath and raised their heads. They weren't going to cower in fear at the end.

The Chosen's officer, a Kurgan in full armor, walked between his men and the prisoners. "You will not die here," said the officer in understandable English. "You will go to a new camp to work for the Empire."

A Chosen sergeant walked alongside the officer and smiled. He placed his hands on his hips and said, "I want all of you to take a seat and not try anything foolish or you will be shot for attempting to escape. A transport ship will be arriving in the hour to move you to your next and final camp."

"Where will that be?" called out one of the prisoners.

"Klatt, it's a prison planet. If you're not used for target practice, you'll spend the rest of your miserable lives mining perlinium for the Kurgan war effort. Now, no more questions. The next person who bothers me will be beaten for insolence."

Wendy held Tarina's hand so tight that it hurt. Tarina leaned over and said, "Let go of my hand before you break it."

"Sorry," whispered Wendy, releasing her grip

Together they sat down on the wooden floor of the gymnasium. Tarina wrapped an arm around Wendy and pulled her close. "I guess we knew this day would come. As we always say, at least we're still together."

"I'd hoped to be rescued by now. I guess no one's coming for us."

"Wendy, you can't think that way. You know that if our friends knew where we were, they'd risk their lives to free us."

"I guess so. It just seems that we've been out here for so long and things just keep getting worse."

Tarina squeezed her friend in her arms. "I need you to keep up your spirits. As long as we're alive and together, there's always hope. You'll see, something will turn in our favor. I know it will."

"Can I have your word on that?"

"Yeah, you can have my word on it."

Tarina knew she was just saying what Wendy wanted to hear. The rumors she had heard about Klatt were horrific. Brutal guards, starvation rations, disease, and overcrowding all combined to give a prisoner there a six-months-to-a-year lifespan. She closed her eyes and rocked Wendy in her arms, all the while praying that someone somewhere would hear her prayers and rescue them before it was too late.

5

With the flick of a switch, Master Sergeant Cole turned on the lights abruptly ending Michael Sheridan's deep sleep.

"Wake up, sleepy head, the captain wants to see us," said Cole loud enough to wake the dead.

Sheridan rolled over and pulled his pillow over his head. "This is unfair," he protested, holding up his bandaged arm. "Can't you see I'm wounded?"

"Yeah, whatever, sir. Now get your lazy arse out of bed. We're wanted in the operations center."

Sheridan sat up and blinked at the bright light blinding his eyes. "You're serious, aren't you?"

"Trust me, this isn't a joke. Something is going on. We've come out of our jump early."

"Why?"

"I have no idea. However, the captain does, and she wants to talk to us."

A minute later in the ops room, Captain Vilar, the captain of the *Orleans*, motioned for the two Marines to join her by a computer. She quickly typed in her personal passcode and stepped back. "This top secret message was sent to me. However, it is for your eyes, Mister Sheridan."

"That's odd," mused Sheridan as he took a seat in front of the computer and began to read the communique.

It wasn't addressed to Cole, but that didn't stop him from reading it over his friend's shoulder.

A minute later, Sheridan turned in his chair and looked up at Vilar. "Ma'am, I take it this is this why you interrupted our jump?"

"You are correct. We are currently in orbit above Aramus-3. Captain Killam, the Sixth Fleet's Operations Officer, has ordered me to support you with all you may need."

"What do you think?" Sheridan asked Cole.

"A Kurgan distress beacon has to mean that there is a ship somewhere on the planet's surface. I didn't think they ventured into this region of space."

"Neither did I."

"And neither, evidently, did Captain Killam," added Vilar. "That's why he wants you to capture the craft and any survivors, so we can find out what they were doing so far from the border before they crashed."

"Do we have a fix on the vessel?" asked Sheridan.

"Yes, it's in the northern hemisphere," explain Vilar as she brought up a holographic image of the planet's surface. She pointed at a red dot on the picture. "It looks like it came down in one piece in this forested area. Our scanners say the vessel looks like a long-range scout ship."

"If they all survived the landing, there won't be more than eight of them down there," said Cole. "Ma'am, is there any indication of a Kurgan rescue ship on its way here?"

"None."

Sheridan said, "Well, I guess we had best get a move on then. What is the atmosphere like down on the planet?"

"Temperate. It's quite Earth-like."

"That's a bonus," said Cole. "Indigenous life, ma'am?"

"The planet does not appear to be inhabited by intelligent life. It was last surveyed almost one hundred years ago. According to our ship's computer records, the animals they encountered were reptiles, very large reptiles."

"Great. We're going hunting for Kurgans, a deadly reptilian species, on a planet infested with dinosaurs," quipped Cole.

Sheridan drummed his fingers on the table while he brought up a video taken during the last visit to the surface a century ago. He stood up and looked at the image of a large predatory animal. It stood almost five meters tall and was well over ten meters in length. It had a long snout full of razor-sharp teeth and two long arms for grasping and holding its prey while devouring it.

"We're gonna need to take some bloody big guns with us," said Cole. "I recommend that we equip every second man with an anti-tank weapon. If we bump into one of these nasty little buggers, small arms ain't going to do us any good."

Sheridan nodded and turned to face Vilar. "Ma'am, a large detachment of Marines will just draw attention. Can you spare ten Marines for the mission?"

"Are you sure you only want that few? I have fifty Marines at your disposal."

"With Sergeant Cole and I, we'll have plenty of people to pull off this assignment and still make it home in time for breakfast."

"Yeah, unless one of them critters decides to make you its snack," said Cole.

The landing shuttle quietly touched down in a small clearing surrounded by tall pine trees. The side door slid open and Sheridan stepped out with a assault rifle in his hands. He took a quick look around through his night vision goggles and saw that they were alone.

"Sir, there's nothing on my screen," said a Marine to Sheridan as he studied the small device in his hand.

Cole exited the shuttle and established a secure perimeter before walking over to the young Marine with the tracker. "What about man-sized beasties? Do we have many of them nearby? I did some reading and their eyes are designed for hunting at night. Big or small, almost everything here thinks you're its next meal."

The Marine widened the search on his scanner. "Found something. It looks like there's a small party of creatures moving along the side of a lake."

"How many, and how far away?"

"Five of them, and they're seven-point-three klicks from here."

"We should be okay," said Sheridan. "However, just to be safe, tag them and track them."

"Yes, sir," replied the Marine.

A cool wind whipped through the clearing stirring up the tall grass. Sheridan watched as one of his men opened up a case and took out a small ball-shaped UAV. Within minutes, the drone was airborne. It took less than five minutes for it to reach the downed Kurgan vessel.

"Any sign of movement?" asked Sheridan, looking at the thermal image sent back by the drone.

"There's a fire and one . . . no, wait, there's two people moving about throwing wood on the fire," said the Marine. "I'd say that by the difference in their heights that one is a Kurgan and the other is a Chosen warrior."

"Okay then. Time to get to work." Sheridan waved Cole to his side. "We'll head out right away. It shouldn't take us more than an hour to reach the crash site."

"Sounds about right," said Cole. "The sooner we're off this planet, the better, as far as I'm concerned. This place gives me the creeps."

Sheridan chuckled. He turned to a Marine lance corporal. "You've got the lead. Take your time. We don't want to walk into an ambush or stir up a sleeping predator."

"Got it, sir," replied the Marine.

Aside from the swarms of mosquitos that seemed to hover around the Marines, the march to the crashed Kurgan ship went by uneventfully. Two hundred meters from the site, Sheridan stopped the patrol and took a quick break.

After ensuring that everyone was covering their arcs, Cole quietly moved up to Sheridan's side. "Aside from giving a pint of blood to those horrid flying bloodsuckers, I'd say things have gone smooth so far."

Sheridan nodded. He tapped the Marine controlling the UAV on the shoulder and took the controller from him. Sheridan ran a finger over the screen, moving the drone's camera around. The Kurgan camp hadn't changed. He could still only see the two survivors sitting by the fire. He knew that there could be more of them inside the ship. Unfortunately, there was no way to know until they got there. He handed back the device.

"I take it you're going to go on ahead and take a look?" Cole said.

"Yeah. I'll take Lance Corporal Moore with me. I expect we'll be back in twenty minutes or less. If we're not, carry on without us."

"Watch for booby traps and alarms. I'd lay some if I were in their shoes."

Sheridan tapped his friend on the shoulder. "I'll keep a sharp eye out for them." With that, he and Moore left the rest of the team behind and moved off toward the Kurgans. They moved as quiet as they could, careful not to step on anything that might make a noise. It did not take long for Sheridan to smell the smoke from the burning fire wafting through the air. He slowed his pace and took cover behind a tall rock. Sheridan brought out his binoculars and looked through the trees at the crashed vessel. The light from the fire lit up the side of the craft. He could see that the Kurgans had landed hard. The landing struts underneath the ship were crushed. There was a long, jagged breach running almost the length of the vessel. It was easy to see that it was going nowhere ever again. He waited five minutes to see if there were any more survivors. When he was satisfied that they were only facing two Kurgans, he pointed back the way they came and led Moore back to the rest of the patrol.

Sheridan briefed Cole and the rest of the Marines before leading everyone back to the rocky outcropping he had used to observe the crash site. There, the Marines broke down into two teams of six. One was led by Sheridan and the other by Cole. Cole's group would cover Sheridan and his team as they attempted to take the camp and the two enemy soldiers alive. It was a long shot. Kurgan officers would rather die than surrender. However, if they could wound either enemy soldier, they might be able to take them both alive for interrogation.

As they crept closer, Sheridan's heart began to beat faster. He could feel the adrenaline rushing through his system. When they were less than thirty meters from the fire, Sheridan stopped for a moment to make sure that they had not been observed. He was about to continue when all hell broke loose. Someone in Cole's team had accidentally set off one of the Kurgan's early warning traps. An illumination device lit up the woods as if it were daylight, blinding everyone wearing night vision equipment. Before Sheridan could yell the order to take cover, the Kurgan officer swung his rifle around and opened fire on the silhouetted Marines.

A man cried out in pain as he tumbled to the ground.

Sheridan swore, ripped off his NVGs, and brought his rifle up to his shoulder. He took aim at the Kurgan and went to pull the trigger. He never got the chance to fire. Hidden in the trees above them were two automatic anti-personnel mines that were triggered two seconds after the light came on. With a loud explosion, the mines detonated. Hundreds of small metal balls shot through the air, striking down two more Marines. Sheridan felt one of the projectiles hit his chest. This time, he was wearing his body armor, saving his life. He cursed and opened fire in the direction of the Kurgan camp. With their cover blown, Sheridan led his men in a headlong rush at the enemy. He saw the officer fall with a hole blasted in the side of his head. The Chosen warrior with him dropped to the ground, struck several times in the arms and chest.

In seconds, the surviving Marines were in the camp. Cole grabbed the Chosen's dropped weapons and tossed them into the woods. A private, cross-trained as a medic, hurried over and checked on the warrior's wounds.

Sheridan rushed over and stuck his head inside the crashed vessel. He was surprised to see that it was empty. If there were other Kurgan survivors, they weren't in the camp. He turned about and saw Cole help two of the Marines hit by the mine to sit down. With them was a Marine with a gunshot wound to his left arm. Thankfully, none of the wounds looked life threatening. "What's the score?" he asked Cole as the light from the traps faded away. The flames from the open fire lit up the small camp.

"Hodges was struck in the arm, Jones in the leg, and Rodriguez in the face by several of those ball bearings. Once Gunther finishes with the Chosen soldier, he can fix these guys up. They should be able to make it back to the shuttle on their own two feet."

Sheridan nodded. They had been lucky and he knew it. Things could have gone far worse than it had for them. He looked over at Lance Corporal Moore. "Go through the Kurgan ship and grab everything that looks even the remotest bit interesting. If you need help, ask for it. We came here to gather intelligence, and I'm not leaving until we find some."

"Yes, sir," replied Moore.

"Hey, sir, you should check this out," said Cole as he shone his light on the face of the dead Kurgan officer. "Have you ever seen anything like this before?"

Sheridan bent down and examined the officer's face. He was surprised to see that the left half of the face was covered in intricate tattoos. His eyes lit up the instant he realized what he was seeing. "My God, this officer is from the *Kyycha*. I read about them when I was at the academy. I never would have expected to see one out here in the middle of nowhere."

"Sorry, you've lost me."

"The Imperial Guard. He's from the Kurgan Imperial Guard."

Cole let out a low whistle. "I bet the intel boys back at headquarters are going to lose their minds when they learn about this. No one has seen these guys in over a century. I wonder what the hell they were doing in this system."

"I can't tell by the tattoos if he's a member of the Old or Young Guard Corps, but he's definitely a guard's officer." Sheridan dug out a small recording device and took several pictures of the dead Kurgan and the markings on his face. He quickly checked the body for anything of value and found a small, slender tablet in a pouch on the dead officer's belt. Sheridan took it and put it away into his pocket until it could be examined later.

"How's the Chosen doing?" Cole asked Gunther.

The young Marine shook his head. "He's fading fast. I gave him something for the pain. It's the best I can do for him."

"Okay, leave him and deal with our people." He moved over and propped the warrior up against a tree. In the dark, the soldier appeared deathly pale. Cole knew that the man would soon pass on.

Sheridan bent down and looked at the mortally wounded warrior. "Can you tell me what happened to your ship?" he asked in Kurgan.

The warrior held out his hand. Barely above a whisper he said, "Water."

Sheridan gave the man his canteen. He held it for the warrior as he took a sip. "You speak the word of the lord. How do you know our language?"

"There isn't time to explain. Who are you, and what are you doing out here?"

The warrior coughed up blood as he struggled to catch his breath. "My name is Sergeant Kaladas. We were on a scouting mission when our ship's engine failed. We were pulled into orbit by the gravity of this planet." The man took another sip of water and coughed. "We were lucky to survive our landing."

"Are there any other survivors?"

"No. The animals got everyone else." The man let out a wet, bloody cough. Sheridan helped him to wipe the blood from his lips.

"What were you scouting for?"

"Perlinium."

Sheridan translated the conversation for Cole.

"Makes sense," said Cole. "This is a quiet region of space. They could set up a mine here and no one would be the wiser. It's not the first time the Kurgs have done this on our side of the border."

Sheridan went to ask another question but saw that the warrior was not breathing; his eyes wide open. He reached over and closed them. He let out a tired sigh, stood up, and looked around. It was time to leave.

Moore waved over at Sheridan. "Sir, I think I can pry the ship's computer free. Should I take it?"

"Yes, and be quick about it. I want to get out of here as soon as possible. All this noise will undoubtedly have made some of the inhabitants of the forest quite curious."

Cole asked, "What do you want to do with the bodies?"

"If we had the time, I'd cremate them. However, we don't, so we'll just leave them where they are and let nature deal with them."

The march back to the shuttle was slowed up by the wounded Marines and the need to avoid any predators. In the night sky, directly above them, hovered their UAV keeping a watch on the surrounding woods for any sign of movement. The more they trudged through the forest, the more curious Sheridan became about the dead officer. He suspected that the Kurgan was an engineer sent into Terran space to find uninhabited planets that could be exploited for their natural resources. He began to wonder if this were a sign that Kurgans were having a hard time keeping up with the voracious fuel demands of their fleet. But why send an officer from their elite Imperial Guard? His thoughts were interrupted when Lance Corporal Moore brought up a hand to stop the patrol.

"What's up?" Sheridan asked.

"About one hundred meters shy of the shuttle craft is what looks like a family of large herbivores. I can't tell how many of them there are from here."

Sheridan waved for the UAV operator to move to his side. He took the controller and studied the picture on the screen for a minute. There were eight large animals with four smaller ones. His blood turned cold when he saw a small pack of predators making their way through the woods toward the plant eaters. If they spooked the larger animals and caused them to stampede, there was no way to judge the damage the tank-sized creatures could do if they struck their ship.

"That doesn't look good," said Cole, studying the picture over Sheridan's shoulder.

"I'm open to suggestions."

"Get the shuttle to take off and move to the alternate LZ to the east. It'll add a klick to our trip, but I'd rather hike the distance than be trapped down here for who knows how long until another ship is sent down. Whatever we're going to do, sir, we need to do it fast as the sun will be coming up in an hour or two, and that's when the larger predators begin to stir."

Sheridan nodded and relayed the order to the flight crew. A minute later, they all heard the sound of the shuttle's engines as it flew over them and headed to the new pick-up point.

"Lead on and pick up the pace slightly," Sheridan said to Moore.

They hadn't gone more than a hundred meters when they heard a loud bellow from the direction of the herbivore pack. As one, the patrol froze in place and turned their heads to look behind them. Another creature cried out in fear, followed right away by several more.

Sheridan knew in that instant that the predators had struck. He was going to tell Moore to push on when he heard the sound of animals crashing their way through the forest. The noise grew louder by the second.

"They're coming this way," cried out Cole.

Sheridan took a quick look around and saw that there was no high ground around they could seek refuge on. There was only one thing they could do, he yelled, "Run!"

The patrol turned and sprinted as best as they could through the woods. Uninjured Marines wrapped their arms around their injured comrades and helped them keep up. Behind them, the sound of the terrified animals charging through the underbrush filled the air.

Sheridan had an idea. He stopped in his tracks, brought up his rifle to his shoulder, took aim at a tree about fifty meters away, and fired a high explosive grenade at it. With a loud explosion, the tree split apart from the blast and toppled to the ground. If he thought the noise and light would make the animals turn and run in another direction, he was sadly mistaken. The pack was fixated on one thing—survival. He lowered his rifle and ran after the rest of the patrol. He had almost caught up with Cole when the world around Sheridan seemed to explode as a large three-horned beast burst through the forest. He glanced out of the corner of his eye as the massive creature, followed closely by a couple of smaller ones, ran straight past him. Sheridan never saw the tree root that caught his right foot and sent him tumbling to the ground. He rolled over and moved to one side just as another herbivore ran right over the top of him; its enormous feet barely missing his head. Just when it seemed the last of the giant beasts had passed him by, their tormentors burst through the woods. They had long snouts filled with razor-sharp teeth. The predators were covered in feathers and ran on their two hind legs. Sheridan watched as one tried to pounce on one of the smaller herbivores, only to be struck by the tail of a larger beast, sending the attacker flying off into the dark.

In a matter of seconds, it was over. Sheridan could still hear the wild melee going on somewhere in front of him, but for now, he was safe where he was. He sat up and reached for his rifle. He was about to get up when he realized that it was quiet. Not even the omnipresent swarms of mosquitos could be heard.

He was being hunted.

Sheridan reached down with his thumb and changed his rifle's setting from safe to full auto. As quiet as he could, he got up to his feet and looked around. He couldn't see whatever it was that was stalking him, but he knew it was out there waiting for a chance to strike. Sheridan activated the thermal sight on his weapon and moved around slowly trying to acquire his target. He wasn't sure if the creatures were warm or cold blooded. He just hoped that they showed up in his sights.

The thought of being eaten alive turned Sheridan's mouth dry with fear. Facing an enemy in battle was one thing, but being hunted by a creature that wanted to devour you alive was another thing altogether. Tension gnawed at Sheridan's insides. A couple of seconds had passed before he saw a bright green shape moving slowly through the woods, trying to get around behind him. He followed it through his sights until it came to a complete stop. He watched it lower itself as it prepared to charge him. Sheridan knew that he had mere seconds to bring it down before it was on him. He placed his weapon's reticle pattern dead center of the predator and began to take up the slack on his trigger. The attack, when it came, still managed to surprise Sheridan.

With a loud hiss, the creature charged out from behind a giant fern and leaped up into the air with the razor-sharp talons on its feet aimed straight at Sheridan. He pulled back on the trigger and fired off a long burst into the attacking predator. The rounds tore into the beast's exposed stomach and came out its back. Sheridan turned and moved to one side as the monster landed on the ground precisely where he had been standing a second ago. The creature let out an angry hiss and turned to look over at Sheridan. He was stunned to see that it was still on its feet. Without aiming, he emptied what was left in his magazine into the predator. Blood and feathers flew as the bullets ripped the animal to pieces. Its eyes rolled up into its head as it tumbled to the forest floor. Sheridan, still expecting it to be alive, edged forward and kicked the carcass with his foot. When it didn't move, he let out a breath and rushed to change the empty magazine on his rifle for a full one.

The buzzing from the mosquitos returned. Sheridan had never been so happy to hear them in his life. He took their return as a good sign. He turned his head and listened. In the distance, he could hear the noise of the larger animals running through the forest beginning to fade. He took a quick look around to make sure that he truly was alone before heading off after his teammates.

It took less than a minute before Sheridan ran into Cole. "What kept you?" asked his friend.

"I tripped over a root and then found myself being eyed as the main course for one of the raptors," replied Sheridan, remembering the term for the creatures. "Where is the rest of the patrol?"

"Moore has them. We came out in a clearing, so Moore's guiding in the shuttle as we speak. Come on, sir, let's get the hell off this planet."

"I couldn't agree more, Sergeant." With that, they jogged to rejoin their comrades. Minutes later, the shuttle closed its side door and began to lift off into the star-filled night. Exhausted, Sheridan sat back in his chair. The adrenaline that had been keeping him going was starting to fade. He reached into his pocket and pulled out the slender tablet he had found on the dead Kurgan. He turned it over in his hands. Sheridan had never seen anything like it. He read the lettering on the back of the device and saw that it was a gift from the Kurgan's father to Lieutenant Kulon on the day of his commissioning in the Kurgan military. A small pang of remorse came over Sheridan. He had never thought of his enemy as having a family. To date, he had only seen them as cruel and sadistic opponents who had started a war that had already seen hundreds of thousands of casualties on both sides. He put the tablet away and closed his eyes. It did not take long for sleep to wash over his tired body.

Cole saw his friend begin to fade, smiled, and reached for a headset to drown out the loud snoring he knew was seconds away.

6

Heat, hotter and more oppressive than anything Tarina had ever felt in her life rushed inside the cramped landing craft the moment the doors slid open.

"Get out and form up in three ranks," barked a Chosen sergeant at the prisoners.

Tarina and Wendy moved outside. Overhead, in a cloudless sky, the late afternoon sun baked the sand and the rocks at close to fifty degrees Celsius. They were already sweating by the time they joined their comrades.

A grizzled-looking Kurgan officer with several deep scars down his face stood on a platform, staring down at the assembled prisoners. He moved over to a microphone and spoke. His voice was instantly translated. "I shan't welcome you here to Klatt, as this is where you will remain until you die. My name is Commandant Kodan; it is my job to make sure that for however long you remain alive, I get the most out of you. You are alive for one reason and one reason only: to mine perlinium. The day you stop working is the day you die." With that, the Kurgan officer turned and strode off the platform.

Wendy and Tarina glanced at one another, exchanging a worried look.

"You will follow me," ordered the sergeant. He led the new group of captives toward a tunnel dug into the side of a rocky hill. As soon as they stepped inside, the temperature seemed to drop twenty degrees. For several minutes, the Chosen warrior steered them through a maze of tunnels until they came out into a large cavern. There were several Chosen soldiers standing there holding whips in their hands. They stared at the newcomers.

The sergeant raised his hand and yelled, "Halt."

The cold, uncaring expression on the faces of the men with the whips frightened Tarina. They looked like they were used to dishing out pain with little or no remorse for their actions.

"I can only echo what the commandant has told you," said the sergeant. "You cannot escape. Even if you could, you would be dead in a day or two on the surface of the planet. Work hard and you will be treated fairly. Work poorly and my men will make your life a living hell." As if to reinforce his words, an emaciated man in rags was dragged from a side tunnel and thrown on the ground at the sergeant's feet. He stepped back and made room for two of his men to work. They uncoiled their whips and before the poor wretch could plead for his life, they began to take turns flogging him to death.

Tarina cringed each time the whip made a sharp cracking sound as it cut through the air. Beside her, Wendy struggled not to cry.

In a matter of minutes, it was done. The man was dead and blood covered the ground where his body lay. "Let that be a lesson to all of you," said the sergeant. He turned and snapped his fingers. A man with long, greasy hair and a thick red beard dressed in what was left of his Marine Corps uniform walked over to the warrior. The sergeant announced, "This man will be your group supervisor. You will answer to him and he in turn answers to me. Your lives are now in his hands."

The man nodded to the sergeant and walked over until he was only a couple of meters from the prisoners. "Listen up, my name is Travis. I don't care what your rank is. From here on out you will call me Master Travis. If you fail to do so, all I have to do is point at you and you will receive twenty lashes for insolence. If I bother to talk to you, you will not look me in the eye, as that is another sign of insolence that I will not tolerate. Now, follow me and I will show you where you will sleep and eat."

In silence, the prisoners made their way past several caverns dug out of the rock. Inside each were hundreds of bunk beds along with dozens of wooden tables and chairs. There wasn't a soul to be seen in any of the living areas.

"This will be your new home for as long as you live," said Travis, pointing to a cave filled with empty beds. "Remember this, your dwelling is called Black-Three. If you get lost or you are detained, say my name as well as Black-Three and you will be brought right back here for punishment."

Wonderful, thought Tarina. There was no way in even her worst nightmare could she have thought up a spot as sad and unforgiving as this.

"As the work details will be returning from the mines in the next few minutes," said Travis. "I want all of you to take a seat at the tables in the middle of the room and sit there until the remainder of Black-Three returns. Supper will be served at precisely eighteen hundred hours. The lights are turned off at twenty hundred and reveille is at five in the morning. Work begins an hour later."

Tarina pointed at a nearby table. She and Wendy took a seat. The mood among the prisoners was despondent. Barely anyone uttered a word. Most just sat there staring at the walls.

"This place is a living hell," whispered Wendy.

"We just got here. Wait until we've been in the mines working under the lash for twelve hours a day. We've got to figure a way out of here while we still have our strength."

"You heard that Kurgan, we wouldn't last more than a couple of days on the run in the heat."

Tarina shook her head. "I don't care, two days on the run is better than waiting down here to die. Besides, we might get lucky and steal a transport shuttle. I'm willing to give it a try if you are."

Wendy smiled. "I'm with you. However, we'll never get past all the guards at the entrance to the mine. So I suggest we look for another way out when we are taken down into the mine to dig for perlinium tomorrow morning."

Tarina squeezed her friend's hand. It was done. No matter what happened, they were going to try and make a run for freedom.

The sound of dozens of feet shuffling across the rocky floor brought the conversation to an abrupt end. Both women looked at the entrance to the cavern and were shocked to see the other occupants of Black-Three staggering toward them. Their bodies were skin and bones. What little clothing they wore was torn and dirty. They looked right through the newcomers. It was as if they didn't exist.

Tarina stood and let out a gasp when she thought she recognized someone. "Angela, is that you?"

The woman turned her head and looked over with eyes that had seen too much death and horror.

Tarina looked deep into the woman dark blue eyes. She had no doubt in her heart that she knew the person in front of her. "Angela, it's me, Tarina. Don't you recognize me?"

"Tarina, my God, it really is you. Am I dreaming?" asked Angela.

Tarina put a hand on Angela's dirt-covered skin. "I'm sorry, you're not dreaming. I'm here with you."

"Here, sit down," said Wendy, making room for Angela on the bench.

Everyone sat. Tarina made the introductions before asking, "When were you captured?"

"My ship was boarded after a battle over Hyperion-Six. We did not have many Marines on board to help repel the attack. They fought hard but were quickly overwhelmed. The Kurgans took most of the crew alive. Unfortunately, they also got the ship's cargo of ammunition for themselves."

"How long have you been here?" Wendy asked.

"What is the date?"

"April tenth."

A glassy look came over Angela's eyes. "I'd lost complete track of time. I've been here for almost five months now."

Tarina saw the miserable look in her comrade's face, reached over, and placed a hand on Angela's shoulder. "I'm sorry."

"I'm the lucky one. Of the forty-eight men and women taken prisoner, there are only four of us left alive. Some died of exhaustion, others from disease, while many more were killed by the guards. They see us as subhuman and not worthy of pity. Keep your head down and whatever you do, don't let Travis take a liking to you."

"Why?" asked Tarina.

"Because he likes to rape women right in front of everyone else. When he's had his way, he gives the poor soul over to the guards who take turns with her until they grow bored and kill her."

"God, no," Wendy uttered.

Behind them, a cart rolled into view. It had three large steel pots on it.

Angela saw the cart and stood. "Hurry, or all you'll get is broth." Tarina and Wendy followed her to the wagon. The lids were lifted off the pots and a foul odor wafted out.

"That smells awful," said Tarina, waving a hand in front of her nose.

"You'll get used to it. We only get two meals a day. Breakfast and supper, and it's always the same thing. Force yourself to eat it or you'll soon begin to fade, and you'll be unable to work. Always keep thinking to yourself that if you don't work, you'll die."

They took their bowls of foul-smelling food back to their table. Tarina spotted a few people who had come with her still sitting down. "Get some food into you," she said to the people.

"I'm not hungry," replied a dejected-looking man.

Angela shook her head. "Forget him and anyone else who won't look after themselves. If you try to help them, all you do is draw attention to yourself. I know this sounds horrid, but you have to care about yourself and only yourself from now on. If you don't, you won't last a week here."

Tarina saw Wendy eyeing the gray soup in her bowl. "Close your eyes and pretend you're back home on Earth in a fancy restaurant in Paris having a scrumptious meal."

Already, Angela was halfway through her meal. She looked up and said, "Eat it fast. I've seen people killed for their food."

Tarina dipped her spoon in the soup, scooped some up, and placed it in her mouth. She almost gagged on the repulsive-tasting broth. She closed her eyes and willed herself to eat the meal no matter how inedible it may taste. If she were going to make a run for it, she knew she had to consume whatever was put in front of her.

7

Sheridan read over his report one last time before saving it. It was only a first draft of what had happened during his time undercover with the smugglers. As was his routine, he would have Cole read it to make sure that he hadn't forgotten anything before sending it on to Captain Killam and the operational staff of the Sixth Fleet Headquarters. The after-action review of the incident involving the downed Kurgan craft had not taken long to write. Sheridan knew that the intelligence personnel would be salivating to get their hands on the computer taken from the ship and all the other devices that they had brought along with them. He glanced down at his watch and saw that they would be coming out of their jump in less than an hour. It would be good to be back home with the fleet and his father, the commanding officer of the Sixth Fleet. He stood up, stretched up his tired muscles, and went to give a copy of his report for his friend to review.

They shared a room with several dozen boxes filled with spare supplies and provisions. It was tight, but at least it was warm and dry. Sheridan stepped inside the cramped quarters. "Master Sergeant, are you awake? I've got a copy of my report for you to look over."

There was no reply.

Sheridan had no idea where Cole could have gone. It wasn't time for supper. He shrugged and tossed the papers down on his cot. He sat down, reached underneath, pulled out a small metal box, and opened it. There should have been a bottle of Scotch inside. Instead, there was a note. Sheridan picked up the paper and read it. There was one sentence: *Sir, I think we need to talk.*

The door to the room slid open. Cole walked in and stood in front of Sheridan.

"Sir, I saw you coming down the hallway and waited a minute. I knew if you didn't find me here that you'd reach for your bottle. Captain, I turned a blind eye to your drinking when your girlfriend was first declared missing. I also kept my mouth shut when we were operating undercover in the smuggler colony. But I'm not going to be silent anymore. You should have come to me before you decided to deal with your feelings by yourself. Did you honestly think that I wouldn't notice you'd been drinking to excess?'

Sheridan sat there confused, ashamed, and angry all at the same time. He did not know what to say to his friend.

Cole sat down across from Sheridan. "You're not alone. I've been in your shoes. The irritability, the inability to fall asleep, the hypervigilance, they're all signs of PTSD. Trust me on this one, self-medication is not the answer. I lost my family because I did precisely what you're doing. Michael, you're only twenty-four. You've got your whole life in front of you. I see potential in you that I've never seen in an officer so young as you. Don't destroy your chance to live a good life."

"I can deal with it," replied Sheridan.

"Sir, you can't bullshit a bullshitter. No one can deal with it by themselves. I'm not going to let you self-destruct. I know that you've gotten more alcohol hidden in your gear. I want you to stand up and give it all to me."

"And If I don't?"

"Then you can find yourself a new master sergeant. My job goes beyond the usual duties of dress, discipline, and deportment. I'm here to give you advice, even if you don't like what I'm saying. Captain, don't let foolish pride blind you. Let me help you."

Sheridan sat there staring over at the man who had become his closest friend. He could not believe that Cole would make him stop drinking.

Cole's voice turned serious. "Michael, if you don't give me all of your booze, and I do mean all of it in the next ten seconds, I'm going to speak with your father and demand a transfer."

Panic began to build in Sheridan's chest. He was conflicted. In his mind, the alcohol was the only thing stopping him from breaking down. Whenever he closed his eyes, he saw Tarina's face or the dead body of his friend, Harry Williams, lying on the ice moon where he had killed him.

Cole stood and turned to leave.

"No, wait," pleaded Sheridan as he jumped to his feet and moved over to his barrack box. He rummaged around for a few seconds before pulling out a couple of bottles. His hands shook as he handed the bottles to Cole.

Cole's eyes narrowed. "The flask in your pack as well, sir."

Sheridan nodded, dug it out, and gave it over. "How the hell did you know about the flask?"

"Sir, you're an amateur compared to me. Remember, I told you once that I used to hide my booze in the bathroom so no one would see me drinking. I was so good at it that people did not even know I was drunk when I was at work."

Sheridan felt his legs give out. He collapsed down onto his cot. Tears filled his eyes. He hung his head in shame. "Oh God, Master Sergeant, what have I done?"

Cole sat down beside Sheridan and placed a hand on his shoulder. "Sir, you haven't done anything wrong. You're human and you've made a bad call. Hell, we all do. You're not the first, and you won't be the last person to do what you have done. Trust me when I say that I'm here to help you get through this. Talking about how you feel is better for you than a dozen bottles of alcohol. Today is the first day of a new life for you."

Sheridan nodded. He did not raise his head. He had never felt so low in his entire life.

Cole examined the bottles. He was surprised at the assortment of alcohol his young friend had accumulated. "Sir, where did you get the vodka from?"

"The ships' supply petty officer has a stash."

Cole stood up and let out a resigned sigh. "Sir, from here on out when you feel the need for a drink, just come see me instead. As for that petty officer, he and I are about to have a one-way conversation that will end badly for him."

Sheridan wiped his eyes and stood up. "Thanks, Master Sergeant. I owe you."

"Sir, this isn't about owing anyone anything. This about doing the right thing. Now hand me that report to read, your last one was full of grammatical errors."

Sheridan gave a fake look of indignation. "Hey, I'm the one with the degree."

"That does not mean you know how to write."

8

Michael Sheridan stood outside the door to his father's private quarters. He made sure that his new uniform was neat and tidy before pressing the buzzer on the wall. A couple of seconds later, the door slid open and his father stood there with a smile on his weathered face. Like his son, Admiral Robert Sheridan was tall and fit, with green eyes and black hair that was now graying around the temples. Right away, his father reached out and hugged his son. The years of estrangement between them had long vanished and a strong bond of respect and admiration had replaced it.

"It's good to see you again, Michael," said the admiral.

"You too, Father." He moved into the room and saw that the dinner table was already set for two.

"Come, let's sit down and have a bite to eat. We can talk over dinner. Unfortunately, I have a conference call with Admiral Oshiro in just over an hour."

"Something up?" asked Sheridan as he took a seat at the table.

"It's my usual weekly chat with the admiral . . . at least, that's what I think it is."

Sheridan smirked when he saw the usual bottle of wine that accompanied all his father's dinner meals was missing.

"Yes, I see you've noticed," said the admiral. "My steward received a message from Sergeant Cole that I was not to serve you any alcohol with your meals anymore. Is there something you want to tell me, Michael?"

Sheridan felt his cheeks flush. He fought the feelings of guilt and shame in his heart and looked up at his father. "Dad, Master Sergeant Cole is just looking out for me. I hit the bottle pretty hard after Tarina went missing. It's for my own good that I abstain from any alcohol."

Robert Sheridan smiled. "Michael, you've got the best damned NCO in the entire Marine Corps. If you won't have any, neither will I from now until this blasted war is over."

"Dad, you don't have to do that. I'm the one with the problem."

"You're right, I don't have to, but I want to. Now dig in, your fish is getting cold."

Sheridan took a fork full of salmon and savored its taste. After almost two months of eating rations or poorly cooked food, he was happy to enjoy a decent meal with his father. A couple of minutes later, Sheridan set his fork down and asked, "Sir, how is the offensive going in the Titan system?"

The admiral shook his head. The bitter look on his face told Sheridan that things had not turned out as Fleet Headquarters had predicted. "I hate to say it, but things there went spectacularly bad for the First and Third Fleets. We lost two carriers and over two dozen other vessels trying to take back Titan Prime. The Kurgans did not come off much better. However, the much hoped for breakthrough in that region has not happened. To make matters worse, an enemy counteroffensive managed to take back two planets and inflict over thirty thousand casualties on the Marine and Army divisions involved in the fight."

Sheridan knew that friends he went through the academy with could easily be among the thousands of killed and wounded. It tugged at his emotions. The first thought that flashed through his subconscious was that he could use a drink. Sheridan took a deep breath and cleared his mind. He had vowed never to drink again, and he was not about to give in to temptation.

"If we've stalled in the Titan system, what's next for the fleet?"

"I don't know. I hate to say it, but I've been told by a reliable source that some politicians back home are talking about entering into negotiations with the Kurgans."

"Father, they can't. If they do, all of this will have been for nothing. Did they not learn anything from the last war? All the people the Kurgans have taken will be forced to become citizens of the Empire. I, for one, don't want Tarina to be brainwashed into becoming my enemy. Hell, you and I both know it, we'll end up fighting them again in a few generations. We have to end this war on our terms."

"Michael, you and I serve at the discretion of our civilian leaders. If they tell us to pull back and let the Kurgans keep what they've already taken in exchange for peace, then that is precisely what we will do."

Sheridan bit his lip. "What does Admiral Oshiro think about this latest development?"

"I honestly don't know. I suspect that this is something we will discuss when he calls."

"Can I come by later? I'd love to hear what the admiral had to say."

Robert Sheridan smiled and sat back in his chair. "Michael, after my teleconference, Captain Killam and I will go over what was said to make sure that we understand what it is Admiral Oshiro wants us to do. You may be my son, but until I announce what is going on at the morning staff briefing, you're going to have to remain in the dark like everyone else."

Sheridan felt foolish for pushing his luck. His father was right; he would have to wait to learn what was going on.

The admiral said, "Look, why don't you and Sergeant Cole sneak in the back of the morning brief and listen in. Most of it is routine fleet business, but there may be a new tidbit or two you may find interesting."

Sheridan nodded. "Thanks, Dad. Any news is better than listening to the rumor mongers spinning their tales every time you go to eat in the mess hall."

"Oh, before I forget, Captain Killam was speaking to the head of fleet personnel and has asked that you and Cole be assigned to a raider battalion. Looks like your stay with us could be coming to an end."

Sheridan tried not to look too happy; however, a position with a deep space raider unit was something he had been agitating for with Killam for months. "Any idea when the transfer orders may come in?"

"No. Why don't you speak with Captain Killam after the brief and see if he's heard anything?"

"Will do."

"Now if you'll excuse me," said the admiral as he stood up. "I want to meet with Killam in the ops room. We need to go over our notes before the teleconference begins."

"Yes, of course, sir," replied Sheridan. He held out his hand to shake. "I'll see you in the morning after the briefing."

"Sounds good. Perhaps we can have a coffee together. You, me, Cole, and Killam should be able to find a quiet corner to chat in."

Sheridan turned and left his father's quarters. He looked around to make sure that the hallway was empty before jumping up into the air and letting out a triumphant cry. After months away from a combat unit, he was finally heading back into the fight with Marines under his command. He could not have been happier.

9

Tarina fought back the tears as she sat down on her bunk. Her entire body ached. She had bloody scars across her back from being struck by the guards. She let out a whimper when she brought up her right foot so she could look at the bottom. Ever so slowly, she unwrapped the blood-and-sand-caked cloth that she had put there earlier in the day after her sandals had fallen apart. Tarina gritted her teeth when she saw that the bottom of her foot looked like raw hamburger.

"Here, let me clean that up before it gets infected," said Wendy as she poured some water over Tarina's feet to clean the dirt and sand from her wounds.

Tarina grimaced in pain and tried to block the agony from her mind. They had only spent two full days in the mine, and she was already beginning to doubt that she could last another week.

"Let me see the other one," Wendy said, lifting up her friend's left foot onto the hard, wooden bunk. It was as bad as the first. She got to work cleaning and bandaging Tarina's bloodied feet.

Angela walked over and sat down. She made sure no one was watching before reaching under her shirt and bringing out two pairs of wooden clogs. "Put these on your feet. If you don't, you'll both fall behind and be targeted for punishment by Travis and his goons."

Wendy took them and tried a pair on her feet. They barely fit, but they would have to do. She left the other pair on the bed beside Tarina. "Let your feet heal a bit more before putting these on."

"Thanks," said Tarina to Angela. "Where did you get these?"

"I took them from a couple of dead workers. They don't need them anymore, and I knew that you two would. That's how I got mine," she replied, pointing down at the clogs on her feet.

"How ghoulish," said Wendy.

"You do what you must to survive."

"Yes, you do," said Tarina. "And we're both grateful to you for your help."

Around them, the other prisoners began to stir. "Food's here," announced Angela. "Stay where you are. Wendy and I will get you something to eat." With that, the two women hurried to get as close to the front of the food line as possible.

Tarina laid on her side in the bunk and closed her eyes. She tried to recall the past two days moving through the tunnels on their way to and from the mine. So far, she hadn't seen a prospective escape route and if one didn't materialize soon, she knew that their chances of successfully getting away would lessen each day. She was not about to let that happen. She would rather die trying than allow herself to succumb to their jailers. It was all just a matter of luck and so far, she had only experienced bad luck. Tarina heard her friends coming back. She sat up and forced herself to smile as Wendy handed her a bowl of soup.

"*Bon appetit*," said Wendy, trying to lighten the mood. "Only the best food is served at this five-star resort."

"Yes. I'll have to recommend it to all my friends when I get back home," added Tarina.

Both women looked at one another and broke out laughing.

"You're both nuts," said Angela. "Has anyone ever told you that?"

"Yeah, I can think of a couple of people who have over the past year," replied Tarina.

Wendy devoured her food. When she was done, she looked over at Tarina and said, "I wonder what the colonel and the rest of the squadron are up to?"

"It's been over four months since we were captured; they could be anywhere by now. Hell, they could even be back home on Earth for all we know."

"Thinking about such things won't do you any good," interjected Angela. "Forget about your past lives and worry only about today. It'll help you from losing it down here."

Tarina nodded. "Sound advice."

"Give me your bowls and I'll return them to the wagon," said Wendy.

Tarina and Angela handed her their empty bowls and watched her hobble over to the food cart. On her way back, one of the older male prisoners reached out and grabbed her by the arm. "Give me a kiss," said the man as he leaned his head down toward Wendy.

"No," she replied, struggling to break from his hold.

Tarina tried to stand up, but the burning pain in her feet almost made her black out. She fell right back down on her bed. Unable to help, she cried out, "Somebody, do something!"

Not a single prisoner moved to help Wendy. Most of the men who had seen this kind of thing before sat quietly or turned their heads away pretending not to see what was going on.

Wendy's attacker grabbed a handful of her long red hair and pulled her close to him. He reached under her shirt and groped her. She cried out in fear. Panic quickly took hold of her. She looked over at the Chosen guards standing nearby, praying that they would help her. They smiled at her and began laughing at her predicament.

"Don't move or say another word," warned Angela to Tarina. A second later, she was on her feet. She walked toward the man holding Wendy. "Anderson, let the girl go!"

"Screw you. You're only here because you want her for yourself. Well, you'll just have to wait until I'm done with her."

"Wrong answer." In a flash, Angela pulled a wooden spoon that had been sharpened into a weapon from behind her back. She jammed it hard into the man's side and twisted it. A second later, she pulled out the bloody shank and prepared to thrust it into his ribs once again. The assailant gasped in pain and released Wendy from his arms.

"You pig!" yelled Wendy, shooting her right foot into the man's crotch, doubling him over.

Angela grabbed Wendy by the shoulders and hauled her back to Tarina's bunk. "You'll be safe now. No one will try that with either of you ever again."

"What about him?" asked Wendy, looking over at the man as he rolled about on the ground in agony.

"He's no good to anyone anymore. When Travis hears about this incident, Anderson will be taken outside and flogged to death. You're not the first woman he's tried to have his way with."

Tarina could tell by the sound of Angela's voice that she hid a pain deep inside of her. She also knew better than to ask about it. Instead, she placed a hand on the woman's shoulder. "Thank you for saving Wendy's life. I owe you."

"You don't owe me a thing. Just be more aware of your surroundings from now on." With that, Angela left them and climbed up into her bunk.

"How are you doing?" Tarina asked her friend.

Wendy sat there staring at the man who had tried to rape her. Hate filled her eyes.

"Wendy, I said, 'how are you doing?'"

"I'm okay," she lied. "I'll be good once they haul him out of here and kill him."

Inside Tarina cringed. They had been together since the beginning of the war and she had never heard Wendy talk so coldly. It was obvious that life was cheap in the mines. She did not want to lose her dearest friend. She vowed to herself that every waking minute from now on would be dedicated to getting them home safely. Tarina did not know how or when, but she knew that she was not going to let her friend down.

10

Sheridan and Cole quietly slipped into the back of the briefing room and took a seat. The room was already full of high-ranking officers and chief petty officers busy chatting with one another. Sheridan wasn't familiar with most of his father's staff. He knew there would be people there representing the fleet's personnel, operations, plans, training, communications, intelligence, logistics, finance, and civil liaison sections. A full colonel from General Denisov's forces on Illum Prime sat at the table as well.

At precisely nine o'clock, Captain Killam and Admiral Sheridan, accompanied by his aide, Commander Roy, walked into the room. Everyone stood and waited for the admiral to take his customary seat up front before sitting.

"Good morning, everyone," said the admiral.

"Good morning, sir," replied the group.

For the next hour, the section heads brought everyone in the room up to speed with what was happening. For Michael Sheridan, it was as much fun as having his teeth extracted. He knew it was important, but he figured some of the people in the room liked to hear the sound of their own voices. Thankfully, Killam would speed a person along if the presentation was starting to drag.

Just as Cole was beginning to rubberneck, Admiral Sheridan thanked everyone for their work and stood up. He moved over to a podium. Commander Roy reached for her tablet and activated the holographic projector. An image of the Titan system appeared.

"Ladies and gentlemen, for reasons of operational security, what I am about to divulge to you cannot leave this room," said the admiral. "A stalemate has developed in the Titan system. Both sides are worn down. Our forces there are leery of starting another action which could further deplete their limited number of capital ships. Skirmishing and raids, however, do continue on a daily basis. Intelligence intercepts indicate that the Kurgans are in as bad a shape as we are and are also taking this pause to rebuild their strength."

"Sir, would this not be the ideal time to strike the Kurgans while they are weak?" asked the captain in charge of the Sixth Fleet's logistics.

Admiral Sheridan shook his head. "The forces there need to save their strength for another day. Only ours and the Fifth Fleet are in any shape to conduct offensive operations. Fleet headquarters has made it clear to me that until a new strategy can be found, we are to restrict ourselves to economy of force operations and avoid anything that could bring on a major fleet engagement."

"Sir, what of the news that the Federation Council was deliberating a motion to begin exploratory talks with the Kurgans that could lead to a negotiated peace treaty?" asked another officer.

"Admiral Oshiro was called to the federation president's office yesterday and told that if a bill was brought before the president asking him to authorize a peace mission that he would personally veto it. Even though there's a war on, the political machinations back home never stop. We are about to go into an election year and the president wants some good news to give to the voters back home, and we are the people who will give it to him."

A loud murmur ran through the room.

Admiral Sheridan raised his hands to quiet the room. "Folks, the president has authorized Admiral Oshiro to conduct a raid inside Kurgan territory. The reason for this action will become clear during Captain Killam's presentation."

Killam stood up and moved over to the podium while the admiral took his seat. An image of the Kurgan border was brought up for all to see.

"Ladies and gentlemen, approximately two weeks ago a Kurgan directive relating to the treatment of prisoners of war was intercepted by one of our long-range satellites deployed along the border. From now on military personnel taken in battle will no longer be sent to re-education camps. Instead, they will be flown directly to a prison on a planet called Klatt to mine perlinium. Until the planet was mentioned in the intercept, we had no idea that such a place existed."

"Captain, I can't find Klatt on the star map," said one of the staff.

"That's because until a few hours ago, we had no idea where the planet was located. During a recent investigation into a crashed Kurgan ship, a veritable treasure trove of information was discovered. It's taken days to sift through everything, but we have been able to pinpoint the exact location of Klatt."

A planet appeared on the chart.

"Sir, that planet is deep inside enemy space," pointed out one of the chief petty officers sitting at the table.

"I know. That's why logistics, not combat power, will make or break our attempt to free our personnel currently being held on Klatt."

Michael Sheridan nearly fell off his chair when he heard the news. His heart began to race. After months of wondering where Tarina was and if she was still alive, he was being presented with a chance to find out. His transfer out of the fleet could wait. There was no way he was going to miss out on this mission.

"When are we planning to conduct this operation?" asked the fleet's logistics officer.

Admiral Sheridan looked at the faces of his staff. "Ready or not, we go in five days' time. I'd go earlier if I could, but we need that time to prepare ourselves. Don't be under any illusions; there will be no one coming from Earth to help us. We go with what we have."

"Sir, no one has ever penetrated into Kurgan space," pointed out the Marine colonel. "What do we know about this prison?"

"Or the Kurgan strength in that sector," added another officer.

"All valid concerns," said the admiral. "That is why orders were issued last night for satellites to be positioned in orbit above Klatt."

Michael knew that only one outfit in the fleet had the ships and the experience to pull it off. It would be Tarina's friends flying into the unknown.

"Sir, how many prisoners are we looking at rescuing?" ask the Marine colonel.

"If the intercepted reports are correct, the prison population is just shy of fifty-two hundred."

A commander leaned forward and looked over at Admiral Sheridan. "Sir, with all due respect, an operation like the one you are proposing will take weeks, not days, to plan and outfit properly. Why the rush?"

Captain Killam cleared his throat, telling everyone that the discussion was over. "If we had the time, Commander, we would take the time needed to plan this down to the last detail. However, time is not on our side. An additional piece of information recently fell into our laps that has forced our hand. It would appear that eleven days from now the Kurgans intend to use some of the prisoners during a *Kahtak* ritual."

Michael bolted out of his seat. "Lord, no!"

The room turned silent as all eyes turned to look over at the younger Sheridan.

Admiral Sheridan shook his head. "Is there something you wish to add to the discussion, Mister Sheridan?"

Michael could feel his cheeks turning red. He had opened his mouth without thinking. All he wanted to do now was shrink back down onto his seat.

"Way to go, sir," murmured Cole with a wink.

"Captain Sheridan, can you elaborate on the Kurgan *Kahtak* ritual?" asked Killam, giving the young officer an opportunity to make up for his outburst.

"Yes, sir, I can," replied Michael. "*Kahtak* is the ritual by which a young Imperial Guard warrior moves from the ranks of the Young Guard to the Old Guard. It is a bloodletting ceremony in which a soldier thrusts his knife deep into the bowels of his enemy, killing him. No one can gain admittance to the Old Guard without performing this ritual. In the past, this was a conducted right after a battle. The prisoners would be rounded up and brought for execution by those young warriors chosen for their bravery in battle or by family connection to join the Old Guard."

"Thank you, Captain. That was succinct and informative," said Killam.

Michael took his seat.

Cole shook his head. Under his breath, he said, "Good thing you went to school or you'd look really foolish right now."

Killam continued. "As you can see, if we don't launch in five days' time, we will arrive too late to help the thousands of men and women who will be slaughtered by the Kurgans. This operation will be known as Trident Fury. Trident for the fleet component, and Fury for the ground forces involved."

Admiral Sheridan said, "Captain Killam will be forming a tiger team to help him plan the operation. If he asks you for one of your people, you give him or her to Killam or you'll be hearing from me. To mask our true intentions, I want a training exercise to be planned for the fleet. It will commence six days from now. Commander Thomas, from the plans section, will take the lead on this. I can't stress enough the need for secrecy to be maintained throughout the fleet. If anyone asks what is going on, refer them to Commander Thomas' section."

With that, the meeting ended. People rushed from the room to put in motion the subterfuge. Admiral Sheridan tapped Killam on the shoulder before steering him to the back of the room where his son and Cole were standing.

"I see the academy's history lessons weren't wasted on you," said Admiral Sheridan to his son.

"I wish I had kept my mouth shut," replied Michael.

"Nonsense," said Killam. "Your concern will undoubtedly motivate the staff to move heaven and earth to see that this mission succeeds."

"Sir, how did you learn the date of the ritual?" asked Cole.

"I can answer that," Killam said. "It was in the personal tablet found on the dead Kurgan officer at the crash site. All his personal information was on there, including a note to himself to be back inside Kurgan space in time to take part in the ritual. A major security infraction on his behalf and an intelligence coup on ours."

"Sir, I don't want to be a pain, but has anyone considered that the information found on the tablet is false?" said Michael.

"I did, but there are too many other pieces of the puzzle that have also fallen into place for it to be a ruse," replied Killam. "No, it's the genuine article."

"I take it you no longer want that transfer out of the fleet?" said the admiral to his son.

"No, he doesn't," answered Cole. "If there's going to be a rescue mission to help free our friends, then we both want in on it, sir."

Killam smiled. "I knew you two would feel that way. The instant we start to receive live feed from the satellites soon to be in orbit above the prison, I'm going to dispatch you with a reconnaissance team to the planet. An eye in the sky is fine, but nothing beats having someone on the ground who can scout out the terrain and help guide in the ground forces when they arrive."

"You can count on us," said Michael.

"I'm starting my mission estimate here in this room in one hour. I'd like you both to come in and give me your wish list for the task. Remember you can only use what we have on hand."

"Yes, sir."

Admiral Sheridan nodded his concurrence. He masked his fear for his son's life behind his eyes. Once more, he was sending his son into battle with only the slimmest hope for survival. Nevertheless, he could not think a better pairing than the two men standing before him. If anyone could pull it off, it was them.

When Sheridan and Cole returned an hour later, the briefing room looked as if a tornado had plowed right through it. Maps, books, charts, laptops, and tablets were strewn everywhere. People were huddled in small groups trying to work out what was needed for the mission. Sheridan saw Killam talking to a short Marine lieutenant colonel with a bald head. He walked over and introduced himself and Cole.

"Good day to you, too. My name is Lieutenant Colonel Kimura," said the officer. "I have been tasked by General Denisov to help plan the ground force composition for the raid. I've heard good things about you two from the general. I understand that you will be leading a reconnaissance team to Klatt ahead of the main body."

"That is correct, sir," replied Sheridan.

"Do you have your wish list figured out?" Killam asked.

"Yes, sir. If the admiral's shuttle crew is available, I'd like to use them again."

"We figured you'd ask for them. They're busy getting the shuttle craft reconfigured for the long jump into Kurgan space."

"Also we'd like to keep the team small," said Cole. "The fewer people we have bumbling around on a Kurgan planet, the better."

"I'd like you to take a fire effects as well as an aerospace control officer with you," said Kimura. "They'll be invaluable to the ground force once it begins its drop to the planet's surface."

Sheridan handed a note to Kimura. "Sir, we thought of that too. In total, the team we need will consist of only ten personnel. The two officers you've mentioned, along with two communications specialists, and four other Marines for close protection are all we require."

Kimura raised an eyebrow. "This is an awfully small team. I can round up more if you need them."

Sheridan shook his head. "This will be plenty. If you can find any who speak Kurgan that would be a bonus. One other thing, before I forget, sir. Master Sergeant Cole and I read over the Kurgan intercepts. The people going with us need to be prepared to work on a harsh desert planet that gets as high as fifty degrees Celsius during the day and below freezing at night."

"I'm sure I can find suitable volunteers for you from the forces on Illum Prime."

"Thanks, sir."

"When do you need them?"

"The sooner they get here, the sooner we can begin training."

Kimura nodded. "Well, it looks like you two know your jobs. I'll make that call to Denisov's staff right away."

Killam said, "I hope all of our other concerns are solved that quickly. Somehow I doubt it."

Sheridan knew that was his cue to leave. He came to attention, saluted, and turned to leave. He and Cole walked out into the corridor and exchanged a look that said, *what have we just gotten ourselves into?*

"Come on, sir," said Cole, "let's go chat with your father's shuttle crew and see what they are up to. I'd hate for their ship to suddenly develop engine issues deep inside Kurgan territory."

"I didn't know that you knew a thing or two about jump engines."

"I don't and neither will they. It's an old NCO trick. I just want them to think I do. It'll make them pay closer attention to what they're doing. Being captured and sent to a prison planet for execution is not high on my to-do list."

11

Colonel Wright ran his hand down the length of his ship, stopping to check out the modifications his crew had made to the engines.

"It may not look pretty, but it'll get you home, sir," said a technical sergeant as he torqued up a bolt.

Wright tapped his jump ship and stepped back. "She's never failed me and neither have you people," said Wright to the four men and women in coveralls clustered around the back of the craft.

"Thanks, sir," replied the sergeant.

"Are the satellites secure and ready to be deployed?" asked Wright, popping his head underneath his ship to check on the payload secured there.

"They sure are, sir," answered a young female technician with a strong Irish accent.

Wright smiled. "I knew they would be. Just checking."

"When do you leave, sir?" asked the sergeant

"We're leaving in just over an hour."

"Good luck, sir."

Wright nodded and turned to check out his wingman's ship. Although they had been declared missing months ago, he wished it was Tarina and Wendy going on the mission with him. He had trusted them more than any of his other flight crews. They thought alike and had always shown a willingness to take risks to get the job done. For this assignment, he had selected Captains Fong and DeGrasse. Both were competent, brash officers who had arrived in the squadron a few months ago and had yet to see any real action.

Fong and DeGrasse were at their ship joking around with their technicians. Wright was going to speak to them but decided to leave them alone for now. There'd be plenty of time to talk once they transferred over to the transport ship.

"Sir, do you have a couple of minutes?" called out a female voice.

Wright saw Lieutenant Colonel Laura Tolinski, his deputy commander, walking toward him with a tablet in her left hand. With short black hair and porcelain white skin, she always reminded Wright of someone who tried their best to avoid the sun at all costs. He waited until she was only a couple of meters away before saying, "Sure, XO, what's up?"

"I just wanted to make sure everything was going as planned."

"XO, your reputation for being able to fly by the seat of your pants will remain unblemished. As per, we are on time and ready to deploy."

"Well, I will be amazed if this comes off without a hitch."

"I hope it does. I'm one of the people going out there."

"Sir, you know what I mean. From receipt of the order to deployment into Kurgan space with untried technological upgrades to our ships in under twenty-four hours is nothing short of miraculous."

"Yes, and you made it all happen."

Tolinski looked around the flight deck. "Sir, where's your navigator? She should be here by now."

"First Lieutenant Eskola is with the padre. She'll be along soon enough."

"She's had time for that," said Tolinski, her tone left no doubt in Wright's mind that she had no time for religious activities. He, however, couldn't care either way. If it made Eskola feel better, he was all for it.

"Do you have the flight plan with you?" asked Wright, changing the discussion.

Tolinski nodded and brought up her tablet. She pressed the screen and a picture of their intended flight path appeared. Wright took the device from her and studied the image. From Illum Prime, they would be jumping to an asteroid belt halfway to Klatt. The transport ship would use the asteroids to hide in. From there, the two jump fighters would make their way to the prison planet, deploy their satellites, and then repeat the journey back home. From the beginning to the end, it was a one hundred hour round trip. For almost half of the flight, he would be stuck inside the cockpit of his ship. It had been years since he'd had to wear a diaper under his survival suit. It was an experience he was not looking forward to.

First Lieutenant Eskola walked over. She was carrying a flight bag along with her helmet under her right arm. "Good evening, sir," she said to Wright.

"Evening," he replied.

"Are you finally ready to deploy?" Tolinski asked Eskola.

"Yes, ma'am," she replied, looking away from the XO.

Wright could sense the tension between the two women. He couldn't have two of the people he depended on to keep him alive having issues with one another. He decided to let it go for now. There were far more pressing issues to deal with. He would wait until they had returned safely to find out what was going on.

"Say, who feels like a coffee before we begin the pre-flight checks?" asked Wright.

"None for me, sir," said Eskola. "I know we're just moving between ships, but I'm nervous enough as it is. Coffee will only exacerbate things."

"I'm okay. I already had a few cups," replied Tolinski.

Wright shrugged. "Suit yourselves. I live on this stuff. I'm going to the galley to grab a cup. I'll meet you both back here in a few minutes."

"I'll walk with you, Colonel," said Tolinski.

Perhaps the discussion can't wait, thought Wright.

When they were alone in the corridor, Tolinski turned and looked over at her boss. "Sir, I bet you're wondering what is going on between Eskola and me?"

"Yes, I had. But I thought it could wait until we return home. However, here we are, so what's on your mind?"

Tolinski hesitated for a couple of seconds as she tried to decide the best way to describe what the problem was. Finally, she said, "Sir, Eskola and I are a couple. We've kept it very quiet so people would not feel that she was receiving easy assignments due to our relationship. Colonel, I'm worried about her safety. We've never attempted anything as dangerous as this, and I'm scared for her."

Wright smiled. He wasn't a fan of couples within the chain of command, but he was also a realist. Things just happened. "Well, thank God for that. I thought you were going to tell me that you doubted her skills as a navigator. Look, XO, I'm not going to tell you who you can and cannot spend your time with. It would be hypocritical of me to give you any advice on the subject. Hell, I've been married and divorced twice. All I ask is that you two continue to keep it quiet, or I'll have to reassign one of you away from the squadron. As I respect both of you, I don't want to have to do that."

"Yes, sir."

Wright placed a hand on Tolinksi's shoulder. "Laura, trust me, I'll bring Miss Eskola home in one piece. I promise."

"Thank you."

"Now how about one more coffee?"

12

Pain had become such a constant part of Tarina's bleak life that she found herself growing numb to it. She stood in line with the rest of the people from Black-Three waiting for her work assignment to be called out. She stared straight ahead through tired eyes that had already seen far too much death and suffering.

Out of the dark walked their tormentor, Travis. He was mumbling something to himself as he walked over to the ever-shrinking group of prisoners. His eyes lingered too long on Tarina for her liking. He placed his dirty hands on hips and said, "Today, we're going to do something a little different. We're not going to haul rocks to the transports. Instead, we're gonna play a little game. You will all be loading the ore directly onto the train at the far end of the mine. As you will be up against the prisoners from Black-One, I expect all of you to work extra hard today. If you don't and they manage to load more perlinium onto the train than you do, you won't like the consequences."

Tarina felt a shiver crawl up her back. She and everyone in her group were already tired. She knew deep down that the day was going to end badly.

Travis smiled and snapped his fingers. The prisoners turned and with their heads held low, they followed him down into the depths of the mine. The sound of dozens of people shuffling their feet filled the air.

Angela leaned over to Tarina and whispered, "Whatever you do today, don't stop for anything or anyone. If you do, you'll be whipped."

"Do they do this very often?" Tarina whispered back.

"About once a month they like to pit us against one another. The guards take bets as to which cell block will win. Last time we did this they whipped five people to death."

"Good God," uttered Wendy. "This prison is worse than hell."

"That it is," agreed Angela.

After the attempted assault on her body, Wendy had cut her hair as short as she could with a sharpened piece of glass that she had found on the ground under her bed. Once she was done, she hid the glass away just in case she needed it again.

It took them almost an hour of walking before they stepped inside a vast cavern dug out of the rock. At the far end was a train platform. Tarina saw that the train floated just above the tracks. Propelled along by magnetic levitation, she did not doubt that it could easily do five hundred or more kilometers an hour. Her heart sank when she observed that there were empty ore cars for as far as the eye could see.

Travis raised his hand and everyone stopped walking. "Look over to your right and you will see the wretched scum from Black-One."

Like everyone else, Tarina looked down the platform and saw an equally tired and ragged-looking group of people.

"The ore will be here in the next five minutes," explained Travis. "You will put it in the empty cars on the train until there is no more to load. It is that simple. Work hard and you will live. Fail me and your back will feel the end of a whip."

Tarina closed her eyes and said a quick prayer for herself and Wendy.

The rumbling sound of transports backing up was the signal that the macabre game was about to begin. The Chosen guards yelled at the prisoners the second the vehicles stopped and dumped their loads onto the platform. Whips cracked in the air as the warriors herded the two groups toward the piles of perlinium.

Tarina lifted a heavy rock and let out a grunt as she turned and shuffled to the nearest train car. She hurled the rock down inside and without hesitating, she made her way back to the ore and bent down to pick up another stone. Her back hurt already from the days of relentless digging for perlinium in the shafts dug throughout the mine. They had barely begun when a few people tripped over their feet and fell to the ground, only to be kicked or whipped by the sadistic guards.

Tarina bit her lip to stifle a cry. *It was going to be a long day*, she thought.

An hour into the demeaning competition, a man who had been in the prison for months dropped to his knees and hung his head down. Travis walked over and pushed the man to the ground with the heel of his boot. "Can't you get up, Sergeant? You're not so tough now, are you?"

The man lay on the ground, silent and unmoving.

With a snarl, Travis hauled off and kicked the man in the ribs. Even from where she was near the train, Tarina heard several bones break from the savage blow. "I said get up!" screamed Travis. His eyes lit up like fires in the pits of hell.

"Go to hell," replied the man as he struggled to get up on his knees.

A momentary look of hesitation flashed in Travis' eyes. Tarina saw the look and right away knew the man was nothing more than a bully and a coward. He wasn't used to people fighting back.

"Screw you, Sergeant." With that, Travis stepped back and pointed at the wounded man. Two Chosen guards unfurled their whips and before anyone could move, they took turns whipping the man until the flesh on his body was torn open and blood flowed like a river on the ground.

Tarina stood there helpless as the sergeant died right before her eyes. She turned her head away so she wouldn't have to look at the body.

"Oh no you don't, sister," said Travis as he strode toward Tarina. He put a calloused hand on her and yanked her head around. "Take a good look at him. That could be you. I could think of more pleasurable things to do to you, but don't think for on second that I won't have you killed for being lazy and insolent like Sergeant Lowe was."

Anger and hate burnt in Tarina's heart. She had never hated someone so much in her entire life. For a brief moment, she wished she could break free and kill her tormentor with her bare hands. Travis let go of her head and spat on the ground before pushing her back in line with the others.

"Work, damn you!" yelled Travis at the prisoners.

Angela was the first to move. She picked up a rock and started to walk to the train. One by one, the rest of the people followed her lead and got back to work.

Out of the corner of her eye, Tarina could see Travis standing there staring at her. The maniacal look in his eyes made her cringe. It was obvious that the man was insane. She lowered her head and focused all of her attention on her feet. If she was going to survive the day, it was going to be by putting all other thoughts out of her mind and acting like an automaton following in the steps of the person in front of her.

The march back to the quarters turned out to be just as horrible as the day's toil. Exhausted and weak with hunger, the prisoners shambled up the steady incline, dragging their feet on the rocks and the sand. Two people had been whipped to death by the guards during the hellish competition. One more, a woman with a bad leg, fell back from the group. No one stopped to help her. The only thought in all of their minds was getting to their cell block alive.

The sound of a whip striking flesh echoed up the long tunnel. Tarina pretended not to hear the pitiful cries of the woman as she was mercilessly flogged to death. She hated herself for not turning around to help the woman; it ran contrary to everything she believed in. However, she knew that there was nothing she could do. It was taking all of her willpower just to keep moving.

When their makeshift quarters came into view, the group began to move a little bit quicker as if there was safety to be found on their uncomfortable, wooden beds. Tarina collapsed down on her bunk, gasping for air. The hardest day of basic training had never even come close to the physical and mental anguish she had just gone through. She rolled over and looked over at Wendy in the next bed. Her friend's hands were shaking. She looked like she was on the edge of a nervous breakdown.

"Hey, there. A penny for your thoughts," said Tarina.

"I'd kill for a beer right now. It doesn't even have to be cold," Wendy replied.

Tarina chuckled. She hadn't been expecting that. "Me too. Or perhaps a strawberry margarita by the pool."

"Sounds delicious."

"You'll have to settle for water," said Angela as she sat down on the edge of Tarina's bed and handed over two cups of water.

"Thank you," said Tarina. She took the water and gulped it down in seconds, as did Wendy.

"I'll get you both some more."

Wendy sat up and looked over at Tarina. "How does she do it? She looks as if she barely broke a sweat today."

"I was just thinking the same thing as well. I've got to be honest. After they had killed the sergeant, I kept my head down until we got back here."

"Me too." Wendy took a quick look about for Angela and saw her standing in line to get more water. "Tarina, can I tell you something?"

"Sure," she replied, reaching out for her friend's hands.

"I know this is going to sound terrible, but I was happy when the other group began to fall behind and the guards paid more attention to them and not us. God, this place makes me feel and act like an awful person."

Tarina saw the sadness etched on Wendy's dirty face. "I'm not proud to admit that I felt the same way as you. We need to find a way out of here before we lose our humanity."

"How well did you know Angela at the academy? I don't seem to recall seeing her around."

"We did boot camp together. She was also in some of my third and fourth-year classes. If I remember right, she was as quiet as a mouse. She most assuredly was not like the person you see here today."

Angela returned and took a seat. All three women sat there quietly drinking their water. It was Tarina who spoke first. "Angela, don't take it the wrong way, but how have you managed to survive down here for so long? Wendy and I are near dead and you look as if nothing seems to bother you. What gives?"

"I was wondering when you were going to ask me that. When I arrived here, I was taken under the wing of a Chosen woman who had been here for months. You see, before the Kurgs turned this prison into a death camp for us, the inmates here used to be Chosen civilians who had committed heinous crimes. My guardian angel, for the lack of a better title, was a Kurgan woman. She had been imprisoned here for the rest of her natural life for killing her husband. According to her, he deserved it, but I could never tell if she was being honest with me or not."

"Are there any other Chosen prisoners still here?" asked Wendy.

Angela shook her head. "Those that did not die under the lash were moved to the ore processing plant out in the desert to finish serving their sentences. The last one left about a month ago. This wonderful little camp is now just for us human POWs."

Tarina asked, "What happened to this woman?"

"Travis killed her one night after he'd been drinking with the guards. The man is a psychopath. He feels nothing for the people he has killed. He used to be a lance corporal, now he lords over us as if he were a king."

"Yes. He's a monster all right."

"Before she died, she taught me how to act, how to survive in this hellhole. More than that, she showed me a way out of the mines."

Tarina's eyes widened. She moved close to Angela and lowered her voice. "Are you telling me that you know a way out?"

Angela nodded.

"Why haven't you tried to escape?" asked Wendy.

"Because until a short while ago, I didn't have the right people here with me to try an escape with. I'm not a pilot and I'm most definitely not a navigator. I'm a logistician. I need you two with your unique skill sets to get off this planet and back home."

Tarina glanced around to make sure that no one was paying any attention to them. "What are you proposing?"

"In a couple of days' time, when everyone is asleep, I'll take Tarina with me and show her the way out."

"Why not tonight?"

"I doubt that you could make the climb after what you've been through today. Besides, there's no need to hurry; the general in charge of the Kurgan penal system won't be here for another ten days. He comes at the end of every month for an inspection of the facilities. It's his ship that I propose we steal."

"What about me?" asked Wendy. "How come I have to remain behind?"

"I think it's better if we do this one at a time. We can't risk drawing the guards' attention."

"It makes sense," added Tarina. "Don't worry, we won't leave you behind."

Wendy pretended to pout. "You'd better not."

"Supper's here," announced Angela as the food cart arrived. With their muscles aching all over their bodies, Tarina and Wendy grimaced as they hauled themselves off their bunks and up onto their tired feet. As fast as they could, they made their way over to the food lineup.

There's a light at the end of the tunnel, thought Tarina. Still, something nagged at her subconscious telling her to be careful. She could hear her father's words in her head telling her that if something appeared too good to be true, then perhaps it was.

13

"Officer on deck," belted out a young sergeant as Sheridan and Cole walked into the room. The ten Marines with him came to attention.

"There's no need for that. At least not while I'm leading this mission," said Sheridan. "Everyone, please take a seat so we can proceed with the introduction." He looked at the faces of the men and women who had volunteered to come with him to Klatt. Aside from the fire effects and the aerospace control officer, all of the enlisted Marines looked barely out of their teens.

"All right, my name is Captain Michael Sheridan and the man to my right is Master Sergeant Alan Cole. I'll learn your names over the next couple of days. So when you talk, please state your name and hopefully it'll sink into my thick skull. What I need to know right now is if you people were told the purpose of the mission that you've all volunteered for."

The fire effects officer, a young female first lieutenant, stood up. "Sir, my name is First Lieutenant Helen Toscano. I can't speak for anyone else, but I was told by my commanding officer that this is a deep reconnaissance mission. I missed the fight on Illum Prime and jumped at the opportunity to do something other than sit around and wait for the war to come to us."

"I was told the same thing," said the sergeant. "Oh, sorry, I almost forgot. My name is Sergeant Patrick Urban."

"How many of you have seen combat?" Cole asked.

Only four of the ten Marines raised a hand.

Cole looked over at Sheridan and shook his head. "I thought the total would be higher."

Sheridan pointed to an open door. "Marines, before I tell you what the true nature of this mission is, I'm going to give each and every one of you the opportunity to leave this room. No one will fault you if you leave now."

None of them moved an inch.

Cole walked over and closed the door so no one could eavesdrop on the conversation.

Sheridan grabbed a chair and took a seat. "Okay then, welcome to Operation Trident Fury. Our part in this mission will be to fly ahead of a fleet task force to scout out a POW camp deep in Kurgan space on a planet called Klatt."

"Sir, Second Lieutenant Viktor Skylar, did you say that we're going inside Kurgan territory?" asked the aerospace control officer.

"Yes, I did. After chatting with Captain Killam, the fleet's operations officer, we should expect to be on our own for approximately forty-eight hours. In that time, we must recce the prison and determine suitable landing sites for the ground forces who will be coming to secure and then evacuate over five thousand people."

"Good Lord, has anyone ever tried anything like this before?" asked Sergeant Urban.

"Yeah, but not in our lifetime. It's an ambitious and highly risky operation that could easily end in disaster. I don't know about any of you, but Master Sergeant Cole and I know people who are prisoners of the Kurgans, and we're going to do all we can to get them home alive."

Urban said, "Sir, I honestly don't know if any of my friends are on that planet. But you can count on me."

"You can count on all of us," stressed Toscano.

Urban raised a hand. "Sir, what is our call sign for the mission?"

"Ghost One."

Urban grinned. "I like the sound of that."

"So do I," added Toscano.

"Okay then, consider yourselves confined to this ship until we leave," said Sheridan. "As this mission is deemed to be top secret, you will avoid talking to anyone about why you are here on board the *Colossus*. In fact, you will not discuss this assignment outside of this room, even with each other. Do I make myself clear?"

"Yes, sir," replied the Marines as one.

"While Master Sergeant Cole checks your gear and sees what you might need, I'm going to speak to our flight crew." With that, Sheridan exited the room and made his way to the landing bay where Admiral Sheridan's private shuttlecraft was housed. He found the crew tinkering with the engine modifications that had been installed only hours ago. The flight crew consisted of only two men. Captain Parata, the pilot, was a short, muscle-bound Maori, who had recently grown a thick, black goatee. His co-pilot and navigator was Captain Mercier, who had a thin face and gold-rimmed glasses perched on his nose.

"Ah, there you are," said Parata when he spotted Sheridan. "You've got to tell whoever is running this farce that we need the mechanics back here right away."

"Why's that?"

"The mods they made to the jump engine aren't going to be enough. We can get to Klatt, but we won't have enough fuel left in the perlinium rods to make another jump back to the fleet once we drop you and your team off."

Sheridan looked at the pilot with a stone-faced visage.

"Oh, crap! You knew that, didn't you. So, when were you going to tell us?"

"I only found out myself this morning. The problem is that your ship's engine is just too small to make any more modifications to it. I'm sorry, but you're both going to have to come along for the ride. We'll only be on our own for a couple of days. After that the fleet will arrive and we can all go home together."

Parata looked over at Mercier, his co-pilot and friend. "Aren't you going to say anything?"

"No. If this is the way it must be, then so be it."

"Great. I'm glad you can roll over and accept your fate without batting an eye. But I won't. Is there anyone we can talk to about this?"

"Yes, me," replied Sheridan.

"Okay then, Captain Sheridan, son of Admiral Sheridan, I hereby lodge a verbal complaint against the assignment that we have been given."

"And I acknowledge your complaint and plan to do nothing about it."

"Well, that settles that. I'm done bitching. I just wanted to get that off my chest. I take it Sergeant Cole will be visiting the quartermaster to procure us the necessary weapons, supplies, and equipment?"

"Yes, he will. I expect that he'll swing by sometime this afternoon to get you two to sign for the equipment."

"I take it that you'd like to do some practice runs somewhere out of sight on Illum Prime before we deploy?" asked Mercier.

"Yes, I do. Can you be ready to go first thing tomorrow morning?"

Mercier nodded.

"Good. I'll see you both at eight o'clock sharp to begin training. If there's nothing else we need to discuss, I'll leave you two to get on with your work." Sheridan turned and left the hangar. He knew that Parata was just pushing his buttons to see if he could get a rise out of him. Parata could be a pain in the ass when he wanted to be, but he was also the best pilot in the Sixth Fleet. Sheridan felt himself lucky to have Parata and Mercier along as part of the team. It was one less thing, among dozens of others floating around in his mind, to worry about.

Light-years away, halfway to the prison planet, Colonel Wright gently applied power to his ship's thrusters and flew his craft out of the open hangar doors into space. For as far as he could see, an asteroid field composed of tens of millions of rocks and boulders, some as tiny as a pebble and some kilometers in width, filled the heavens. The transport ship had come out of her jump behind a small moon and was using it to hide behind. They waited an hour to make sure that they had not been spotted before launching the two deep reconnaissance vessels.

Wright looked down at his instrument panel and made sure that everything was working as it should. "Okay, Miss Eskola, how are things back there?"

"Sir, my nav computer is fully operational. I can confirm that my calculations are correct and we are ready to make our jump."

"Sounds good." Wright looked out the glass window in his cockpit at the other ship about to make the jump. He saw the pilot wave over that he was also good to go. As they were in enemy space, both ships were operating on comms silence.

"I'm ready when you are, sir," said Eskola.

Wright took one last look up at their support ship. He had made dozens of combat jumps since the war had begun. Yet none of them had seemed as important as the one he was about to make. He reached over and set a hand on a picture of his girlfriend back home on Earth. It was a good luck ritual that he had done on every mission. It hadn't always worked perfectly, but he figured the odds were still on his side. He knew that while they were gone their support ship would be deploying another satellite to act as a relay station for the information that would be streaming back from Klatt once the two satellites there went operational. Wright keyed his mic. "Okay, Miss Eskola, we're in your hands now."

"Roger that, sir." She began her countdown. "Five-four-three-two-one."

Impenetrable darkness engulfed the two ships the moment they jumped beyond the speed of light and began their twenty-four-hour flight to Klatt.

Crap, thought Wright as his bladder reminded him that he shouldn't have had three cups of coffee before climbing into his cockpit. He tried to get comfortable in his seat. The only consolation he could think of was that he hadn't forgotten to put on his diaper. He shook his head. It was going to be a long couple of days.

14

Sheridan and Cole grabbed some food before making their way to the back of the dining room. They took a seat at a table far away from anyone else so they could talk.

"Anything new from Captain Killam?" Cole asked.

Sheridan shook his head. "Not since the last mission brief this morning. Looks like the task force will be built of a slimmed down carrier battle group with a couple of battalions of Marines to act as security and to help evacuate the POWs as fast as humanly possible. The longer we spend in Kurgan space, the greater the chance of them counterattacking."

"What do you think of the people we were given?"

"They're eager enough. Like my father said, we go with what we have, or they would have sent a Special Forces team to do this assignment."

Cole scrunched up his face. "Special Forces . . . bah! Just more prancing prima donnas like the parade ground soldiers in the First Div. I'd rather go with what we have than be forced to rely on people living off a reputation earned a century ago."

Sheridan set his knife and fork down. "I take it by that little tirade that you don't like them."

"Sir, a few years back we had some working with us during an armed stand-off with some disgruntled miners on a mining colony, and they only made things worse. Rather than just simply wait the miners out, they launched a raid, unbeknown to the rest of us, to capture the leader of the rebels. It was a complete and utter disaster. When their extraction transport developed engine problems, we had to go in and rescue a team of special operators trapped in a building that was surrounded by a couple hundred of really pissed off miners. When the dust settled that night, we had lost six men, and the miners considerably more. It left a sour taste in my mouth that has never gone away."

"Perhaps they've changed. I'm sure they had to answer to the chain of command for what went wrong."

Cole chuckled. "You can put lipstick on a pig, but when all it is said and done, you're still left with a pig. Sorry, sir, but I don't trust them and never will."

"Good to know," said Sheridan, wishing he had never mentioned them at all.

A female voice announced over the ship's intercom, "Captain Sheridan, Master Sergeant Cole, please report to the briefing room immediately."

Sheridan glanced down at his watch. They weren't scheduled to meet with anyone. "I wonder what that's all about?"

"I dunno," replied Cole standing up. "I suspect that the good Captain Killam wants to talk to us about something."

"This isn't fair. I didn't get to eat my spaghetti. It's my favorite."

"Duty calls. You can always grab a bite to eat later if you're still hungry."

A couple of minutes later, they walked into the briefing room. Sheridan saw right away that the people there had not taken a moment's rest since they began planning the operation. Half-drunk cups of coffee and junk food wrappers were everywhere. Captain Killam had a couple days' growth on his face and looked as if he could sleep for a week. By his side was Lieutenant Colonel Kimura. They appeared to be deep in discussion.

"Sir, you wanted to see us?" said Sheridan to Killam.

"Ah, good, you're here. That didn't take long."

"We were in the mess hall."

Killam placed a hand on Sheridan's arm. "Let's all find a quiet corner so I can tell you what's up." They moved to the back of the crowded room. Killam looked over and asked a couple of people standing nearby to take a five-minute break.

Sheridan could see that something was on the operation officer's mind.

"Captain, if I were to ask you, how soon can you depart?" asked Killam.

Sheridan looked over at Cole. "No more than a couple of hours. I think we're just waiting on a few things from the quartermaster."

"Like what?" queried Kimura.

"The night vision gear we received was damaged, and I still want an armorer to check the new arrivals' weapons before we depart. I wouldn't want them to fail in the middle of a firefight," explained Cole.

"Not a problem. I'll have the equipment you need flown over to the *Colossus* within the hour, along with an armorer."

"Thanks, sir."

"Captain Killam, I take it that you want us to go early?" said Sheridan.

Killam nodded.

Kimura explained the situation. "Gents, Colonel White, the ground assault force commander for the mission, is concerned that forty-eight hours on the ground won't be enough. He's asked that you go as soon as possible."

Sheridan looked down at his watch. "If everything runs smoothly, I think we can leave three hours from now."

Kimura looked relieved. "That's excellent news. I'll pass that along to Colonel White. I know he'll be happy to hear that."

Sheridan said to Killam, "Sir, the original plan was for the shuttle to be carried on board another ship with the rest of the task force to the halfway point. Once there, we were to fly the rest of the way there on our own. We can't possibly make it to Klatt from here on our own power."

"The plan's changed. A modified transport ship will be here soon enough to take your shuttle into Kurgan space. You'll be using the same route as Colonel Wright and his team. By the time you reach the asteroid field, you should be receiving feed from the satellites currently being positioned in orbit by Wright. Hopefully, it'll help you choose your landing site on Klatt."

"Once you're there, you can relay information back to the fleet via the satellites," explained Kimura.

"I guess we had best get our butts in gear if we're to shove off in a few hours," said Cole.

Sheridan asked, "Gents, do either of you have anything else for us?"

"No, except to say good luck," replied Killam offering his hand.

"Thanks, sir," said Sheridan, shaking Killam's hand.

In the hallway, Cole looked over at his friend and shook his head. "Sir, I didn't want to say anything in front of the two senior officers, but changing the plan on the fly, as complicated as this one is, is a good way for things to cock up. We haven't had the time to see what our people can do under stress. This is unlike anything we have ever done before. A couple more days would have been ideal."

"I agree but what can we do? If I were in Colonel White's shoes, I'd also be screaming for intelligence on the enemy dispositions."

"Oh well, 'once more unto the breach.' I guess I'll go round up the rest of the Marines while you track down the flight crew. Knowing those two, they'll be in the officer's mess already."

"God, I hope they haven't started drinking. We need them sober and fully alert."

"I guess you had best find out."

The last thing Sheridan needed right now was a couple of drunks. If they were in the mess, there was going to be hell to pay.

15

"Get out of bed and form up in two ranks out here," hollered Travis as he flicked on the lights in the cavern.

Tarina groaned, rolled over, and sat up. The bright lights bothered her. She reached up and rubbed the sleep from her eyes.

"Don't make me angry," added Travis to make the prisoners move faster.

After slipping her clogs on her feet, Tarina joined the rest of the prisoners as they shuffled over and formed up in front of Travis. She had no idea what time it was, but her tired and aching body told her that she hadn't slept enough to recover from yesterday's work.

"What's up?" whispered Wendy.

Tarina shook her head. She was as mystified as her friend as to what was going on.

"Now stand up straight as if you maggots were on parade," ordered Travis.

Tarina and everyone else tried their best to comply. Most were just too exhausted and hurt to raise their heads up.

Out of the corner of her eye, Tarina spotted a Kurgan officer walk out of the dark and move over beside Travis. The Kurgan had tattoos on one side of his face. She grew curious, having never seen any markings whatsoever on a Kurgan's face before.

"Now don't any of you move while Colonel Kuhr inspects you," barked Travis. Slowly, the colonel and Travis walked down the rows of prisoners checking each one individually.

When the colonel came to Tarina, he stopped and looked down at her. She felt her skin crawl as he lowered his head to look into her eyes. He said something to Travis that she did not understand.

"She's an officer and a pilot," said Travis to the Kurgan.

Tarina's heart skipped a beat when the colonel reached down and squeezed her arm tightly.

The Kurgan again spoke to Travis. "Yes, sir, she's a hard worker," he replied. "She and a bunch of the prisoners haven't been here that long. They're still healthy and fit. Shall I write her name in the book?"

Colonel Kuhr studied Tarina's face for a few seconds before nodding. Travis dug out a small book and wrote Tarina's name inside of it.

She had no idea what had just happened and was not sure that she wanted to know either. For several minutes, the colonel went up and down the two ranks of tired prisoners. More names were added to the growing list. Wendy's name, however, was not written down. Tarina overheard Travis saying that Kuhr found human redheads abnormal and wanted nothing to do with Wendy. Finally, the inspection was over, leaving the prisoners of Black-Three with more questions than answers.

"All right, you can go back to your beds and get another hour's sleep if you want," said Travis to the group. "Those of you whose name I wrote down in my book had best take special care and not injure themselves in any way over the next few days. If you do, you'll have to answer to the colonel."

"Master Travis, could you tell us what that was all about?" asked Angela. She had her head bowed so their jailer would not take offense.

"Let's just say that the ten of you whose names I wrote down will be going on a little trip soon and none of you will be coming back." With that, he put his book away and laughed to himself as he walked off into the dark.

"I saw him put your name in his book," Wendy said to Tarina. "Something bad is about to happen, I can feel it."

"So can I," replied Tarina.

"Has this kind of thing ever happened before?" Wendy asked Angela.

She shook her head, "No, and I've never seen a Kurgan with half of his face covered in tattoos before, either."

Tarina asked, "What the hell is going on?"

"I wish I knew. All I do know is that we can't afford to waste any more time. I'll show you the way out tonight and Wendy tomorrow. Three nights from now, we'll make our escape and hope that the ship we need is there. If not, all my planning will be for nothing."

"Better to die on our feet trying to escape than to wait to die down here."

"Amen to that," added Wendy.

"Okay then, it begins tonight," said Angela with a gleam of hope in her eyes.

High above, two ships suddenly appeared on either side the planet.

Klatt, the desert world, loomed large beneath Wright's vessel. "Any Kurgan military ships or satellites in our local area?" he asked Eskola.

"None," she replied. "There is not a single electronic signature in a one hundred thousand kilometer radius. We are free to deploy the payload."

Wright reached over and flipped a switch on his control panel. Their satellite detached and began to float free in space. Guided by its thrusters, the spy satellite moved into orbit right above the prison.

"Sir, I'm getting a good signal from the satellite," reported Eskola.

"Excellent."

"Sir, my return flight calculations have been inputted into the navigational computer."

That was all Wright needed to hear. He said into his helmet mic, "Begin the countdown."

"Roger that, sir. Jumping in five-four-three-two-one."

Again a cold, dark bubble surrounded their ship as they began the long flight back to the asteroid belt.

Wright checked the time. It had taken them less than thirty seconds to deploy their satellite. He doubted that their presence above the planet had been detected by any of the orbiting enemy satellites. The only thing that he had no control over was the other team. He would have to wait until they reached their transport ship in twenty-four hours' time to know if they had succeeded in their mission. He sat back in his seat and took a deep breath. If he thought that the flight in was boring, now that the excitement was over, the next day was going to be the longest and most tedious day of his life.

16

The flight to the drop off point near the asteroid belt had gone by far too fast for Sheridan's liking. He had barely had a chance to acquaint himself with the other members of the reconnaissance team.

Up front, the shuttle flight crew were fast asleep in their chairs so they could be ready at the drop of a hat to jump into Klatt's atmosphere. It was planned to land the team in walking distance of the prison. Sheridan hadn't found them in the officers' mess back on the *Colossus*, in fact, they had been going over the updates to their ship for the third time with an exasperated-looking technician.

Master Sergeant Cole had taken Sergeant Urban and the five other close protection Marines off to a quiet part of the transport's cluttered hangar and ran them through instinctive shooting drills with a floating target drone. They were keen and focused. It didn't take them long until they could react without hesitation. Once he was satisfied, Cole took a couple of hours and inspected everyone's weapons and equipment to make sure that it was all working as it should be. There wouldn't be any quartermaster stores where they were going. If something failed in battle, it could cost the life of one or more of the team, and Cole was not about to let that happen.

Sheridan left the two officers to get to know their communicators. Normally, the officers would carry their own communicators and speak directly with the asset they were controlling. However, as Sheridan had learned the hard way several times, comms is life. If you cannot call for fire or help, then you risked being overrun and killed. The Marines carrying the secondary radios were backup in case the first comms devices failed, which they had a bad habit of doing the instant you met the enemy in combat.

A metallic-sounding voice came over the ship's PA system. "Captain Sheridan, to the bridge, please. Captain Sheridan, please report."

Sheridan had to chuckle; the ship from bow to the stern was only one hundred meters long. It was a glorified engine with a small hangar bay to move goods around in. The bridge was in the next room. He pressed a button on the wall and stepped inside the cramped room. There were three people operating the ship's controls. Everyone had two jobs. The captain was also the pilot. The co-pilot was also the navigator, and the last person there was the engineer and comms specialist.

"What's up, Master Chief," asked Sheridan.

A man with thinning blonde hair looked over. "Sir, we're going to be at the drop point in just over one hour. We're receiving feed from only one of the satellites above Klatt."

"Well, one is better than none," replied Sheridan philosophically.

"Sir, it gets worse. The signal keeps coming and going. There could be any number of things to explain that, from faulty equipment to sun spots to enemy jamming. I've had the live feed forwarded to your shuttle's computers to help you plan your jump."

"Thanks."

"Sir, if I were you, I'd plan my jump now. My gut tells me that we're going to lose both satellites before too long."

"I'd rather you were wrong, but I've also learned to trust my gut as well. Thanks, Master Chief. I'll get my people up and working on the jump calculations right away." He turned and left the bridge, making his way to the shuttle to wake up Parata and Mercier. While they shook themselves awake and got to work, Sheridan opened up a computer console and studied the images sent back of the prison. The only things visible on the surface was a processing plant over three hundred kilometers from the prison and a small landing site near a cluster of buildings at the mine's entrance. He wanted to find them a place to land that afforded them cover and was not too far from the prison. A couple of minutes later, he chose a spot in a canyon fifteen kilometers from the mine. To go any closer was to risk being detected by the prison's scanning devices, he reasoned.

"Here, I want to come out of our jump right above this spot," said Sheridan to Mercier.

Mercier leaned over and took down the coordinates.

"Can you do it?" asked Sheridan.

Mercier shrugged. "I've never plotted a jump this far in my life. Ask me when we get there."

17

I'm being smothered, thought Tarina as she fought to take a deep breath. She opened her eyes and tried to sit up but found that she was being held down. In the near pitch-black room, she began to panic and reached for the arm pinning her to her bed.

"Ssshhh," said someone in the dark.

Tarina instantly recognized Angela's voice. She relaxed and turned her head to see her friend kneeling beside her bunk.

Angela removed her hand from Tarina's mouth. "Come on, the guards have gone to get a bite to eat. They won't be back for nearly an hour."

"How do you know?"

"I've been watching and studying them for months. Trust me, they're creatures of habit. Today is Tuesday, and the late shift always sneaks off around this time for a bowl of soup and a drink or two."

Tarina swung her legs down, slipped on her clogs, and followed Angela to the entrance of the cavern. They paused for a moment to make sure that there wasn't anyone still lingering around in the tunnel before making their way down the corridor to a boarded up shaft. Angela got down on all fours and pulled the bottom three wooden boards free. She turned and waved for Tarina to follow her as she disappeared into the opening. With her heart racing, Tarina hurried to join her accomplice. The inside of the air shaft was dark and foreboding.

"Take this," said Angela, handing Tarina a small flashlight. When she turned it on, she saw that it had a red filter on it, making it hard for anyone to spot them.

"This is an air shaft. It used to be open when I first arrived," explained Angela. "They closed it and opened another one farther down the mine. It took me forever to loosen the bottom boards so I could easily sneak in here."

"Where does it lead?"

"It comes out on a rocky ledge that overlooks the administration buildings and more importantly, the mine's landing strip."

Tarina looked up but could only see darkness. "How long of a climb is it?"

"It takes about ten minutes. Just stay close behind me and climb where I climb and you'll be okay."

Tarina nodded and began to climb up the wooden rungs. She might as well have been blindfolded as she could barely see more than a meter in front of her. Dirt and dust trickled down into Tarina's eyes from above as Angela led the way up. She stopped for a couple of seconds to rub the dirt from her eyes before continuing the climb. Less than a month ago, she could have made the ascent without breaking a sweat. Now, however, after the abuses her body had taken, she had to force herself to keep going. It actually took twice the time Angela had said it would to make it to the top of the shaft.

Angela reached down and helped her friend climb the last few rungs before letting her catch her breath. "We don't have a lot of time to waste up here. We still have to climb down and make it back to our bunks before the guards get back."

Tarina took a deep breath and nodded.

Angela turned off her flashlight, reached above her head, and pushed the top cover aside. Light from outside flooded inside. She tapped Tarina on the head and whispered, "Stand up."

Tarina stood. The fresh night air felt warm and refreshing. It reminded her of having a shower with Michael after having made love.

"Look over there," Angela said, pointing toward a brightly lit landing port. "That's where the Inspector General will land. Unless they've changed how they do business, the shuttle will be moved to a bunker dug into the side of the mountain. His inspections usually last two to three days. We'll steal it on the first night he's here and make our run for it."

"How do we get there from here?"

"There's an old path that leads down to the far side of the landing strip. From there we can use a dry riverbed to mask our movement to the shuttle. I'm sure that we can make it the whole way there without being seen."

Tarina raised an eyebrow. "How can you be sure that it is an unobserved approach?"

"Because the guard towers are all facing the mine's entrance. They don't expect anyone to be moving around behind them. Their arrogance is their weakness."

Tarina couldn't fault her logic. "Do you have any homemade weapons? I doubt that they'll let us simply walk onto a Kurgan shuttlecraft and hijack it without trying to stop us."

"Watch your head," said Angela as she bent down and pulled the cover back over the shaft.

Tarina got below and switched her light back on. She was surprised to see the small stash of supplies and equipment that Angela had acquired. There was a set of NVGs, a couple bottles of water, a few rations packs, and most surprisingly, a Kurgan pistol with a full clip. Her father's voice echoed in her mind . . .

'if it looks too good to be true, then it's too good to be true.'
"Angela, how did you get all this stuff?"

"We can talk about that later. We have to get going or we're going to get caught."

"No, now!" said Tarina, grabbing Angela's arm.

"I did things I'm not proud of. There, are you happy now?"

The bitterness in her voice told Tarina that she had asked the right question, just the wrong way. "I'm sorry, Angela, but I had to know."

"Can we go now?"

"Yes, of course. Lead on."

Tarina felt sorry for making Angela confess her sins, but with her and Wendy's lives on the line, she wanted the truth no matter how unpleasant it may be to learn or admit. At the bottom, Angela made sure the way was clear before sliding out into the tunnel, closely followed by Tarina. They moved like a pair of cats hugging the shadows for cover all the way back to their cavern.

"Thanks for trusting in Wendy and me," whispered Tarina, trying to make up for her earlier remarks.

"Who says I trust you? You're a means to an end. I need you and you need me; that's all there is to this arrangement. Don't confuse what has happened between us with friendship." Angela turned her back on Tarina and made her way to her bunk.

Tarina shook her head and climbed into her bed. She kicked off her clogs, pulled up her blanket to the shoulders, and tried to make herself as comfortable as she could. Something nagged her tired mind. She couldn't put her finger on it, but she knew she would eventually, just not tonight. In a matter of hours, they would be woken up for another day's toil in the mines. Within seconds, fatigue washed over her and she was fast asleep.

18

With a loud crash, Colonel Wright flung his helmet to the hangar bay floor, cracking open the glass faceplate. "Just what the hell are you telling me?" He could barely hold back his brewing temper.

"Sir, things aren't working as they should. One of your satellites only lasted one hour and three minutes before failing," explained a red-faced technician. "The other cuts in and out. I'm sorry; I don't understand what could have gone wrong. Both of the satellites were tested and double-checked before being loaded onto your ships."

Wright ground his teeth as he looked over at the other flight crew as they got down from their vessel. Forty-eight wasted hours flashed through his mind.

"Sir, these things happen from time to time when new technology is rushed into operation without sufficient testing," said a senior technician.

Wright yelled. He lashed out with his right foot sending an empty container flying against the wall.

"Colonel, something is better than nothing," Eskola said, trying to get her boss to calm down. "Perhaps it's a small glitch that the computer techs can fix from here?"

Wright clenched his fists. He knew it wasn't the technicians' fault. He took a couple of deep breaths to calm himself down. He looked over at the senior tech. "Petty Officer, do you have any more satellites onboard?"

The man shook his head. "No, sir. There was insufficient time before we left to acquire a spare."

"This is a bloody nightmare. Can we get two more satellites brought to us? Surely there are more back with the fleet."

"That's not going to happen, sir," said Lieutenant DeCarlo, the ship's captain, as she joined the conversation.

Wright turned and saw the slender young officer standing there holding his shattered helmet in her hand. "Why can't we, Lieutenant? We're already in Kurgan space. It wouldn't be too difficult for anther transport to bring us two new satellites."

DeCarlo handed Wright his helmet. "Sir, while you were gone, a couple of things came up that changed everything."

"Like?"

"First off, we have detected a Kurgan listening station barely ten light-years from us. As we are running under strict comms silence, I don't think they have detected us. However, the longer we spend in Kurgan space, the greater the possibility that they will find us and vector fighters to our location."

"And the second thing?"

"The only other transport ship configured like mine in the Sixth Fleet for a deep space jump has just appeared off our port bow. It looks like they are preparing to launch a vessel. If I did not know any better, I would suspect that a ground reconnaissance team will be heading for Klatt in the next five minutes."

Wright shook his head. "Jesus, if the other satellite craps out while they are in flight, they'll have nothing to help guide them in when they arrive over the planet."

"That is a distinct possibility, sir. Now if you'll excuse me, I need to ensure that everything is as it should be on the bridge. I suggest that you and your people make themselves as comfortable as possible as we will be jumping back to the fleet as soon as my executive officer's calculations are verified by the navigational computer. It's going to take us the better part of a day flying at maximum speed to reach the nearest friendly vessels." DeCarlo saluted Wright, turned, and left the hangar.

"This is how disasters begin," said Wright. "The entire mission hinges on those satellites; without them, anyone heading to Klatt will be flying in blind."

Eskola said, "Sir, I suggest that we both climb out of our survival suits. I don't know about you, but I smell awful. After a shower, we can grab something to eat and try to brainstorm the problem. There may be an easy fix that we can't see right now."

Wright nodded. He turned and handed off his helmet to one of this ship's technicians. Another issue was already being played out in his mind. As far as he knew, the Kurgan listening station had never factored into any of Captain Killam's planning. It was one thing for small transport ships to hide among the clutter of an asteroid field—a task force was another. If his mission to deploy the satellites over Klatt had not worked out as planned, perhaps he could do something about the Kurgan post to help the fleet. In seconds, Wright's mind started to process the new problem and come up with a surefire way to overcome it. Time was not on his side. Separated from his staff, he would have to come up with a solution all by himself. Tired or not, he relished the chance to pay back the Kurgans for all the suffering they had put his people through.

19

"Okay, we're going to come out of our jump in the next five minutes," said Parata to Sheridan. "The feed coming from the only working satellite in orbit has crapped out again. We know where you want to land, but without the live feed from the satellites there are no guarantees that we can put you down precisely where you want to go."

"What's the margin of error?" asked Sheridan.

"Give or take five hundred meters."

"That doesn't sound so bad. What's the problem?"

"Michael, your landing site is at the bottom of a canyon. Right now, there is a sandstorm covering the land for hundreds of kilometers around the mine. I've never seen one like it. It's a monster of a storm. It reaches up almost five kilometers into the sky. I'd hate to come out of the jump and fly into the side of a mountain or crash into a canyon wall. What I'm getting at is that you have two choices. You can change your landing site or carry on as planned. I'm only the pilot. It's your mission and your call. So what will it be?"

Sheridan looked over his shoulder at his friend. "Master Sergeant, your thoughts?"

"Go for it," replied Cole. There was a fierce look of determination in his eyes. "Sir, a lot of people are counting on us. We don't have the time to abort the jump and wait out the storm."

Sheridan thought exactly the same way; he just needed to hear it from Cole. He looked back at Parata. "If anyone can land us safely in the middle of a storm, with or without satellite guidance, it's you. Carry on, Captain."

"Okay then. Strap yourselves in. It's going to be one hell of a bumpy ride," said Parata as he reached behind his shoulder, pulling down his harness to buckle himself in.

Sheridan and Cole headed back to the shuttle's crew compartment.

"Hurry up and stow your gear; we're about to fly through the belly of a dragon," said Cole to the other Marines who rushed to lock away all of their loose equipment.

Sheridan sat down and hurried to secure his six-piece harness before their ship came out of its jump inside Klatt's atmosphere. He put a headset on so he could hear what was happening in the cockpit. With one last quick check of his watch, he saw that they had less than thirty seconds before he found out if he had made the right decision or not. Sheridan took a couple of seconds to look around the cabin at his teammates' faces. Some were scared, some tense, while a pair of the younger Marines seemed excited. The butterflies in his stomach told him that he was not made of stone. It was okay to be worried. He knew that the day he no longer feared death was the day he would start to make bad decisions. He reached into a pocket, grabbed his mouth guard, and popped it in just as the shuttlecraft ended its long jump.

The light in the back of the shuttle turned from white to red. Automatically, the artificial gravity switched off and the body harnesses tightened to keep everyone in place.

"Hang on!" hollered Cole as Klatt's gravity took a hold of the shuttlecraft and pulled it toward its surface. The sudden jolt shook loose anything not properly stowed away. An assault rifle flew from its rack and smashed into the face of one of the Marines, breaking his nose. Blood streamed down the stunned man's face. Until the pilots managed to get the vessels' sublight engines running, the ship fell like a rock.

A second later, the lights flashed on and off in the back of the shuttle. In his headset, Sheridan heard Parata swear. He had to fight the urge to ask what was going on while the two men up front struggled to keep their craft from crashing into the ground. The last thing they needed was a passenger asking a lot of annoying questions.

Without warning, the ship banked over hard to the right. Sheridan groaned as he felt the gravity pull against his body. Again the lights flickered. It was obvious that something was wrong.

"Jesus, sir. What the hell is going on?" yelled out Cole.

Sheridan shook his head just before the shuttle righted itself and then turned over on its left side. The lights went out, plummeting the back of the shuttle into darkness. A woman's voice cried out in fear. Sheridan couldn't take it anymore. He reached up and pressed his headset mic. "What's going on up there? We're being tossed around like ragdolls back here."

"We've lost the starboard engine and most of the avionics," replied Parata, his voice tense. "They failed the second we came out of our jump. Without the guidance and terrain awareness warning systems, we're well and truly flying blind in this storm. We can't see more than a few meters in front of the ship."

Sheridan bit his lip. "Can you climb out of the storm?"

The ship began to shake up and down as if being buffeted in the back of a bucking bronco.

"No! We don't have enough power left in the one engine still running. Hell, we'll be lucky if it doesn't seize up before we land."

"Okay, do what you can." Right away, Sheridan regretted his choice of words. Of course, they were already doing their best.

"Well?" said Cole, yelling to be heard over the turbulence.

"We may have made the wrong call on this one. We're flying blind."

"Bloody hell," said Cole.

For close to thirty seconds, the shuttle rocked so hard that Sheridan thought it was going to fly apart. When it seemed to find a pocket of calm air, the craft righted itself and stopped shaking. Sheridan allowed himself a moment to relax.

In the cockpit, the pilots never saw the jagged peak of a rocky hill obscured by the swirling sand until it was too late. With a loud crash of metal tearing apart, the portside wing of the shuttle was torn right off. In the blink of an eye, the craft began to plummet to the ground. It had fallen less than two hundred meters when the shuttle hit another rocky outcropping, tearing open a large jagged gash in the side. In the back, dust and sand rushed inside.

In the pitch-blackness, Sheridan heard voices calling out in fear and pain. His hands gripped his harness as tight as he could. His heart jackhammered away in his chest. He closed his eyes and prayed that their ordeal would soon end.

Seconds later, with a crunch of buckling metal, the nose of the shuttle hit the hard ground sending the vessel cartwheeling through the air. It went end over end three times before coming to a halt against a tall stone spire. The sudden stop threw Sheridan's head flying back onto the headrest of his seat, knocking him out.

The haze in his mind slowly began to fade. For a few seconds, all Sheridan could hear in his ears was the pounding of his own heart. Gradually, it was replaced by the wailing sound of the wind rushing inside the stricken craft. Right away he knew that something wasn't right. His chest felt as if it were being crushed. He opened his eyes, reached into a pocket, and pulled out a small flashlight. He turned it on and saw that he was hanging upside down. The shuttle had come to rest on its roof. The crew compartment was a mess of broken seats and twisted metal. A quick glance told him that he had lost at least three of his team. Their bloodied and broken bodies were strewn in the wreckage.

"Here, let me help you down," said Cole.

Sheridan swung his light over and saw his friend standing there with a deep gash on his forehead. His face was covered with dust and blood. "You okay?" Sheridan asked.

"Yeah. This is nothing. Looks worse than it is."

Sheridan unbuckled his harness and fell down into Cole's arms. He placed his feet down and felt something soft under his boots.

"Don't look down," warned Cole. "Half of Mister Skylar is at your feet. The other half is still strapped into his seat."

"How long was I out?"

"I dunno. Four, maybe five minutes."

Sheridan shone his flashlight around. "Did Miss Toscano make it?"

"I don't know. I haven't had a chance to take a good look around."

"I'm over here," called out Toscano.

"Where?" said Sheridan, trying to see where the voice was coming from.

"I'm still in my chair. I think I'm trapped under the weapons rack. I can see your flashlight beam."

Cole and Sheridan carefully made their way to where the weapons had been stored.

"You're right next to me," said Toscano. "I can see your boots."

Sheridan bent down and shone his light under the long metal rack. He smiled when he saw First Lieutenant Toscano wave back at him. "Hold on, we'll get you out of there."

"Let me help," said Sergeant Urban as he bent down with Cole and lifted the metal frame up. Sheridan reached over, unbuckled Toscano's harness before grabbing a hold of her closest arm and pulling her free.

"Thanks," said Toscano as she brushed the sand from her face.

"Are you hurt?" asked Sheridan.

"No, sir. Apart from a few bruises and being scared out of my mind, I think I'm okay."

"Good. Now grab a light and search the wreckage for your Marine comms specialist."

Toscano nodded, dug out her light, and turned around to see if the young private was still in his chair.

"Okay, I'm going to check on the pilots," announced Sheridan. "Master Sergeant Cole will see to whoever is still alive back here while Sergeant Urban checks outside the shuttle for survivors. Make sure that you don't wander too far. If you do, you'll get lost in this storm and become another fatality."

Urban nodded his understanding.

Sheridan moved as best he could through the debris as he made his way to the cockpit. He found walking on the roof was a disorienting experience. Luckily, the door to the cabin was still open. Sheridan popped his head inside and moved his light around. He grimaced when he saw that a long metal beam had impaled itself into Mercier's stomach, killing him. He turned and looked over at Parata and nearly jumped out of his skin when he saw the man sitting there strapped into his seat staring back at him.

"Guess we made the wrong call, eh, Captain?" said Parata.

"We can worry about that when this is all over."

"I think I broke my arm," said Parata, showing Sheridan his badly mangled limb. "How's Mercier?"

"He's dead. Let's get you down from there," said Sheridan as he helped Parata to escape his restraints.

"He was a good man," Parata said, looking over at his dead friend.

"Yes, he was, but we've got a job to do." Sheridan tore off a strip of Mercier's uniform and made an expedient sling for Parata's arm. He had to help guide Parata out of the cockpit. It was clear that the man was in shock. In the crew compartment, Sheridan left Parata to take a seat on a box while he went to speak with Cole.

"What's the damage?"

"Sir, Mister Skylar and two other Marines are dead. As for wounded, one has a broken leg. Sergeant Urban can't find one of the comms specialists. I think he was thrown out of the ship when it was ripped open."

Sheridan shook his head. "It gets worse. Mercier is dead and Parata is in shock. Not an auspicious start to our mission."

"Do we even know where we are?"

"No. Until the storm lifts or the satellite starts working again and sends a signal to our GPS, we're trapped here."

"Well, if we're going to be here a while, we might as well make things as comfortable as possible. I'll get the hole blocked up as best I can. No point in letting any more sand in here. Sergeant Urban can work out a sentry roster."

"Sounds good." Sheridan stepped back and took a seat on an overturned container. He looked down at the GPS tracker he wore on his left wrist. When he saw there was no signal available, he swore under breath. He knew from experience that sandstorms could last for days, if not weeks. Staying in the wreck wasn't an option, nor was blindly walking out into a storm. He needed some good luck and he needed it fast.

20

The mood inside the packed briefing room aboard the *Colossus* was stressed. The mission to free the hostages, planned in haste, looked to be coming apart.

Admiral Sheridan looked over at Captain Killam. "Captain, you may begin the update brief."

Killam cleared his throat and brought up an image of Klatt. "Ladies and gentlemen, as you have all no doubt heard, Phase One of Operation Trident Fury has not gone according to plan. Only one of the two satellites in orbit above the planet is working. Unfortunately, it keeps cutting in and out. I have been told that it is a software glitch that cannot be corrected in time before the commencement of the raid."

"What about the reconnaissance team?" asked Colonel White, a broad-shouldered Marine officer with a stern visage and smooth shaven head. "Has there been any word from them?"

"None," replied Killam. "They could have landed, or they could have crashed. Without a fully functioning satellite, we may never hear from them until the task force arrives over Klatt."

"Surely, the mission is already a failure," said Captain Hodges, the commander of the missile cruiser *Ford*. "In my opinion, flying into Kurgan space without knowing what is going on around Klatt would be rash and highly dangerous."

Sheridan raised a hand to silence any further discussion. "Please carry on with your brief, Captain Killam."

"Sir, intelligence intercepts have told us that the Kurgan blood ritual has been moved up by a day and up to a battalion of Imperial Guard soldiers will be involved in the ceremony."

Admiral Sheridan fixed his steely gaze on the people sitting around the table. "Folks, let there be no doubt in your minds, this fleet will deploy a task force to rescue those prisoners. My orders are clear; we will launch a raid into Kurgan space with or without proper intelligence preparation of the battlespace. There are, however, two changes to Captain Killam's original plan. First, we will go one day earlier than anticipated, and the second, is that we must also destroy a Kurgan installation as part of the operation."

Off to one side at the back of the room, Colonel Wright smiled. They had accepted his plan.

Admiral Sheridan continued. "Captain Killam will now outline the operational plan."

Killam pressed a button on his lectern and an image of the asteroid field halfway to Klatt appeared. "Trident Fury will be conducted in four phases. "Phase One has already begun. This was the deployment of the satellites and the reconnaissance team to Klatt. Phase Two will involve the deployment of the task force led by the carrier *Saratoga*. It will consist of the fighter carrier with a reduced number of escort and support vessels. We will be bringing with us six battalion-sized landing ships to evacuate the prisoners in. The Marine assault force will be carried in another three craft, and three more will be held in reserve just in case we need them. In order to ensure that the task force goes in undetected, Colonel Wright's team will neutralize the Kurgan listening post on the edge of the asteroid field." An image of the Kurgan post appeared. No one ever mentioned Wright's squadron by name, but everyone suspected that they were a special warfare organization.

Killam switched the picture to the prison planet. "Phase Three will be the ground force insertion phase of the operation and will not be deemed complete until we have rescued as many of the captives as we possibly can. Phase Four will be the task forces' safe return to our side of the border."

"Thank you, Captain," said the admiral. He stood up, moved over to the lectern, and rested a hand on it. "Folks, I said this days ago, this operation is not about combat power, it is about logistics. To mask our true intentions, the task force will be jumping from multiple locations spread throughout our area of operations. The only way this mission could be scrubbed is if we lose too many landing craft. That call will be made by me at the RV point near the asteroid belt."

"You, sir?" said Captain Jackson, the fighter carrier *Saratoga's* captain. The crushed look on his face betrayed his disappointment that he would not be leading the raid.

"Yes, Captain. I will be personally commanding this operation. I have already told my staff to transfer my flag to your ship no later than eighteen hundred hours today. I spoke with Admiral Oshiro earlier in the day and informed him of my decision to appoint Rear-Admiral Julie Foster, my deputy, to acting commander of the Sixth Fleet in my absence. He fully supported both decisions."

"This is highly irregular, sir," said Foster, leaning far forward in her chair. She was a slender woman in her early fifties with short brown hair and coal-black eyes. "What if something should happen to you?"

"Then you'll get the command you were hoping for," replied Robert Sheridan with a smile. "Julie, I have to do this. There is nothing you or anyone else can say that would make me change my mind." Everyone in the room knew that to be true. Once he had made his decision, Admiral Sheridan never wavered from the course of action he had chosen.

"Yes, sir," said Foster, sitting back.

"I want everyone to return to their respective ships and begin your pre-jump preparations. We will commence with Phase Two in precisely twenty-three hours and five minutes' time," said the admiral, glancing over at the clock on the wall.

The meeting adjourned. Everyone stood and began to file out of the room.

"Colonel Wright, if you could stay behind," said Admiral Sheridan.

Wright stood where he was and waited until only he and the admiral were left in the room. "How can I help you, sir?"

"Colonel, can you do what you're proposing to do before the enemy can get off a signal that they are under attack?"

Wright grinned. "Yes, sir. When you come out of your initial jump, there'll be nothing left of the Kurgan base to warn Klatt that you are coming. You have my word."

"Very good, Colonel. I'm keeping you from your people."

Wright saluted, turned, and left the room.

Admiral Sheridan watched Wright leave. He felt the muscles on the back of his neck tense. So many things had gone wrong and they had barely begun the operation. A million more things could go off the rails and he knew it. He ran a hand over his neck. He could tell that he was already heading for an agonizing migraine. A visit to the infirmary for some painkillers was in order as he knew that he would not rest until the task force was back on the Terran side of the disputed zone, days from now.

21

Michael Sheridan's luck began to change a couple of hours after they had crashed on Klatt. The missing Marine, who had been thrown out of the shuttle, staggered into their makeshift camp. He was a mess. Blood and sand covered his face. He had lost an eye and shattered his left wrist, but had somehow found the rest of his team. Sergeant Urban helped the young man into the wreckage of the shuttlecraft and looked after the man's wounds as best he could. The next break came when the storm began to abate. On the horizon, a rose-colored sun started to rise.

Sheridan was ready to rip the GPS off his wrist. Each and every time that he had checked it, it always said that there was no signal. *The second satellite must be down for good*, he thought to himself.

"Oy, you don't need that hunk of junk," said Cole as took a seat next to Sheridan.

"Why's that?"

Cole held up a piece of string with a needle hanging from the end of it.

"What's that?"

"Weren't you ever a Boy Scout? It's an expedient compass. I rubbed one of the needles from the first aid kit with a piece of fabric to magnetize it. Then I hung it from this string and held it out in front of me, and voila, it pointed north."

Sheridan had to smile at his friend's resourcefulness. "If we assume that we landed somewhere near my proposed landing site, then the prison is off somewhere to the east of us. When the sun comes up, we should be able to see the tall mountain range where the mine is located."

Cole looked over at Parata. He looked more like himself after a few hours' rest. In a hushed tone, Cole said, "Sir, what are we going to do about our wounded personnel? They'll only slow us down and will be next to useless in a fight should we bump into a Kurg patrol."

"We're going to have to leave them here. Parata will be in charge until we come back or they are rescued by someone else. We'll take the remainder with us. I spoke with Toscano and she feels confident enough to be able to co-ord fire from the fleet and direct in the fighter-bombers and troop carriers when they drop down from orbit."

"I hope she's as good as she says she is, as we've got no one else."

"How long do you think it'll be before the sun rises enough for us to see the mountains and get our bearings?"

Cole glanced at his watch. "After breakfast we should be good."

Sheridan shook his head. "You and your stomach."

"First order of survival, sir. Get some nosh into you. You never know when you'll eat again."

"Okay, break out the rations and we'll have a quick bite to eat. After breakfast, we need to discuss how we're going to divvy up the kit that we need to take with us."

"Already done. While you caught forty winks, Sergeant Urban and I went through our supplies and made sure that we had enough food and water to sustain us for up to ninety-six hours. We also decided to bring along an extra radio in case the other two fail. Considering how things have been going so far, I thought it prudent to err on the side of caution. Wouldn't you agree?"

"Yes, I would. What about supplies for the people staying back here?"

Cole feigned being hurt. "Please, sir, do you honestly think I wouldn't factor them into my planning. They'll be far more comfortable than we will be with all of the supplies we're leaving behind for them."

Sheridan raised his hands in defeat. "Sorry, I should have known that you would do this."

"Just doing my job." Cole reached into an open box of rations and tossed a meal at Sheridan.

He caught it and read the label. With a sour look on his face, Sheridan said, "Beans . . . you always give me beans for breakfast. For once I'd like to have something different."

"You want to trade?"

"Sure," he said throwing his ration over in exchange for Cole's food. When he turned it over and read the packaging, he shook his head. "Beans!"

"We got a whole box of them. I bet the boys in the First Div don't eat the same meal day after day. In fact, I'm sure of it. Ain't it grand to be on the frontlines? Now, eat up, Captain."

An hour later, Sheridan and Cole lay on their stomachs on the top of a nearby hill. The wind had died down so much that they could see for kilometers in all directions. As anticipated, they could see the mountains to the east. Silhouetted against the horizon, it looked like a devil's pitchfork.

Sheridan lowered his binoculars and looked over at Cole. "The middle mountain is where the prison is located. What do you think . . . thirty klicks?

"Yeah, maybe less but not much less."

"I'd love to launch a drone over toward the mine to see what the ground looks like between it and us."

"Yeah, and if you did that, the Kurgs would know we're here for sure. Their sensors would light up like a Christmas tree if we put something up in the air."

"It's already getting hot," pointed out Sheridan. "Within the hour it'll get up to nearly fifty Celsius. I'd rather wait until tonight when it's cooler to begin our trek, but we don't have the time to waste."

"If we walk slow and steady, we should be all right."

Sheridan nodded. "Okay, let's round up the gang and get going."

22

A thick cloud of dust hung in the air. Tarina waited for the signal to enter the newly blown open mine shaft to grab the rocks and place them in the back of a long transport vehicle that looked like a robotic snake. She had heard a rumor over breakfast that they would be given a new assignment in the next day or two. Angela explained that just prior to the arrival of the Inspector General the prison commandant liked to get the prisoners to clean their living quarters up a bit. It was all smoke and mirrors intended to make it look like he was doing a good job looking after the mine.

A whistle sounded.

Tarina trudged forward. She brought up her dirt-encrusted shirt over her mouth so she wouldn't breathe in the fine dust particles. Beside her Wendy did the same thing. There had been no time this morning for Tarina to ask her how her reconnaissance of the escape tunnel had gone the night before. She had tried to stay awake the whole time the two women were gone but hardly lasted ten minutes before exhaustion took over and pulled her into a deep sleep. Tarina waited a moment for the dust to settle before beginning the arduous and backbreaking work of hauling the rocks out of the debris-strewn tunnel.

For close to three hours, the prisoners worked without respite. Tarina's body was soon covered in sweat and dust. She had grown accustomed to being filthy. In fact, she doubted that she would ever come clean.

Another whistle sounded. Everyone stopped what they were doing and shuffled over to a cart with a large metal pail of water on it. People queued up and waited their turn to get a cup of water. It was never enough to sate the burning thirst in their throats, but it was all they were going to get before the supper meal.

Travis walked up and down the row of prisoners, poking and prodding them with a wooden baton, looking for any sign of defiance. Tarina turned her head to the ground as he got close. A second later, she felt his wooden truncheon against her ribs. She fought the urge to reach over and scratch the man's eyes out. She knew that would be foolish and result in not only her death but that of her friends. She watched his shadow pass only to stop alongside Wendy. Tarina bit her lip and raised her head to see what was happening.

"I bet you don't realize how lucky you are that Kurg colonel never selected you when he was here a few days ago," said Travis to Wendy.

Wendy said nothing. She kept her gaze fixed on the back of the person in front of her.

Travis thrust his baton under Wendy's chin and forced her to lift her head. He kept raising his stick until Wendy was on her tiptoes. He slowly forced her to step out of line with the others. He smiled lustfully at her as he lowered his truncheon. "Look at me, Captain. I'm speaking to you."

Wendy took a deep breath and with reluctance turned her head.

"That's better. Now, do you have any idea why you should consider yourself extremely lucky? Do you, girl?"

Wendy shook her head.

"Believe it or not your red hair saved your life. The Kurgs hate it. I, on the other hand, find it sexy."

Wendy felt her skin crawl as he leaned forward and studied her face.

Travis continued "You're one fortunate girl. For you see, three days from now, my dear captain, all those people whose names are in my little black book will be leaving us and never returning. Do you know why?"

Again she shook her head.

"Of course you don't. It's never happened here before. But I'll let you in on a little secret. The Kurgans have plans for those people. It's called *Kahtak,* and I bet you have no clue what that means." Travis turned his head and flashed an evil grin at Tarina. "I'd pay good money to see what happens, but I'm not allowed to go. It's for Kurgans . . . pure Kurgans only. The Chosen can't even attend."

Wendy kept her mouth shut. Travis was right, she had no idea what *Kahtak* was, but, by the way their tormentor was salivating, she had no doubt that it was not good.

"Back in line," said Travis, pushing Wendy back with his truncheon. He was about to leave when he fixed his gaze on Angela. "You should ask her what *Kahtak* means. She knows. Don't you, girl?" He laughed to himself, spat on the ground, and kept on walking down the line having fun at tormenting the helpless prisoners.

At the water station, Tarina slipped over beside Angela. "What was that all about?" she asked barely above a whisper.

"It's nothing," replied Angela. "He's just messing with our minds, that's all."

"That's a load of crap and you know it. He may be mad, but he knows something about you. I want the truth this time."

Angela hesitated before nodding. "I'll tell you and Wendy everything after supper tonight. Trust me, you aren't going to like what I'm going to tell you."

"By the way Travis was going on, I'm fairly sure that my days are numbered."

Angela didn't respond. She took her cup of water and drank it all down before moving back to the tunnel entrance to get back to work.

"What's going on, Tarina?" asked Wendy. "I'm scared."

"Me too . . . me too."

The women ate their meager meal in silence. The mood between them was somber as if they had all just come back from a funeral. None of them seemed willing to broach the topic of what Travis had been going on about. After placing their empty bowls on the food cart, they walked back to Tarina's bunk and sat down. When they were sure that no one was paying any attention to them, Angela broke the silence. "I guess I have some explaining to do. First off, my name is not Angela, it is Kitan, and I am a citizen of the Kurgan Empire. Angela died two weeks after she arrived here. As I looked an awful lot like her, I assumed her identity. If we are to keep up this ruse, I must insist that you continue to refer to me by my adoptive human name."

"Well, that explains a lot," said Tarina. "But why did you not leave with the other Chosen prisoners when this was turned into a prisoner of war camp?"

"Because my best chance of escaping from here lay with people like you. Pretending to be Angela was my best hope for freedom. If I had never told you this, you'd still think I was her, wouldn't you?"

"I was beginning to have my doubts."

"As was I," added Wendy.

"By Travis' tone, I take it that he knows your little secret," said Tarina.

"Yeah, he does but keeps the information to himself. He's borderline insane. I think he thinks it's hilarious that I would want to hide out amongst my enemies."

Tarina sat up. "So do you consider Wendy and me your enemy?"

"At first, I was leery of all humans. I had been taught all my life that you were a sub-species and since you didn't worship our god that you were all infidels. However, as weeks turned into months in this hellhole, I began to see that we aren't all that different. So to answer your question, no I do not see you as my enemy, just fellow prisoners."

"That's good," said Wendy.

"How is that you can speak fluent English?" asked Tarina.

"I have an ear for languages. I was a teacher and taught Kurgan back home until I was arrested for killing my husband and sent here. Immersed in your tongue, it didn't take me long to pick it up."

Tarina looked her straight in the eyes and asked, "So what were you planning to do once we had escaped from here?"

"I would have told you the truth before we reached Terran space. All I would have asked for in return for helping you escape was that after you were safe, you'd reprogram the shuttle's navigational computer to return me to my home world. I have two children there, and I miss them terribly."

"If you can't fly it, how would you have landed the ship when you arrived at your home world?" asked Wendy.

"I don't know. All I know is that I have to get home to my children. I would have bailed out when I was over land or something like that. Look, I really hadn't thought that part through. But wouldn't you try to reach your children if you were in my shoes?"

"Neither of us has any children, but I guess we would do the same," Tarina replied.

Wendy asked, "Can you explain what Travis meant by *Kahtak*?"

Angela nodded. "It is a bloodletting ritual."

Tarina's eyes widened. "It's a what?"

"It is a ritual that goes back centuries. For a Kurgan to become a member of the Old Guard, the Empire's most elite and veteran soldiers, he must have dipped his blade in the stomach of his enemy. I'm assuming that you and all the other people earmarked by that colonel are going to be sacrificed so that new warriors can join the ranks of the Old Guard. I'm sorry."

"Not as sorry as I am." Tarina could hardly believe what she had been told. It was barbaric. She was an officer, not some animal that could be led to the slaughter to appease some ancient tradition.

Wendy reached over and put a hand on Tarina's shoulder. "This is horrible. We can't let this happen to you."

"I don't plan to die."

"It'll all come down to timing," said Angela. "Hopefully, the Inspector General gets here before they come for you."

"I don't plan to stick around to see who gets here first. Tomorrow night, I say we take our chances. I'd rather die trying to escape than be gutted by a Kurgan blade."

"Me too," added Wendy.

Angela hesitated. She had waited months for the right people to come along; however, now she seemed unwilling to take the risk.

"We'll go with or without you," said Tarina. "If you want to get home to your children, I suggest that you come with us."

Angela nodded. "Tomorrow night it is."

"I think it would be wise to end our conversation," suggested Wendy. "One of the guards is looking our way." With that, they split up and went back to their own bunks.

With a growing sense of resolve in her heart, Tarina laid back on her bed and closed her eyes. In her mind, she saw herself frolicking on the beach with her lover, their bodies were intertwined while the warm water of the Pacific Ocean surged over them. With a smile on her face, Tarina drifted off to sleep. For the first time in ages, she dreamed about her life with Michael and how much she missed him.

23

The setting sun cast long, dark shadows across the bleak desert terrain. Michael Sheridan could not remember a time when he had felt so hot and tired. He had trained in the deserts of Nevada, but it hadn't prepared him for the broiling hot temperatures on Klatt. His desert camouflage uniform stuck to his sweat-soaked skin. He had already gone through four liters of water and still felt thirsty. He couldn't wait for the sun to dip below the horizon, allowing the planet's surface to cool. Behind him, his small band of Marines kept pace. No one complained or asked for a break. Everyone knew what was at stake. What were a few days of discomfort compared to the deprivations that the prisoners in the mines would have suffered?

"Drone," called out Cole from the rear of the column. As one, the Marines dove for cover under any rocky shelter they could find. A couple of seconds later, a large UAV flew overhead and carried on out into the wastelands.

Sheridan waited close to a minute before crawling out from under a ledge and peering up into the cloudless sky. The drone was nowhere to be seen. Thankfully, the rocks, heated by the sun, masked their body heat. It would be harder to hide at night when the temperature would drop to near freezing. With a wave of his hand, Sheridan took the lead once more. He was aiming for a mesa a few kilometers away; he hoped it would give them a good view of the mine.

Two hours later, in the dark, Sheridan brought up his hand. His team stopped, dropped to one knee, and raised their assault rifles to their shoulders. As quiet as he could, Sheridan moved forward on the top of the round, flat mesa. He could see the bright lights from the mining camp illuminating the horizon. It took him less than a couple of minutes to find the ideal spot for them to establish their base camp. Rain had long ago carved a deep crevice into the rock that was wide enough for Sheridan to climb down inside. There he found a small cave. It was ideal as it would provide them with protection from the heat and hide them from prying eyes. He hurried back and brought his people down into the cavern.

Cole ordered Urban to dig out a small camera from his pack and had him leave it at the entrance to the cavern. He camouflaged the device before joining everyone else down below.

"What can you see?" Cole asked.

"For starters, if anyone tries to sneak up on us, I'll see them coming," replied Urban as he moved his finger along the screen of a small handheld tablet. He adjusted the picture until it gave him a thermal image of the world around them. A small rodent ran past the camera; its warm body showing up against the cold rocks.

Sheridan asked, "What about the mining complex?"

Urban moved the camera around. "I can see several buildings and an entrance that is guarded by a couple of Chosen warriors."

Cole said, "I've never seen this type of surveillance camera before. How long are the batteries in your monitor good for?"

"Forty-eight hours. I've also got several spares with me just in case we need them."

Cole nodded. "Okay, I'll make up the duty roster. You're on first. Make sure that the monitor gets handed off to the next person on shift, along with a quick lesson on how to use it."

"Yes, Master Sergeant."

Sheridan lowered his pack to the ground. It felt good to have the extra weight off his back. Aside from his water, rations, and ammunition, he was also carrying a spare radio, batteries, and several anti-personnel mines. He took a seat on the cool, rocky floor, dug out his canteen, and took a long deep gulp of hot water. He swished it around in his mouth for a minute before swallowing it. At least being out of the sun, their water would cool down and make it more drinkable.

"Hey, sir, hand me one of the anti-pers mines," said Cole.

Sheridan opened a flap on his pack, grabbed one of the mines, and gave it to Cole. The device was the same size as a baseball and made to look like a rock. Once activated, it would lay silent until it detected movement nearby. If the mine took the motion to be of something the size of a man, it would launch itself up into the air and explode, sending hundreds of ball bearings into its intended target. "Where are you going to place that?"

"Near the camera. Just to be on the safe side."

"Good idea."

"I know, that's why I came up with it," replied Cole with a wink.

Sheridan propped up his rifle on his pack before moving from person to person checking their feet and seeing if they had any other problems. If they did, they hid them well. Although tired from the march under the hot sun, everyone's spirits were high. Sheridan made his way back to his pack, rummaged around for a ration, and opened it. He sat down and took a sip from his canteen.

"So, sir, what's for dinner?" Cole asked, taking a seat beside his friend.

"Same as breakfast. Next time steal something more than beans from the quartermaster."

Cole shrugged. "Food is food. Besides, the boxes were marked as being something else. Pasta meals, I think. This must be someone's idea of a cruel joke."

They sat and ate their meals in silence. Both men were deep in thought.

"Sir, something is coming in to land," said Urban as he made his way to Sheridan.

"That's a big bastard. I wonder what it is?" Cole asked, looking down at the monitor's screen.

"That's a Kurgan troop transporter," said Sheridan. "By the looks of the size of it, it could easily hold five hundred soldiers."

"Sergeant, you had best make note of when and where it landed," Cole said. "The task force is going to need to know about this. They don't want to try landing on a hot LZ."

"Yes, Master Sergeant," replied Urban, inputting the info into his monitoring device.

"Make sure whoever is on next knows what you have done so there's no confusion later," added Cole.

Urban nodded and walked back to show Toscano the information. He found her helping Private Snow, the Marine comms specialist, take off his heavy pack.

Sheridan and Cole resumed sitting on the cool floor.

"Sir, do you still get those dreams of yours?" Cole asked.

"No, not recently. I did after Tarina was first reported missing. However, as you were right to point out, I hit the bottle a little too hard and the dreams stopped. I've been so busy and tired these past few days that I doubt I dreamt at all."

"So what does your gut tell you? Is she still alive?"

Sheridan sat there for a few seconds before answering. "My gut tells me that we and everyone else involved in this operation are in great danger. If that was an Imperial Guard transport, then they have arrived far earlier than initially expected. As for my heart, it speaks loud and clear to me. Tarina is somewhere in that mine, and I intend to get her and as many of the other prisoners out alive."

"Then we had best get a move on. I'd hate to think that the task force is going to arrive too late to help anyone."

"My thoughts exactly." Sheridan drew his bayonet from its scabbard and ran his thumb along the blade's edge to see how sharp it was. "We'll get a few hours' rest and then make for the mine. I need to know what is going on in there."

"The others?"

"They can stay here. If we are killed or captured, Miss Toscano can still help the invasion force do their job."

"If there is anyone left to help."

"We didn't come all this way to watch our friends be butchered like animals by the Kurgs. As long as I have a breath left in my body, I'm not going to let them kill our people."

Cole nodded. He pitied any Chosen or Kurgan warrior who got between Michael Sheridan and his girlfriend. It was a fight they could never hope to win.

24

"All right, listen up," said Colonel Wright to his assembled personnel. "We've only got one chance to make this work, so split-second timing and precision will be vital throughout this phase of Trident Fury. I volunteered this squadron because I have faith in each and every one of you to do your job and do it well. I know some of you may feel that we haven't had the time to adequately examine the enemy base and its capabilities and others have already voiced their concerns over the lack of rehearsal time. Well, folks, you're all right, but I don't care. We're launching in an hour, so pay close attention to the XO's mission brief."

Lieutenant Colonel Tolinski walked in front of Wright's Avenger jump ship and raised up a remote. The lights in the launch bay dimmed. A second later, a holographic image of a small planetoid appeared. Tolisnki zoomed in on the Kurgan listening station. It looked like a large metal ring. There were numerous towers and antennae spread out along the surface of the rocky asteroid. The only visible weapons were a couple of missile launchers dug into the top of a nearby hill.

"Ladies and gentlemen, the Kurgan base is our target. It is located on a small rocky planet that the fleet has designated as GX 111. As you can see, the base is lightly defended with only a few anti-ship missiles. However, just because we cannot see any more weapons, we should not discount the fact there could be more hidden from view."

"Ma'am, how old is this image?" asked one of the pilots.

"It is almost forty-eight hours old. I strongly doubt that the Kurgs could have substantially altered their defense posture in that time."

"No more questions until the XO is finished," said Wright, his tone told his people to keep their mouths shut.

Tolinski glanced at her watch. "In exactly fifty minutes from now, I, along with my wingman, Captain Zhang, will begin our jump to GX 111. We will arrive there twenty-three hours later. Both of our Avengers will be carrying electromagnetic pulse bombs which we will deploy above the Kurgan base. Once that is done, we will jump back one-quarter of a million kilometers so that we won't be caught in the electromagnetic wave created when the bombs go off. It is anticipated that these two devices will be sufficient to destroy or at the very least cripple the Kurgans' ability to call for help or defend themselves."

She brought up a new image of four teams of two Avengers each. "Thirty seconds later, Colonel Wright and the rest of the squadron will destroy the listening station. Your ships will all be carrying a single Mark V torpedo, specially modified to fit underneath of your vessels. Your targets have already been inputted into your Avengers' computers. Unless something catastrophic happens, you should be over the target for less than a minute. Once you're done, there shouldn't be a soul left alive to report what has happened."

Wright stepped forward. "Once we have flattened that Kurg base, we will all RV with the XO. Our lift home will be waiting for us there. Don't be late as you won't have enough fuel left to make another jump. I can't stress this enough, the success of the rescue mission on Klatt is riding on our ability to eradicate that listening station. Folks, I don't intend to let the task force down, and neither do you."

A chuckle ran through the nervous flight crews. It was Wright's standard line letting everyone know that there was only one outcome possible and defeat wasn't it.

Tolinski turned off the holographic projection. The lights came back on. She looked over at Colonel Wright, who nodded back at her. She clapped her hands in the air to get everyone's attention. "Pilots and navigators, to your ships. Technicians, begin your last minute flight preps. This mission is a go."

A loud cheer erupted from the men and women of the squadron as they shook one another's hands and told their friends that they'd see them again when the job was done.

Wright moved over beside Tolinski.

She held out her hand. "Thanks for letting me in on this one, sir. I thought I was doomed to be stuck behind my desk until the war ended."

Wright shook her hand. "XO, you're the best pilot for the job. If you fail, we all fail. I know that you won't let us down. I'll see you back on the transport."

"That you will, sir."

They smiled at one another for a second, before turning and making their way to their ships. Throughout the launch bay, the sound of people and equipment moving about filled the air. The First Special Warfare Squadron was once again preparing to go into harm's way.

"Sir, the last of Colonel Wright's ships have jumped," reported Captain Killam.

Admiral Sheridan nodded. "Task force status?"

"Sir, the *Saratoga* has reported that she is ready to deploy. The missile cruiser, *Ford*, and the destroyers, *Churchill* and *Algonquin*, are good to go. The support ship, *Arctic*, will be reporting in shortly."

"What about the transports and the ground forces?"

"All twelve landing craft have given us the green light, and Colonel White is already busting my chops asking when we're going to get under sail."

Robert Sheridan chuckled. No one could fault the Marine colonel for his zealous desire to get the mission done. "Please pass onto the good colonel that we'll go when I give the order and not a nanosecond before."

"Aye, sir."

The clock on the tactical display counted down toward zero. Admiral Sheridan glanced over at it and saw that they would begin their jump into hostile territory in precisely forty-nine minutes. He felt a pang of anxiety in his stomach. The men and women who made up the task force numbered close to ten thousand, twice the number of the people they were going to rescue. He had tried to par down the number of people and ships going but each time he did, Killam had a viable answer as to why he thought they needed every last ship and person in the task force. The admiral knew that to go any smaller was to invite failure.

"Sir, I noticed that you didn't leave the operations center for a bite to eat tonight," said Commander Roy.

Admiral Sheridan looked over and saw his aide holding a tray. On it was a sandwich, an apple, and a tall glass of water. "I must have forgotten to eat."

Roy handed the tray over. "Sir, you'll be no good to anyone if you don't keep your strength up. I know you. You're not going to rest until it's all over. So if you must insist on pushing yourself, at least eat something from time to time."

"Thank you," replied the admiral as he took the tray and sat down in his chair.

Roy shook her head and moved over to speak with Killam. Sheridan had no doubt that she was telling Killam to keep an eye on him. He chuckled to himself. He had the best staff in the fleet and he knew it. They had become more like family than any other officers he had ever worked with in his long career. He took a bite of his sandwich and tasted tofu. He made a quick mental note that if Roy was going to look after him, she would have to feed him non-vegetarian food. For now, he would eat his meal and enjoy it.

Forty-nine minutes later, Admiral Sheridan gave the order. On the tactical screen, he watched as the task force jumped away from Illum Prime and sped toward Kurgan space. In roughly twenty-four hours, he would know if the listening station had been destroyed and if it was safe to proceed with the flight to Klatt. He made himself as comfortable as he could and watched the timer countdown. With the task force in motion, there was nothing for him to do but wait. His thoughts turned to his son. He prayed that he was still alive and they would soon be reunited.

25

"All clear," reported Sergeant Urban, looking down at the screen on his monitor.

Sheridan took a quick look at the screen, nodded, and handed it back. He looked over at First Lieutenant Toscano. "Okay, if we're not back by midnight tonight, go with the assumption that we're never coming back and you're in charge. Keep a sharp eye out and keep developing the intelligence picture for the fleet. They're going to need to know the ground truth when they arrive."

"Yes, sir," replied Toscano. "Good luck."

"Thanks. Hopefully, we won't need it."

Cole said, "Stay alert, everyone. The Kurgs aren't stupid or lazy. They found our hiding spot last time using a robotic hunter-killer. It would be like shooting fish in a barrel if they were to stumble upon you lot trapped down inside this cavern."

"I'll keep my eyes peeled," said Urban.

"Well, that seems about it," said Sheridan. "Shall we get going?"

Cole nodded and began to climb out of their shelter. Sheridan quickly joined him. On the top of the mesa, they hunched down and ran for a gully they intended to use for cover. After the scorching temperatures during the day, the nighttime air was a welcome change. Above in the night sky shone millions of stars. None of which looked even the remotest bit familiar to

Sheridan. He was thankful that there was only a sliver of a moon hanging low on the horizon.

Sheridan brought up his thermal binoculars and quickly surveyed the mining complex. Aside from a dozen or so Chosen guards walking around looking bored out of their minds, the camp was silent. He handed off his binoculars to Cole while he pondered their next move.

"I don't think they're going to let us waltz up to the front entrance and ask to see the prisoners," said Cole. "There has to be another way in."

"I didn't see another entrance."

Cole grinned. "Yeah, but I do."

"Where?"

Cole gave back the glasses and pointed. "There's a door about one hundred and fifty meters to the left of the main entrance. Can you see it?"

It took Sheridan a few seconds searching to find what Cole had seen. "Got it. I wonder what it's for?"

"I'm no miner but if I were to hazard a guess, I'd say at one time it was the way in for the foremen and mine owners. Even Kurgs can't be seen rubbing elbows with the prisoners."

"I don't see any cameras or sensors facing that way."

"Neither did I."

Sheridan spoke into his headset mic. "Sergeant Urban, swing your camera over to the mine entrance and then pan to the left about one hundred and fifty meters. You should see a door."

"Got it," replied Urban in Sheridan's earpiece.

"Okay, now search the area for any heat signatures or scanning devices invisible to the human eye."

A minute later, Urban reported, "All clear."

"I guess we just found our way inside," said Sheridan as he put his binoculars away.

As silent as a pair of jaguars on the prowl, Sheridan and Cole made their way down off the hill and over to the closed door. Sheridan keyed his mic, "Urban, can you see us?"

"Affirmative, sir."

"Okay, we're going in. I suspect we'll lose comms once were inside the mine." With that, Sheridan looked over at Cole, who reached over and tried the door.

"Bugger," said Cole. "It's magnetically sealed."

"Step aside," said Sheridan as he reached into his pocket and pulled out a slender plastic card. He inserted it in the door crack just above the door jam and pushed down. A second later, with the electrical circuit interrupted, the door slid open. Both men darted inside a darkened office with their weapons at the ready in case they ran into any trouble.

"Clear," announced Sheridan when he saw that they were alone.

Cole reached back and closed the door. He lowered his weapon. "Sir, you were supposed to leave your ID back on the *Colossus*. Not that I'm complaining right now."

"It's not my ID. It's my ration card. I forgot to take it out my pocket when we left. It doesn't have my name on it, so no harm, no foul, as far as I'm concerned."

"Where did you learn a trick like that?"

"My mother used to go out a lot when my father was away. So she would lock me in my room at night when I was a young boy. It didn't take me long before I figured a way out."

"Thank God for that. Now, what do you want to do?"

"I want to take a quick look around the room to see if we can find a plan of the mine."

As quiet as they could, they dug out their flashlights and began to search the office. It took less than ten seconds before Cole found a schematic of the mine hanging on the wall.

"Bingo," said Sheridan as he studied the diagram. The mine went down for twelve floors. There were dozens of shafts dug out from each level. He was intrigued when he saw at the bottom of the mine there was a train tunnel that led to the ore processing plant hundreds of kilometers away.

"Does it say where the prisoners are being held?"

"It sure does," Sheridan said, pointing to a floor three levels below theirs. "It says they are housed in a series of large caverns. There are thirty-three in all. Some hold about one hundred prisoners while some of the larger ones can accommodate more than one thousand. The guards and administrative personnel are on the first two floors beneath us."

"Yeah, and I bet the Kurgs have the POWs stacked in there like cordwood."

Sheridan pulled the map off the wall, folded it up, and handed it to Cole. "For safe keeping in case we get separated."

"I take it you want to take a look around."

"I sure do."

Cole looked down at his uniform. "I hate to point out the obvious, but we kinda stand out in our desert attire."

"Time to get us some new clothes," replied Sheridan with a glint in his eye. He edged over to a door at the other end of the office and listened for a few seconds before cracking it open. He could see a long, dimly lit tunnel heading down into the mine. He closed the door and stripped off his helmet and tac-vest. He handed it, along with his rifle, to Cole before taking a suppressor and screwing it into the barrel of his pistol. "Master Sergeant, it's best if you stay here. If I'm not back in thirty minutes, head back to the rest of the team with the map."

Cole placed a hand on Sheridan's arm. "Keep your head down, sir, and be back in twenty, or you'll never hear the end of it from me."

Sheridan nodded, opened the door a little wider, and slipped out into the tunnel. He looked both ways before deciding to head down the tunnel and into the mine. He counted on the monotony of guarding sleeping prisoners to act in his favor. With his pistol hidden behind his back, Sheridan did his best to stay in the shadows. After a couple minutes of walking, he heard some men talking as they made their way down the tunnel. It sounded like they were having an argument. They were close, perhaps only seconds away. Sheridan looked around, saw a stack of boxes, and ran to hide behind them. He dropped to one knee and grabbed a hold of his pistol. The voices soon sounded like they were right next to him. Sheridan held his breath, afraid that his ragged breathing would be heard. The two Chosen warriors stood next to the crates and bitched about an assignment they had been given. Silently, Sheridan prayed that they would just do as they were told and carry on down the passage. After what seemed like an eternity, the two men turned and moved away. Sheridan waited until he couldn't hear their footsteps anymore before popping his head up to look around. Once more he was alone.

"Friggin bellyachers," commented Sheridan under his breath.

He was about to carry on when someone in the dark coughed, scaring Sheridan. In one fluid motion, he brought up his pistol and took aim. He edged forward looking for the man who had made the sound. Sheridan was stumped. He couldn't see where it had come from. Again, he heard the unmistakable noise of a man hacking and coughing. It sounded like the man's throat was full of phlegm. A few seconds later, he caught a whiff of a foul odor. Sheridan did not need to be told that the noxious smell was coming from dead bodies. All of a sudden, light shot out into the tunnel as a dirt-encrusted tarpaulin hung from the roof was pushed aside. Sheridan threw himself against the wall and watched as a man stuck his head out and spat on the ground before letting the makeshift door fall back into place.

Although he didn't really want to, Sheridan had to know what was going on behind the canvas. After making sure that no one was around, he walked over and pulled open the tarp. With his pistol held straight out, he stepped inside. In under a second, he regretted his decision. His stomach turned when he saw dead bodies lying in bunk beds that reached from the floor to the ceiling. The hair on the back of his neck went up. The Chosen soldier he had noticed was nowhere to be seen. The smell of death was overpowering. He fought the urge to be sick. There were piles of clothes taken from the corpses lying on the floor. Sheridan had no doubt they would be handed off to new prisoners arriving at the mine. Out of the corner of his eyes, he saw a box on a nearby table. Sheridan moved over and took a quick look inside. His blood began to boil when he saw gold teeth, rings, and jewelry lining the bottom of the container.

"Who the hell are you?" demanded a Chosen soldier as he moved out from behind one of the bunks. He appeared to be about fifty years old, had a couple of days' growth on his dirty face, and looked as if he hadn't washed his uniform in weeks. The man stood there staring at Sheridan. He did not have a weapon in his hand. Instead, he was holding a blood-covered saw.

Sheridan turned his pistol on the man. "What is going on in here?" he asked in Kurgan.

"Why are you out of your cell block?"

"I asked you a question," Sheridan's tone left no doubt that he wanted an answer. "What the hell is going on in here?"

The Kurgan chuckled. "Can't you tell? This is the morgue. Every day people die by the dozens. Someone has to deal with them once they're dead."

"What are you doing with the saw?"

The Kurgan went to take a step toward Sheridan only to have the pistol aimed at his heart. He froze in his tracks.

"The saw . . . what are you doing with the saw?"

"The boxes they give me to put the bodies in are too small, so I have to make the remains fit."

A wave of revulsion washed over Sheridan. "What do you do with the bodies once you have put them in their boxes?"

"Cremation. It happens every third day as the sun goes down. But you should know that." The Kurgan studied Sheridan for a moment. His eyes widened. "May the lord protect me. You're wearing a clean uniform. You're not one of the prisoners."

"Correct," replied Sheridan as he pulled the trigger. His pistol fired without making a sound. With a stunned look on his face, the Kurgan fell to the floor with a hole blasted through his heart. Sheridan walked over to the corpse and nudged it with his foot. He was sure that the man was dead; he just wanted to be positive. Sheridan had no idea when the next cremation ceremony was going to take place, but he doubted the man got many visitors. However, if his body were discovered, the Kurgans would know someone was in the mine. He bent down and dragged the corpse as far back in the room as he could and then stripped the clothes off the dead man's body. He picked up the man and dumped him on a bunk with several other corpses. As much as it made his skin crawl, Sheridan knew that the Chosen's garments would prove to be invaluable. He wiped his sweaty hands on his uniform before picking up the dead Chosen's uniform as well as some of the discarded prison work clothes. He hurried to jam them all into a bag he found on the floor. At the tarpaulin, Sheridan listened for a few seconds before moving back out into the darkened tunnel.

He glanced at his watch and saw that time was not on his side. He had pushed his luck and he knew it. With his pistol in his right hand and the bag of clothes in the other, Sheridan made his way back to the office where Cole was waiting. Rather than barge in and risk being shot by his friend, Sheridan knocked lightly once and whispered, "Don't shoot, it's me." He opened the door, slid inside, and found himself looking down the barrel of a pistol.

Cole lifted his weapon and flicked the safety on with his thumb. "You're cutting it fine. I was getting ready to leave."

"I know. It couldn't be helped."

Cole's face soured. "Jesus, sir, what the hell is that smell?"

Sheridan held up the bag. "These clothes are our way down into the mine."

"Frigg, the smell is making me gag."

"You had best get used to the smell as we're going to be wearing these clothes when we come back."

Cole shuddered. "I guess it's too late to ask for another assignment."

Sheridan shook his head. He took back his combat gear from Cole and rushed to put it on. He moved to the front door and keyed his headset mic. "Sergeant Urban, this is Sheridan, is the coast clear?"

"Roger that. A Kurg patrol walked past your door about a minute ago. However, they're already out of sight."

"Drones?"

"None in sight."

"Thanks. Stay alert. We're on our way back to you. Sheridan, out."

Sheridan looked at Cole. "Come on, let's get back to our people before our luck changes and we run into another Kurg patrol."

Cole opened the door and took a quick look around before stepping aside for Sheridan. They hunched down and sprinted for a rocky outcropping at the base of the hill. When they were a few meters shy of the cover, Cole tripped over a rock, hidden in the shadows, and fell to the ground. His rifle made a racket as it slid along the rocks. Sheridan turned and hurried to help his friend back up to his feet.

"My rifle?" said Cole, looking all about.

"Here," said Sheridan, picking it up and handing it over.

Before Cole could say thanks, Urban's voice boomed in both of their headsets. "Drone! Five hundred meters out and coming in fast."

Sheridan pulled Cole with him as he dove for cover behind the rocks. They tumbled to the ground. A second later, they could hear the whine of the UAV's engine as it closed in on their hiding spot. Both men hugged the rocks, trying to blend in. It was an act born of desperation and they knew it. If the drone saw them with its thermal camera, a missile would be coming their way in mere seconds. The sound of its engine grew close as it flew near. All of a sudden, a spotlight shot down from the UAV lighting up the ground in front of their position.

"They must have seen us," whispered Sheridan.

Cole shook his head.

A voice on a loud speaker drowned out the hovering drone's engine. "Prisoner, stop where you are, or I will be forced to fire."

Cole said, "I don't think that was for us."

Sheridan moved just enough so he could see what was going on. At first he saw nothing, then a man stumbled out of the dark. His clothes hung from his emaciated body. The UAV's light moved over onto the prisoner.

"Halt, or face the consequences," warned the UAV.

The man paid it no heed and kept staggering forward. Each footstep taken was one more toward freedom. Sheridan could see that the prisoner was not going to make it. With a loud whoosh, a missile shot from the drone and exploded right next to the man. His dead body flew up into the air before crashing down onto the rocky ground.

"Poor bastard," whispered Cole.

Sheridan slid back down behind the rocks. Anger filled his heart. He couldn't wait for the task force to arrive so they could pay back the Kurgans for their cruelty. Urban's voice filled his earpiece. "Gents, don't move. A Kurg patrol mounted in two vehicles is heading your way. I think they're coming to pick up the dead guy's remains."

The drone's light switched off. It hovered over the body for a few seconds before flying off to another part of the mining camp.

Pinned behind their rocks, Sheridan and Cole waited for the Kurgans to retrieve the corpse lying less than fifty paces from them. Two eight-wheeled APCs drove out of the camp and stopped right next to the body. A couple of Chosen warriors got out of the back of one of the transports and dragged the shattered remains into the back of their vehicle. A minute later, the APCs left.

Cole whispered, "I'm amazed that the Kurgs didn't see us too."

"We left by an unguarded exit. I bet that poor soul tripped some kind of alarm when he made his escape from the mine. We'll have to be wary and look for laser warning systems from now on."

Cole nodded. "I think we're alone now. Let's get the hell out of here before anything else goes wrong."

Sheridan nodded. As quiet as a pair of church mice, the two Marines crept from their hiding spot and made their way back to the rest of their team. Tired and scared, Sheridan knew that luck more than skill had helped them so far. He couldn't always count on being fortunate in the future. From now on he would have to rely on his and Cole's experience to keep them alive.

26

Lieutenant Colonel Tolinksi's navigator, First Lieutenant Frost, broke the long silence. "Ma'am, we're almost there." His accent had a hint of Scandinavian in it.

Right away, Tolinski could feel her heart begin to race. Although qualified to fly the Avenger, she had only ever flown it on training missions in the Illum star system. Today was her first combat assignment. She sat up in her chair, took a deep breath, and waited for the stars to appear.

Frost reported, "Coming out of the jump in three-two-one."

In the blink of an eye, their ship came out of its long jump precisely where they had planned to. Stars filed her cockpit canopy. Below them was the Kurgan base. Less than five kilometers away, the other ship appeared. Both had survived the long journey into enemy space.

Tolinski reached over and flipped a switch on her control panel. "I'm arming the bomb."

"I have the device on my screen. The signal is good," announced Frost.

"I'm releasing the bomb . . . now." Beneath their sleek vessel, the large circular bomb detached and floated free.

"Ma'am, my scope shows no enemy activity. I don't think they've spotted us."

"They will if we stick around any longer. Get us the hell out of here."

"Yes, ma'am." Seconds later, Tolinski's Avenger vanished as it jumped away from the base.

Tolinski sat back and let out a long-held breath. From the time they jumped in over the top of the base until they departed was less than one minute's time. She chuckled to herself. If she survived the war, she could stand around the officers' mess with a beer in her hand and brag about her one minute of combat.

"Ma'am, we'll be coming out of our jump in less than one minute. Will our transport ship be waiting there for us?"

"They want to be or they're going to get my boot upside their asses if they're not."

"Ma'am, after what happened with the satellites the squadron deployed above Klatt, do you think the EMP bombs worked?"

"I goddamn well hope so, because Colonel Wright and the rest of our friends should be finishing their jumps right about now." She closed her eyes and saw Eskola. With a silent prayer on her lips, she waited and worried.

Like a flock of predators appearing from nowhere, the second wave of Avengers dropped out of their faster-than-light journey. In case the electromagnetic bombs had failed, Colonel Wright had insisted that the squadron end its jump ten kilometers away from the Kurgan base behind a long rocky ridge that shielded them from enemy observation and fire.

"Speak to me, Eskola," said Wright.

"One second, sir," replied his navigator. "Nothing. I've got nothing on my screen; the Kurg base has no power signature whatsoever."

"That's good enough for me." He keyed his mic and spoke to the rest of the assault force. "Reaper Team, this is Reaper Six, you are clear to attack. I say again, you are clear to attack. Follow me onto the base. I want you to fire your missiles and then get the hell out of Dodge. Reaper Six, out."

He turned his helmet slightly so he could see Eskola in her chair behind him. "Ready?"

"Ready," she replied with a confident tone in her voice.

Wright gave a bit of power to the ship's engine. His Avenger sailed up and over the rocky hill. Formed up like a wedge, the squadron flew meters from the ground toward its objective. Without any power on, the Kurg base sat dark on the asteroid surface. Wright checked his targeting computer and saw that it had already identified its target, the base's main complex.

Barely five seconds later, he heard a steady tone in his headset. He announced, "I have a missile lock." Just to be sure that he wouldn't miss, he waited a few more seconds before depressing the fire button on his joystick. With a bright flash, the torpedo shot out from underneath his ship and streaked straight for its target. All around him the other crews fired off their weapons. Wright pulled back on his joystick and climbed away from the base as the long line of warheads sped toward the doomed base. One by one they struck home, blasting the buildings and communications arrays spread throughout the base to pieces. Wright did not think of the hundreds of Kurgans and Chosen he had probably just killed. He had a job to do and that was all there was to it.

He was about to tell Eskola to begin the countdown for the return jump when an alarm sounded in his helmet. "Warning, incoming missile!"

Without hesitation, Wright applied full power to his ship's engine and flipped a switch on his panel, firing off the Avenger's countermeasures. Behind his craft, superheated metal balls shot out trying to draw away the heat-seeking missile locked onto his Avenger.

"Come on . . . come on, take the bait," said Wright as his ship's computer counted down the seconds to the incoming missile's impact.

"I can see it," called out Eskola, looking through the glass behind her. "It's coming up from the surface of the asteroid. It's small. Must be from a man-portable launcher."

Right away, Wright knew that things might just change in their favor. A shoulder-launched weapon had far less range than a missile fired from a missile battery. He waited a couple of seconds before asking, "What's it doing?"

"It's given up. It's turning away from us," she replied excitedly.

Three seconds later the missile exploded destroying one of the decoys with it.

"That was too close for comfort," said Wright.

"Yes, sir. I'd rather not do that again."

"Do you have the return jump calculations confirmed in the computer?"

Before she could reply, half a kilometer off to the right, a bright flash of light told Wright that one of his ships had just been destroyed. He clenched his jaw in anger and frustration. It was obvious that after the Kurgan base had lost power, some of the soldiers must have known what was coming and rushed out onto the asteroid's surface to engage Wright's team. It was what he would have done if he had been in their position.

A voice came over the comms system. "Reaper Six, this is Reaper Four. Reaper Three just exploded. I say again, Reaper Three is gone."

"Did anyone eject?"

"Negative, sir."

"Roger that," replied Wright, his voice was bitter at the loss. "Time to leave. All craft begin your jumps."

"Sir, we're ready to jump," announced Eskola.

Wright felt the loss of the flight team in his chest. *There would be time to mourn later*, he told himself. "Take us back to the RV, Eskola."

She began her countdown. Within seconds, the stars vanished from sight.

Wright bashed his fist against the side of his cockpit. He knew that there was nothing he could have done to prevent the loss of the two men in Reaper Three, but that didn't stop him from being angry. The only consolation he could think of was that the incoming task force would not be spotted by the Kurgans and reported. They had done their job. Now it was up to the people in the task force to do theirs.

"Status report?" Admiral Sheridan asked.

Killam looked away from the tactical screen. "Sir, we have come out of our jump five hundred thousand kilometers from the Kurgan base. Sensors are showing no sign of life or power emanating from the installation."

Admiral Sheridan smiled. Wright's people had come through. "Task force integrity?"

"Sir, all of the ships have reported in. Only one ship has reported any issues."

"Which ship, and what is the problem?"

"Sir, it's LC-432, one of the spare landing craft. The ship's captain has reported that his perlinium reactor is running a bit high but feels that it is nothing to worry about."

Admiral Sheridan shook his head. "Order him home. I don't want his engine to fail when we are over Klatt. We still have two spare landing craft at our disposal; more than enough to get the job done.

"Aye, sir," replied Killam as he quickly typed out the order. "Message sent and acknowledged."

"Open a secure channel to the task force," said Sheridan to his communications specialist.

"You're on, sir," replied the petty officer.

"Ladies and gentlemen, this is Admiral Sheridan, we have successfully jumped into Kurgan space. The first leg of our journey is now complete. In a couple of minutes, we will begin the second and most hazardous part of this operation. I need not remind you that the lives of over five thousand of our fellow soldiers, fleet members, and Marines hang in the balance. To steal a quote from Admiral Nelson, 'I expect that everyone will do their duty.' End of speech; let's get to work."

"Sir, the task force has indicated that they are ready to jump to Klatt," reported Killam.

With a determined look in his eyes, Admiral Sheridan placed his hands behind his back and nodded.

Killam gave the order. On the tactical screen, all of the ships vanished within seconds of one another.

Sheridan began to pace the deck. He knew that there was no turning back now. They were committed to their chosen course of action. For better or worse, there was going to be a battle in the next twenty-four hours which would seal the fate of the men and women languishing in the mines.

27

Tarina didn't sit down on her bunk as much as collapse onto it. She let out a moan when her arm, bruised earlier in the day, hit the hard wooden sides of her bed. Another long day in the mine had taxed her to the breaking point. She doubted that there wasn't a muscle on her body that did not ache. She closed her eyes for a few seconds and felt herself drifting off to sleep. As much as she wanted to she couldn't afford herself the luxury of a quick nap. Tonight was the night that they intended to escape. She needed all the nourishment she could get, even if it were from the awful Kurgan soup. She muttered, "Get up, you lazy lump."

"Did you say something to me?" asked Wendy, looking as tired as her friend was.

Tarina smiled. "No, just talking to myself again."

"You know that's not a good thing. Soon you'll be answering yourself."

"At least it'll be the right answer."

The people in the bunks began to stir. Tarina looked over and saw the food cart pull up. Her stomach growled. She swung her feet down and slid them into her clogs. With Wendy and Angela by her side, Tarina joined the lineup. After getting their supper meal, they made their way back to Tarina's bed and sat down together.

Angela dipped a piece of dry bread in her soup before devouring it in one bite. She licked her lips and then her fingers, not wanting to waste a morsel of food. She took a quick glance around and said, "I heard a couple of the guards say that the Inspector General is due to arrive later tonight. I hadn't expected him for a few days. Perhaps he's here to witness the bloodletting ceremony?"

A shiver ran down Tarina's back. "If he's here for that, he's a ghoul."

"Ghoul or not, things have just fallen into place for the three of us," interjected Wendy. "Just think, in a matter of hours we could be heading home."

"Let's not get ahead of ourselves," said Angela. "One thing at a time. I think it would be best if we waited until sometime after midnight before sneaking out of here."

Tarina nodded. "I agree. If we go too early we run the risk of someone coming around, finding our bunks empty, and sounding the alarm. It's better to wait until the guards have a belly full of liquor before trying to escape."

"I'll never be able to wait that long," Wendy said, nervously tapping her feet against the side of the bed. "I'm already too worked up."

"You'll just have to try and force yourself to relax," said Angela. "You're supposed to be downtrodden and defeated, not excited and happy."

"You're asking for the impossible."

Tarina patted her friend on the shoulder. "You once told me that you were involved in your high school's drama program. Well, for the next few hours you're going to have to channel your inner actress."

Wendy chuckled at the thought. "Can do."

Travis appeared at the front of the cavern. With him was a squad of Chosen warriors. This time they were carrying rifles, not whips. He spat on the ground at his feet. "All right, you lazy sons of bitches, get up off your asses and form up in three ranks in front of me."

Tarina could sense that something was amiss. The prisoners put down their food and slowly got to their feet.

Travis' expression turned ugly. "Hurry up or I'll have the guards shoot some of you for being slow!"

A murmur ran through the prisoners as they shuffled over and got into three ranks.

"Keep you mouths shut," hollered Travis. "Now listen up, you maggots; I want the following people to fall out and move over beside the guards. For the rest of you, take a look at 'em as they ain't ever coming back."

Tarina's heart began to beat wildly as the names were read off one by one. When hers was called, she could have cried. Instead, she held her head up high, walked over, and joined the other prisoners. She looked back over at Wendy and saw the tears in her friend's eyes. Tarina tried to smile to comfort her but found that she couldn't; she was scared out of her mind.

"The first person who tries something stupid dies as does the person standing next to them," threatened Travis to the selected prisoners. He smiled sadistically at the people he knew he was sending to their deaths. "You'll be joining the other volunteers at the loading platform. Behave yourselves and try to have a nice day."

A captured Marine sergeant broke from the group and ran at Travis only to be shot down before he got a little more than five paces. Less than a second later, another shot rang out and a woman who had been in line with the sergeant fell to the ground dead with a hole in her head.

"God damn it. I warned you, didn't I. I've got a quota I have to fill. I got to find me two more volunteers." He spun about and glared at the cowering prisoners. He quickly picked out two of the fitter and healthier-looking people and had them dragged over to replace the two dead ones.

A terrified young crewman was pushed in line beside Tarina. He was shaking like a leaf and looked no older than eighteen years old. She tapped his arm. Quietly, she said, "Stay calm. If we get the chance, you and I are going to make a run for it."

The young man looked over and nodded. He was too afraid to speak.

Travis dismissed the other prisoners and marched himself to the front of the small column. "No more funny business," warned Travis as he led the prisoners away from their friends.

Wendy stood fixed to the ground as if her feet were made of lead. She watched in horror as Tarina vanished into the darkened tunnel. For the first time in months, she was alone.

A hand reached out and grabbed her arm. "Come on, let's go back to the bunks or the guards will make you move," said Angela.

Wendy hesitated, unsure of what she should be doing.

"There's nothing you can do. She's gone."

Wendy turned. "No! I don't believe you. There must be something we can do to help her and the others."

Angela shook her head. "There is nothing you or I could do that would help Tarina. If we tried to stop them, we'd end up dead like the others."

With her head bowed, Wendy shuffled back to her bunk and collapsed onto her mattress. She brought up her knees to her chest and began to sob. She felt as if someone had just thrust a dagger deep into her heart.

"Let it out," consoled Angela, sitting on the edge of the bunk.

For several minutes, she cried until she rolled over and wiped the tears from her face. "This is horrible beyond words. Poor Tarina; we were so close to getting away."

"I'm sure that she'd still want us to try."

Wendy couldn't believe what she was hearing. Her closest friend had just been taken away for execution and Angela was treating it as a minor setback. She shook her head. "Unless you're a pilot and a damn good one, we're not going anywhere."

"I'm no pilot. I thought perhaps you could give it a try."

Wendy looked Angela in the eyes and said, "In your dreams."

Angela stood up and shook her head. "Then I guess we're stuck here until you die or I find us another pilot, whichever comes first."

28

"Okay, it's nearly 2300 hours; Master Sergeant Cole and I are going to take a better look around this evening and try to learn what we can," explained Sheridan to Toscano. "If we're not back by 0300, carry on without us. The task force isn't due for another day, so you have plenty of time to mark and record all of the LZs for them."

"Right, sir," replied Toscano.

"Are you sure you don't need another set of eyes?" asked Urban, chafing to help.

Sheridan shook his head. "No, Sergeant, you have to remain here. Two people may be able to move about without drawing too much attention, three might be pushing it. Besides, I only brought back enough clothes for two people."

"You're welcome to mine," said Cole, waving a hand in front of his nose. "It's gonna take a week of long, hot showers to wash the smell of my body."

"Sergeant, you can't go anywhere. I need you to help me coord the incoming fire," pointed out Toscano.

Urban knew that he didn't have a leg to stand on. He relented and nodded.

Sheridan said to Toscano, "We'll see you in a few hours."

"Good luck, sir."

"How come no one ever says good luck, Sergeant?" groused Cole.

"Because it would be wasted on you," replied Sheridan. With that, he led Cole out of their hiding spot and back out into the open. Both men took cover and looked up into the sky trying to see if there were any drones flying about.

"The coast looks clear," said Cole. "Let's get a move on, sir."

Sheridan hunched down and led them into the darkness. It took them less than ten minutes to make it back to the office door they had used the night before. Sheridan quickly jimmied the door open. Only Sheridan had a weapon on him. As Cole was playing a prisoner, he wasn't carrying one. The room, as before, was quiet. All of the lights were off. Sheridan dug out his flashlight and turned it on.

"Okay, from here on out, unless we're dead certain that we're alone, we cannot talk to one another," explained Sheridan. "As I'm supposed to be escorting you somewhere in the mine. I'm going to speak Kurgan to the guards and the odd word to you in English to move you along."

"Sounds par for the course," said Cole with a grin on his dirt-covered face.

"If, for whatever reason, we get split up, head straight back to the cavern and let the others know what has happened."

"Yeah, whatever, sir. I ain't letting you out of my sight. So quit stalling and let's get a move on. My skin's crawling. I think these rags are infested with lice or whatever pests they have on this godforsaken rock."

Sheridan shuddered at the thought of the little parasites and scratched the back of his neck. "I don't think mine are much better."

"Don't change the subject," Cole whispered, sliding over to the door leading out into the tunnel system. When he didn't hear anyone moving about, he opened the door.

Sheridan stepped out and grabbed his pistol, a Kurgan one that he had kept from the fight on Illum Prime, and pointed it at Cole. "Walk," he said in his best attempt at a Kurgan speaking English. Which sounded to him more like poorly spoken Arabic than anything else.

With his hands by his sides, Cole began to walk down the long sloping corridor. When they came to the tarpaulin screen, Sheridan stopped and poked his head inside. Bile rushed to his throat when he saw at least twenty new emaciated bodies lying on the ground in a heap. Some of the men and women had their eyes open looking up at him. It appeared that the Kurgans didn't care if the Chosen warrior who looked after the dead was around, they just kept dumping the bodies. Sheridan pulled his head back and took in several deep breaths to calm himself and to rid his nostrils of the vile smell from the room.

"You okay?" whispered Cole.

Sheridan nodded and pointed down the corridor with his pistol. They carried on for another minute before coming to an open elevator shaft. Sheridan stepped up to a metal bar secured to the wall to prevent people from falling down into the shaft and looked down. He could only see a few meters below them, after that, it was as dark as pitch. He moved back, pushed the button, and waited for an elevator to arrive.

Just as their lift arrived, a voice in Kurgan called out, "Hold, please."

Sheridan turned and saw a Chosen sergeant running toward them. He raised the bar and motioned with his weapon for Cole to step back. The sergeant stepped into the elevator as did Sheridan and Cole.

"Where are you taking the prisoner?" asked the sergeant.

"The third level," replied Sheridan, recalling the mine schematic on the map.

The sergeant nodded and looked down at this watch before saying, "Your prisoner looks healthy enough. Is he going to join the others?"

Sheridan had no idea what the sergeant was on about. Rather than keep talking and potentially revealing that they weren't what they appeared to be, Sheridan shook his head.

The sergeant shrugged and pressed the down button for the third and eighth floors. With a shudder, the elevator began to descend. Cole and Sheridan looked over at one another as if to say that they had dodged their first bullet of the evening. Less than thirty seconds later, the elevator came to a halt. Sheridan nodded at the sergeant before escorting Cole out onto the third floor. He stopped for a moment to get his bearings.

"The nearest duty station is to your left," said the sergeant just as the elevator continued on its way.

Sheridan waved and waited for the sergeant to disappear from sight. The second he was gone, Sheridan lowered his weapon and indicated to the right with his head. It didn't take them long before they came to the first cavern filled with sleeping prisoners.

Cole saw a painted sign. "What's that mean on the wall?"

"It says Red One. I think they color and number code the caves."

"The schematic said that there were thirty-three caverns, did it not?"

Sheridan nodded. "Let's see how long it takes us to walk the length of the tunnel; see if there are any exits along the way we could use when the time comes."

With Cole in the lead, they walked in silence studying every nook and cranny of the long passageway. Every detail, from the size of the caves to their exact location, was memorized.

A hushed voice seemed to float on the air. Wendy rolled over and did her best to ignore it. Her tired body craved sleep. Again the sound of a woman's voice invaded her subconscious. For a split second, she saw Tarina standing there next to her bunk. Her heart began to race. Pulled out of her deep slumber, Wendy opened her weary eyes, turned over, and sat up. Instead of her friend standing there, her eyes focused on Angela's face. "What do you want?"

"I know what you said earlier, but I think that we should still try to escape tonight while we still have the chance."

Wendy shook her head. "I already told you. I don't know how to fly a ship."

"I know but what if we forced one of the shuttle's pilots to help us? I know that you can't read Kurgan, but I can. I could assist you with the ship's navigational computers."

Wendy sat up and hung her feet over the side of her bunk. As much as it pained her, she knew that there was nothing she could do to help Tarina. Perhaps Angela was onto something. Wendy knew that without her friend to help sustain her courage that her days were probably numbered. Escape seemed the only logical thing left to do. She slipped her feet into her clogs and looked over at Angela. Feeling as if she was about to betray her best friend, she said, "Okay, let's do this."

"What are you two deceitful bitches up to?" asked Travis as he slipped out from the shadows. Neither woman had heard him sneak into the cavern. Both looked over at him with a look of horror on their faces.

He pulled a long knife from behind his back. "I said, what are you two bitches planning to do?"

"We were just about to go to the bathroom," replied Angela. "After the guards have been drinking, it's not safe for a woman to go there on her own."

Travis stepped closer. He twisted the blade around in his hand. "You're lying. I can see it in your eyes, you Kurgan witch."

Angela moved Wendy behind her, protecting her with her body. "I'm not lying."

With a move that surprised both women, Travis shot his hand out and grabbed Angela's left wrist and twisted it hard over. She grimaced in pain and dropped to her knees. Before Wendy could help, Travis shot a knee straight into Angela's head, knocking her out cold. With a lustful look in his eyes, Travis grabbed Wendy and pulled her close to him. The smell of alcohol on his breath made her turn her head away.

"What's wrong, Captain? Don't you like enlisted men? When I get finished with you, you're never going to forget how much fun you had tonight."

"No!" pleaded Wendy as she squirmed in his arms trying to break free.

He reached up and forced a grubby hand over her mouth. "Don't fight it, little girl. Hell, with a man like me, you may even like it."

No matter how hard she fought, she could not escape his hold on her. She tried to bring her knee up to hit him in the groin, but he had already placed his hip there blocking the move. The thought that he knew what he was doing terrified Wendy. Travis chuckled and pushed her back against her bed. They fell back and Travis landed on top of her. His hands began to tear at her clothes. Fear filled her mind. She knew that no one was coming to her aid. Even if any of the other prisoners were awake, they were all too scared of Travis to lift a finger. She closed her eyes and blocked what was about to happen out of her mind. All of a sudden she heard Travis gasp in pain. A second later, she felt his body being pulled off of hers. She opened her eyes and saw two men standing beside her bed. One was a Chosen soldier who held

Travis' knife in his left hand while the other man, holding Travis by the neck, was dressed as a prisoner.

"Are you okay?" asked the prisoner.

"Yes," she replied. She turned her head and saw that the Chosen warrior seemed to be examining her face. Something about him made her look deep into the man's eyes. Her eyes widened and her heart leaped for joy when she recognized the man standing before her. "I know you. You . . . you're Michael Sheridan . . . aren't you?"

"Shhh," said Sheridan, bringing a finger up to his lips. Quietly he asked, "How do you know me?"

"I'd know you anywhere. You may not remember, but we've met before. Not to mention, Tarina has your picture all over her room and in the cockpit of our old Avenger."

Sheridan's pulse began to beat faster at the sound of Tarina's name. Right away, his mind took him back to a cold, fog-filled morning on a distant world when he and Cole had rescued a handful of downed pilots from a Kurgan patrol. A smile crept across his lips when he recognized Wendy. He was aghast at her condition. Her clothes were ragged and torn. Her face was covered in weeks of dirt and grime. It looked as if she had lost fifteen kilos since he had last laid eyes on her.

"My God, I do remember you. Your name is Wendy. Where's Tarina? Is she here?"

Wendy shook her head.

Just as Sheridan was about to ask where Taina was, a woman at his feet moaned and tried to sit up. He bent down and helped her up.

Wendy jumped from her bunk and swung an arm around the woman. She looked up at Sheridan and said, "It's okay. Her name's Angela; she's my friend."

"Who's this then?" asked Cole as he tightened his grip around his captive's neck.

"His name is Travis," replied Wendy, with hate in her voice. "He's nothing more than a traitor. He sent Tarina and some of the other prisoners away to be butchered by the Kurgans."

Sheridan's gut felt as if he had been sucker punched. The ceremony was not supposed to happen for another couple of days. "When was she taken?"

"I'm not sure; some time after five this evening."

Sheridan turned on a dime and took a hold of Travis's dirty uniform collar and pulled him toward him. "Where did you send her, and how do I get there?"

Travis looked from Sheridan to Cole. His days as master over the lives of his fellow service personnel had just ended and he knew it. "You're both Marines, ain't ya? What are you doing here?"

Sheridan tightened his grip on Travis' collar and began to choke him. "Answer my bloody questions."

Travis began to quiver. He gasped for air. "Look, sir, I was only doing what needed to be done to stay alive."

"Where is she, and how do I get there?" Sheridan asked, inches away from Travis' face.

"They were marched down to the train loading platform for movement out to the Kurgan camp in the desert. It should be leaving in the next few minutes. You'll never get there in time."

"I'll be the judge of that." With that, Sheridan pushed Travis back into Cole's arms. He looked over at Wendy. "Where's the nearest elevator?"

"Head out of the cavern, turn right, and it should be no more than one hundred meters away on the left-hand side of the tunnel."

"What do want me to do with the traitor?" Cole asked.

"Kill him," said Sheridan.

Travis' eyes widened. He went to speak but found that Cole had wrapped his arm tightly around his neck. Like a boa constrictor, Cole began to squeeze the life out of the collaborator. Sheridan was surprised that neither woman looked away. Instead, they seemed to relish watching Travis flail about as he lost the fight to live and died in Cole's powerful arms. After less than a minute, it was over.

"Where can we dispose of the body?" Cole asked Wendy.

"Leave him here with us," said Angela. "I know plenty of out-of-the-way spots to stash his body where it will never be found."

Cole laid Travis' body on the ground before looking up at Sheridan. "Now what, Captain?"

"I'm going to try and stop the train. If I can delay its leaving for a full twenty-four hours, then they'll be here when the task force arrives."

"The fleet, it's coming here?" asked Wendy.

Sheridan nodded. "You have to keep it quiet. Your lives require that secrecy be maintained."

"I think I can keep my mouth shut for a day or two."

Cole stood. "Okay, then it's done. Let's go."

Sheridan shook his head. "Master Sergeant, I need you to stay up here with the prisoners. I can blend in with the Chosen soldiers and do what I must. You, on the other hand, can do more good by remaining back here. Someone needs to help the prisoners when the Marines arrive."

Cole hesitated a second before offering his hand. He did not want to split up from his friend but knew that he was right. He forced a smile. "Good luck, sir. I'll see you in a twenty-four hours."

Sheridan shook his friend's hand. "It's a deal. Try not to be late."

With a look of fierce resolve in his eyes, Sheridan turned and ran for the nearby elevator. His mind fixed on saving Tarina before it was too late.

Cole looked over at Wendy. "Would either of you two ladies happen to have a weapon on you?"

"Actually, we might just be able to help you, Sergeant," said Wendy. She looked at Angela. "Why don't you go and retrieve your pistol and anything else you think might help us from your hiding spot?"

Angela looked up at Cole with genuine fear in her eyes.

"Don't worry, I'll protect you," said Wendy, trying to reassure her worried comrade. "Trust me, everything will work out. You'll be home with your children before you know it."

Angela patted Wendy on the hand, stood up, and walked out into the darkened tunnel.

"What was that all about?" Cole asked.

"She's just worried, that's all."

"Aren't we all? How many prisoners would you say we can count on should things turn ugly?"

"You just met them. Everyone here is too afraid or too tired to lift a finger to save anyone but themselves. You saw what was about to happen to me and not a one of them could be bothered to help me."

"Jesus, an army of three people. That is not what I'd hoped to hear."

"Sorry. Anyone who pushed back or showed any spark of life was killed within days of getting here. Most of the people left alive are emotionally broken wrecks."

"It's not your fault. Aside from the tunnel that leads to the next level, do you happen to know how many elevators there are on the third level?"

"Six. Why?"

"Just a thought," replied Cole, his voice trailing off while he pondered his next move.

29

At the bottom of the mine, a long line of prisoners snaked down a darkened tunnel and then out onto the train platform. Heavily armed Chosen guards walked up and down the column pushing and beating the people to keep them from trying to escape.

"I don't understand why they are doing this to us," said the frightened teenage crewman at Tarina's side.

"It's some Kurgan ritual," replied Tarina. "What's your name?"

"Crewman Jones, ma'am."

"I think we can dispense with rank. What's your first name?"

"Mike. My name is Mike."

"Mine is Tarina. Pleased to meet you, Mike." Tarina looked away and smiled. She wished that it was her Michael standing there. If he were, she had no doubt that things would turn out differently.

A voice boomed out of a speaker mounted on the wall. "Move forward slowly and enter the train cars. Do not attempt to escape or you and the people around you will be killed."

"I guess this is it," said Tarina.

"I don't want to die," stammered Jones.

Tarina took his hand in hers. "We're not going to die. I won't let that happen."

"I'm glad I'm with you, Tarina."

The line began to move.

Tarina said, "Keep your head up and never let them see you looking scared."

Jones nodded and put on his best face. He went to take a step when the sound of gunfire cut through the air. People screamed and dropped to the ground as a Chosen warrior shot down a couple of men who had attacked another warrior.

Tarina felt Jones grip her hard so tight that it hurt. She couldn't blame him; she was scared too.

"On your feet!" yelled a Chosen sergeant. "Keep moving!"

Together, they walked forward as calm as they could, knowing that each step brought them closer to their deaths.

The instant the elevator touched the ground, Sheridan jumped over the metal safety bar and sprinted down the tunnel. The sound of distant gunfire reverberated off the rocky walls. Sheridan picked up his pace. He had no idea what he was going to do when he got there, all he knew was that he had to stop the train from leaving. Up ahead, he could see the light shining in the tunnel from the train station. He was almost there when two Chosen soldiers stepped out from behind a wooden barricade and waved at him to stop.

"You, there, stop," yelled one of the Chosen.

Sheridan saw the soldier's partner raise his rifle and aim it at him. He gritted his teeth, slowed down, and came to a halt at the barricade.

"Where do you think you are going?" asked the Chosen soldier. Sheridan saw that he was wearing a sergeant's insignia on his collar. "No one can go in there. The ore loading platform is out of bounds until the train leaves."

It hadn't left. There was still time. Sheridan came to attention. "Sorry, Sergeant, but I was told to report to the train. I'm filling in for another man who is sick. If I don't get on the train, my officer will have me punished."

The sergeant shook his head. "I don't care. Orders are orders. The only people who can board the train are those from Captain Katulan's company. Now step back and give me your name so I can check your story."

The sergeant's partner walked closer with his rifle aimed at Sheridan. The sound of the train's engine powering up told him that he had to act before it was too late. Out of the corner of his eye, he saw the barrel of the Kurgan rifle. With lightning-fast reflexes, Sheridan grabbed the rifle barrel and pointed it at the ground. At the same time, he reached behind his back, grabbed a hold of a hidden knife, and threw it into the unsuspecting sergeant's chest. The stunned Chosen soldier tried to pull his rifle free, only to have Sheridan let go of the barrel. The soldier, not expecting the move, staggered backward. Sheridan reached over and pulled the blade from the dying sergeant's chest, spun about, and sent it flying into the soldier's stomach. The man let go of his rifle and reached for the knife protruding from his midsection. His face turned gray as he dropped to his knees with a puzzled look on his face. His last thoughts were: *Why would one of our own attack us?*

Sheridan rushed over and pulled the dead sergeant's pistol from its holster. A second later, he heard the train come to life. He jammed the gun into his belt and ran as fast as he could out onto the station platform. He could see the last train car beginning to move. Like an Olympic sprinter closing in on the finish line, he dug deep and gave it all he could. He ignored the shouts from the other Chosen still standing around on the platform. His mind was focused on one thing and one thing only, getting onto the train. A soldier stepped in front of him and tried to stop him, only to be struck in the chest by Sheridan's shoulder and sent tumbling to the ground.

Within seconds, the back of the train was in reach. Sheridan looked up and saw that the last car was about to enter the tunnel heading out into the desert. He had perhaps five seconds before it was gone. With a yell on his lips, he dove for a metal handrail on the back of the train car. Sheridan felt his fingers take hold. He yanked the rest of his body onto a small railing at the back of the train just as it was swallowed up by the darkened tunnel. He scrambled to grab a hold of whatever he could with his other hand. Sheridan turned his head and took a quick look behind him. He could see a couple of Chosen warriors standing on the platform pointing at him. They grew smaller by the second and then vanished from sight as the train turned a bend in the pitch-black tunnel. With his heart beating wildly in his chest, Sheridan took a couple of deep breaths to calm himself before trying to see if the backdoor on the car was unlocked. He was relieved to find that the door was open.

"In for a penny, in for a pound," he said to himself as he pulled out his stolen pistol and brought it up so he would be ready to react if he ran into trouble. Sheridan pulled open the door and stepped inside. He was surprised to see that the long car was empty. He had expected there to be at least a couple of soldiers sitting there. Rather than dwell on his good luck, Sheridan began to walk forward to the next car. He had no clue how long the train was or where the prisoners were being held. He knew that although trains had become faster, the basic design of trains had not changed over the centuries. Somewhere up front, the locomotive would be controlled by an engineer using a computer to control the train's speed.

A door at the other end of the carriage flew open and two Chosen soldiers stormed in with rifles in their hands. Sheridan never hesitated. He dropped to one knee and opened fire. The lead warrior fell with a hole in his chest. The next tried to bring his weapon up to fire but found it unwieldy in the narrow corridor and died from a shot to the head. Sheridan ran forward and checked the bodies. Both were dead. He rummaged through their uniforms for any ammunition for his pistol before moving to the open door. He took a quick look and saw that the door to the next car was closed. A feeling in his gut told him be wary. He had no doubt they knew that he was here and would be waiting for him. Sheridan turned his head and looked back at the two dead Chosen. When he saw their ammunition belts, an idea popped into his mind.

"What do you think is going on?" Jones asked Tarina as a couple of warriors ran past them to the back of the car and took up positions covering the door.

"I don't know, but something has really gotten them spooked," she replied. All of the prisoners in the car were sitting on the floor. They were being held in three cars that were usually used to transport the ore to the refinery.

She knew that their best chance of escape had just arrived. With the guards distracted, if she could rally enough people, they could try to overpower the soldiers and stop the train before it reached its destination. Tarina looked around the carriage and saw a tough-looking man with tattoos covering his trunk-like arms whom she knew had to be a Marine.

"Stay here," she whispered to Jones before crawling over beside the Marine. She could see him studying the two soldiers by the door. She smiled. He was thinking exactly the same thing she was.

"Hey there," said Tarina to the man. "We don't have a lot of time. Are you a Marine, and are you thinking of making a break for it?"

The man nodded.

"Are there any other people in here you can trust?"

"Yeah, a couple."

"Good. My name is Captain Pheto and when I give the signal, I want you and your friends to take down those guards."

"My name is Sergeant Lee. After we kill them, what are we going to do, ma'am?"

Tarina hadn't thought that far. Before she could say another word, the door at the back of the car erupted in a fiery explosion. Shrapnel flew inward, killing one of the Chosen; the other, stunned by the blast, staggered back from the smoldering debris.

Sheridan was up on his feet and running for the blown-open door. His plan had worked better than he had anticipated. He had taken two hand grenades from the dead Chosen, jammed them against the door's lock, activated the grenades, and taken cover. He ran through the smoke and jumped over a jagged piece of the destroyed door, landing inside the next carriage. He saw a warrior try to bring up his rifle and fired off two rounds into the man's chest, killing him.

"Michael!" called out a familiar voice.

"Tarina, is that you? Are you in here?" replied Sheridan. His eyes searched the crowd desperate to find her.

A second later, from out of the surprised crowd ran Tarina. She dove at Sheridan and threw her arms around his neck and pulled him in tight. Tears began to run down her face. "Oh God, Michael, I thought I would never see you again."

He gave her a hug letting her know that he felt the same way. "It's all right, we're going to get through this together. A task force will be arriving soon to bring all of you home."

"Who the hell are you?" asked Lee, eyeing Sheridan with suspicion as he picked up one of the dead Chosen's rifles.

"Captain Michael Sheridan," he replied, letting go of Tarina. "And you?"

"Sergeant Lee. I was with the Ninth Marines when I was captured."

"Okay, listen up, Sergeant, we've got to take this train before the Kurgs wise up and send reinforcements. For the moment, I think they believe that I'm one of theirs and have gone nuts. So, I'm willing to bet that they still think they can handle the situation."

"What do you want to do, sir?"

"This is a mag-lev train, so climbing outside at over five hundred kilometers an hour is a non-starter. Also, trying to go underneath is no good as there won't be enough clearance from the bottom of the train to the magnetized tracks. We're going to have to take this train car by car until we get to the control room. The faster we do this, the less chance they'll have to organize themselves and stop us."

Lee squeezed his rifle tight in his hands. "Sounds good to me, sir. After a couple of months of hell, I'm ready to give some of it back."

"Does anyone have any idea how many Chosen and Kurgs there are on the train?"

"Perhaps twenty in total," said Tarina.

Sheridan pursed his lips. "Sergeant, round up a couple more people capable of fighting and join me by the door leading to the next carriage. Make sure that you grab the grenades and weapons from these two Chosen," said Sheridan, pointing at the corpses.

Lee nodded before bending down to strip off the ammo belt from the nearest body.

"What do you want me to do, Michael?" asked Tarina.

"There are more weapons and ammunition laying on the floor of the car behind us. Take someone with you, grab it all, and then fall into line behind the sergeant and me. We're going to need all the firepower we can muster if we want to pull this off."

Tarina nodded and looked at her newly found friend. "Come on, Mike, we've got work to do."

Jones stood up and moved over to Tarina's side.

Sheridan looked at the young crewman. He thought about making a wisecrack about being traded in for a younger man but let it go, for now. He turned and made his way through the crowd to the back door. Lee and two more Marines were waiting for him. "When Captain Pheto gets back here with more Kurgan weapons, I want you to place two grenades against the next door's lock and arm the devices. When they go off, we rush the next car and shoot anyone who isn't a prisoner. We keep repeating this until we reach the front of the train."

Lee smiled. "My pleasure."

30

The rich smell of incense wafted through the air. The light from several ornamental torches flickered as a breeze came inside the crimson-colored tent.

Colonel Kuhr knelt before a stone altar with a copy of the Kurgan Scriptures in his hands. He read out loud the prayer for purification before closing his book. He bowed his head, stood up, and carefully placed his holy book on a nearby table. His copy was nearly four hundred years old and had been handed down from generation to generation. Next to his son fighting somewhere in the galaxy with the Kurgan military, it was his most prized possession. He stepped to the tent opening. Outside he could see hundreds of torches burning in the night, each one marking another tent. He had forbidden anything but traditional means to light the camp. All of their transports and fighting vehicles were parked a couple of kilometers away to give the illusion that they had stepped back in time to when the sacred ceremony had first begun. In a matter of hours, just as the sun rose on the horizon, he would oversee the first wartime *Kahtak* ritual in over a century. He felt a certain pride knowing that one hundred of his officers and senior sergeants would soon be ascending into the ranks of the Old Guard.

He put a hand on the hilt of his sword hanging from his waist. Unlike the straight, heavy blades carried by Kurgan officers in line units, those of the Imperial Guard were curved and looked more like a scimitar. His had been his father's when he had loyally served the empire. Colonel Kuhr had received special permission to bring his entire regiment, all four battalions, to witness the bloodletting ceremony. He intended to form them up so they could watch and rejoice in the ritual as their peers, one by one, took the life of an enemy combatant.

"Colonel Kuhr, sorry for interrupting," said Captain Kazar, Kuhr's hard-working adjutant.

"What is it, Captain?"

"I have just received a report that fighting has broken out onboard the train filled with the human prisoners."

Kuhr did not like the sound of that. "Captain, what precisely was passed on to you?"

"The train's engineer reported that he had heard gunfire and explosions in the cars behind him."

Kuhr knew that it could only mean that the prisoners had somehow rebelled and gained access to some of the weapons onboard the locomotive. He regretted not sending more Kurgans along, instead relying on the prison's poorly trained Chosen warriors to escort the POWs to the camp. "What is Commandant Kodan doing about this?"

"Sir, I spoke with his deputy and he informed me that a couple of gunships had been dispatched to stop the train."

"Kodan is a drunkard and a bloody fool," said Kuhr. "He can barely manage his prison, let alone try to sort out this mess that he has allowed to happen. Captain, get a hold of Kodan's deputy and tell him not to engage the train with gunfire. If they do, I will personally cut open Kodan and anyone else I can lay my hands on with my blade. I want all of the human prisoners captured alive."

"Yes, sir," said Kazar, turning to leave.

"One last thing, Captain. When is the train due to arrive here?"

Kazar glanced at the watch built into the armor protecting his wrist. "Sir, it should be here in precisely twelve minutes' time."

Kuhr nodded. He watched his adjutant dart away to try and get a handle on the situation. He had hoped for a quiet and dignified ceremony. Now, however, he had to face the facts; he would have to take charge of the situation before it got out of hand. He yelled out, "Sergeant Kurka, report."

A couple of seconds later, a grizzled-looking Kurgan soldier with scars running across his leathery face ran over and stood ramrod straight in front of Kuhr. "Yes, Colonel."

"Sergeant Kurka, my old friend, wake the regiment and have the battalion commanders report to me right away."

"Yes, sir." Kurka turned and let out a deafening cry that was taken up by sentries all around the camp. Within seconds, soldiers rushed from their tents and formed up into their companies and then their battalions.

It took less than three minutes for the four battalion commanders to arrive at Kuhr's tent. He waited outside with his hand resting on his sword. He looked into the golden eyes of the men he had handpicked to be in his regiment and had steered their careers every step of the way. He got straight to the point. "Something has gone wrong. It sounds like the train carrying the prisoners has been hijacked or soon will be. What I want is for the train to be retaken with a minimum number of casualties to the humans on board. We need each and every one of them alive for the ritual."

His assembled leaders nodded their understanding.

Kuhr looked at the youngest one and said, "Lieutenant Colonel Kulk, I want you to stop and seize the train intact. No small arms, swords only."

Kulk stood tall. "You can count on the Fourth Battalion to do what must be done."

"I know. Now report to your battalion and move it to the train station immediately. Don't waste your time giving any speeches. Attack is the order of the day."

Kulk nodded, clicked his heels together, and sprinted off into the night.

Kuhr said to the remainder, "As for the rest of you, I want you to form up your men and be prepared to assist if necessary."

The three other senior officers nodded and left to get their men ready. Kuhr stood alone looking up into the heavens trying to find his home world. When he spotted the flickering speck of light, he closed his eyes and said a prayer asking for victory and a speedy resolution to the crisis.

Sergeant Kurka walked over and waited for Colonel Kuhr to finish. He reported, "Sir, the regiment is ready to move."

"Thank you, Sergeant."

"Sir, what of our aerial transports and ground support vehicles, shall I order the crews to make ready?"

In the rush to get on top of the situation, Kuhr had forgotten about their integral fighting assets. "A wise idea, Sergeant. Have my adjutant pass the order for crews to prepare their equipment for battle. We may not need them, but I'd feel better if I knew that they were ready to move on a moment's notice."

"It will be done, sir," replied the old sergeant as he ambled off to find Captain Kazar.

With the orders given, Kuhr could only wait. Once more he turned his head and stared up at the stars. He spotted a bright light racing across the night sky. It looked like a meteor, but he knew better. It was one of the planet's communications satellites that he had spotted the night before. He watched it streak past only to vanish in the blink of an eye. *How odd,* he thought to himself. *It shouldn't have reentered the atmosphere and if it did, it would have left a bright trail behind it as it burnt up.* For now, he let it go. He had more important things on his mind. When the dust settled, he could ask all the questions he wanted. He looked away and walked to the front of his tent. In the low ground, he could see the warriors of the Fourth Battalion running in step toward the train station. Colonel Kur didn't expect things to take long. His soldiers were more than a match for any escaped prisoners. He looked forward to getting the ritual back on track and enjoying the dawn ceremony.

Above him, another satellite quickly followed by another, vanished. As did his ability to communicate with anyone outside of his camp. Colonel Kuhr did not know it yet, but his troubles were just beginning.

31

Smoke clouded the air. The sound of automatic gunfire in the enclosed space drowned out the voices of the dead and dying that littered the floor of the train carriage.

Sheridan dropped his empty pistol and picked up a Chosen soldier's discarded rifle. The second train car filled with prisoners had fallen quickly. However, the enemy soldiers in the last carriage were not as easily surprised and were selling their lives dearly. Caught in the deadly crossfire were the prisoners who could do nothing more than lay down with their hands over heads and wait for the nightmare to be over.

With a long burst, Sheridan killed a Chosen sergeant who was trying to haul a terrified woman up off the floor to use her as a shield. Standing beside him was Sergeant Lee. Hit three times already, the indomitable Marine refused to step back and let someone else join the fray. Through the smoke, Sheridan could see that there were only a Kurgan officer and one Chosen soldier blocking the way to the train's engine compartment. He had had enough. With a flick of the arming switch, Sheridan activated the grenade launcher on his rifle.

"Everyone down!" hollered Sheridan as he pulled the trigger. In the blink of an eye, the high-explosive shell struck the Kurgan officer in the chest. With a loud boom, it exploded, killing him and the warrior next to him. A shard of shrapnel flew back and hit Sheridan on the cheek, digging a deep groove into his flesh. He was so worked up that he never felt the blood trickling down his face.

Sheridan edged forward over the bodies of several dead Chosen soldiers until he came to the front of the carriage. The Kurgan officer was nowhere to be seen. Blood and gore were splattered on the walls. He opened a door and saw that they had finally arrived at the engine compartment. It had cost at least a dozen lives and twice as many injured personnel to get this far. Sheridan turned his head and called out, "Next team up."

Through the haze, Tarina and Crewman Jones made their way through the debris-filled car to link up with Sheridan and Lee.

Sheridan stepped out of the way to allow Tarina and her partner to place the explosives on the final door barring their way. As soon as the devices were set, Tarina pressed the arm button and hauled Jones back to avoid the coming blast.

In his mind, Sheridan counted down the three-second delay. Right on time, the grenades exploded, shattering the door leading to the engine. Sheridan was the first one inside and saw that aside from a terrified engineer sitting behind his computer console, the compartment was empty. He let out a deep breath. The fight was over.

Sheridan walked over and jammed the hot barrel of his rifle into the man's side. "Stop this train and then take us back toward the prison."

The Chosen shook his head. "I can't. Even if I wanted to, I can't do what you want."

"Why not?"

The man, his hand shaking uncontrollably, pointed to the computer built into the wall of the carriage. "The outgoing route is fixed as is the return one. I just ensure that the train does not go too fast and fly off its track."

Sheridan swore. "Okay, when do we arrive at our destination?"

The Chosen checked the time on the computer screen. "In four minutes and twelve seconds."

They had spilled so much blood to get this far; Sheridan couldn't believe that there was nothing they could do. He looked over at the screen before asking, "Once we stop, can you activate the return trip without waiting to be told to do so?"

"Yes, but why would I?"

"Because if you don't, the sergeant standing behind me will rip your head off with his bare hands, that's why."

When the engineer saw the blood-stained visage of Sergeant Lee staring down at him, he gulped and nodded. Any thought of resistance evaporated in under a second.

Sheridan turned and filled in Lee with what was going on.

Lee smiled, stepped over to the train's engineer, and put his rifle up against the man's temple. "Hello," he said in Kurgan.

"Hello," replied the engineer, positive that he was looking into the eyes of the devil himself.

Sheridan moved back to the last train car and met Tarina and Jones waiting there for him. Both were covered in sweat and blood.

"Michael, you've been hit," said Tarina as she reached over and wiped the blood from his cheek.

Sheridan saw the blood and shrugged. "I hadn't noticed. How are we?"

"We lost fourteen people during the fight," said Tarina, her voice was tired and sad. "A couple more are on their way out. There are plenty of injuries, but most are superficial or light wounds. Aside from that, the remainder of the freed prisoners seem to be doing okay."

He smiled. "We're not out of the woods yet. In only a couple of minutes' time, we're going to arrive at the Kurg camp.

Hopefully, we can get this heap of junk moving back the way we came before the Kurgans manage to put a stop to our little rebellion."

"Michael, I doubt anyone here wants to go back into that godawful prison."

"None of you will. When we're about fifty klicks from the mine, I'll disable the train's engine. We'll head for the hills and hunker down until the task force arrives."

Tarina put her hand on his shoulder. "No matter what happens next, I'm happy that you're here by my side."

He placed a hand over hers. "So am I, Tarina, so am I."

32

Private Snow spat out the food he had been chewing, scrambled to his feet, and ran over to Lieutenant Toscano's side. She was lying on the ground with a blanket wrapped around her "Ma'am, . . . ma'am, please wake up. I'm picking up chatter, a lot of chatter on the radio!"

Toscano sat straight up, pulled off her lightweight blanket, and looked up at Snow. "Are you sure? The task force isn't due for another twenty-four hours."

"I'm positive, ma'am. I've got comms traffic from several fighter groups. I think they're busy blasting the Kurg satellites to pieces."

Toscano nudged Urban with her boot. "Game on, Sergeant, it's time to guide in the assault force."

Urban got right to his feet. As he rubbed the sleep from his eyes, he checked the time. "They're early."

"Early or not, we've got a job to do. And one thing's for sure, we can't do it from in here. Let's grab the comms and laser-marking gear and get up on top of this butte."

With their arms full of weapons and equipment, Toscano, Urban, and Snow climbed out of the cave, ran to the edge of the rocky hill, and set up an observation post.

Toscano grabbed a handset and keyed the mic, "Trident Six, this is Ghost One, over." With her heart beating like a drum, she waited for someone high above in orbit to answer her call.

Within seconds of one another, all of the task force's ships ended their jump right above the prison planet. Admiral Sheridan stood with his hands behind his back and watched the tactical screen as his ships spread out and got to work. The *Saratoga* launched one of her fighter squadrons to destroy all of the Kurgan satellites and any ships unlucky enough to be in orbit. Another squadron took up position around the task force ships to protect it. The last two waited for the order to begin their attack on the planet's surface to clear away any enemy opposition before the landing craft went down. The missile cruiser, *Ford*, had already launched her first salvo of missiles at the communications sites around the mine to prevent the enemy from calling for help. The destroyers, *Churchill* and *Algonquin*, maneuvered to cover the landing craft that would be used to bring the freed prisoners home, while the support ship, *Arctic*, stayed close to the *Saratoga*, ready to assist as needed.

"Sir, Colonel White wants to know if he can begin his descent," said Killam, looking up from his console.

Admiral Sheridan shook his head. "Has there been any word from the reconnaissance team? I don't want White's ground force going in blind."

"Yes, sir. They just came up on the means," replied the communications officer.

"On speaker."

Toscano's voice came in loud and clear. "Trident Six, this is Ghost One, do you read me, over."

"This is Trident Six, we hear you loud and clear, over," replied the admiral. "What is your status down there?"

"We crash-landed but have managed to set up an OP overlooking the mine. We have already sent to you the coordinates for five possible LZs and have also identified several Kurgan heavy weapons' positions."

"Got 'em," said Killam as he rushed to relay the info to the task force.

"Any word on the status of the prisoners?" asked Admiral Sheridan.

"None. We have men inside but have yet to hear back from them."

Robert Sheridan didn't have to be told that it was undoubtedly his son and Master Sergeant Cole who had entered the mine. At least he knew that his son had survived the crash. "Ghost One, good work. Keep your heads down, the fighter-bombers and the Marines are on their way down. Trident Six, out."

"Sir, the assault force is entering Klatt's atmosphere," announced Killam.

"Time to the objective?"

"Fifteen minutes for the fighters and twenty-three for the landing craft."

Admiral Sheridan turned and looked back at the tactical screen. "Have the long-range scanners detected any Kurgan ships in this sector?"

"None so far, sir," replied a young lieutenant from her workstation.

"Keep a close eye on the scanner, Miss Seward. If you spot anything, and I do mean anything, even if it's a lowly shuttlecraft, I want to know about it."

"Aye, sir."

"Sir, when do you want to dispatch the additional landing craft to the surface?" asked Killam.

"Keep them up here for now. I don't want them going down until I know that Colonel White has secured the LZs and the mine."

"Very good, sir."

Robert Sheridan returned to his pacing. It was out of his hands now. Until Colonel White gave the order to begin the evacuation, there was nothing he could do but wait and hope that their raid was still a secret. They had enough firepower to protect the landing craft and that was it. If a Kurgan Fleet were to jump into orbit, his small task force wouldn't last long. He would be compelled to abandon the people on the surface of Klatt, and that was something he was not prepared to do under any circumstances. Their fate would be his as well.

33

"She's been gone nearly an hour. I doubt she's ever coming back," whispered Cole to Wendy.

"Yes, she will. She wants to get off this rock as much as, if not more, than many of the people here."

Without warning, all of the lights came on in the mine and a loud siren sounded.

Cole ducked down. He half-expected to see a squad of Chosen warriors with weapons drawn coming to take him prisoner. Instead, he saw Angela sprint into the cavern. She ran past several inmates and came to a sliding halt at Wendy's bunk.

"Did you cause this?" Cole asked.

Angela shook her head and fought to catch her breath. "No. Something else is up. I thought I heard explosions in the distance, but I couldn't be sure."

"Thunder perhaps?" offered Wendy.

"No, the sky is clear. There isn't a cloud in sight."

"Quickly, before the guards get here, what did you manage to bring back?" Cole asked.

Angela dumped the contents of a small bag onto Wendy's bed. Cole scooped up the pistol and spare magazine. He rummaged through the rest of the stolen equipment until he found an explosive charge with its detonator still attached. He picked it up and saw that it looked to be in perfect working order. "How the hell did you get your hands on this?"

Angela smiled. "The guards aren't that observant. It really wasn't that hard to do. It's pre-set for ten seconds before detonation."

A voice boomed through a speaker on the wall of the cavern. "All prisoners are to remain in their cells. Do not attempt to leave or you will be shot." A couple of seconds later, another announcement was made, this time in Kurgan.

"What did he say?" Cole asked.

"All of the Chosen soldiers have been ordered to report to their duty stations," said Angela. "I think the mine is under attack."

"I thought you said we had another day to wait," said Wendy to Cole.

"Things change. Come on, we've got to keep the Kurg bastards off this floor."

Angela said, "How do you propose we do that?"

"First, we take out the guards and then we disable the elevators."

"I'm a navigator, not a soldier," protested Wendy.

"Wendy, I know that you had to pass basic marksmanship training in the academy. Soon enough, there'll be plenty of Kurgan weapons laying around. They're not that different than ours. Just pick one up, make sure the safety is off, and pull the trigger," replied Cole as he bent down and pulled out a ceramic knife from a sheath hidden under his pants leg. He handed Wendy the knife while Angela picked up one of her own from the pile on the bed.

"Okay, Angela, how many guards are there on this level?"

"There's usually around one hundred around during the day and only about fifty at night."

"We'll never take on fifty soldiers with one pistol and two knives," said Wendy.

"You forget, most of them will be pissed out of their minds," said Angela. "They're probably scrambling about right now trying to find their weapons and gear before a sergeant or a Kurgan officer gets down here to take charge."

Cole liked the sound of that. "Where is their duty station?"

"It's down the hall and to the left," replied Angela.

"How far?"

"At least five hundred meters."

"Okay, let's get to work." He took one last look around at the other prisoners and saw that many had already gone back to their bunks as if nothing was happening. A handful of others stood there staring at Cole and the two women. Their faces were a mix of suspicion and curiosity. Cole checked that his pistol was loaded, moved to the tunnel entrance, and looked both ways before stepping out.

The noisy alarm switched off. An uneasy silence gripped the passageway. With Wendy and Angela close behind him, Cole led the way to the guards' quarters. When they were halfway there, Cole stopped and raised a hand telling the others to freeze in place. On the other side of the tunnel was an elevator shaft. Cole could hear the sound of an elevator descending from above. With his pistol raised, he walked straight at the opening and waited. Less than ten seconds had passed before the elevator came into view. In it was a Kurgan officer with a couple of Chosen soldiers by his side. Cole never hesitated. He shot the officer dead with one shot to the head before turning his pistol on the two warriors trapped inside the cramped elevator. By the time the elevator came to a stop, it was over and all three lay dead. Cole moved the safety bar aside, grabbed the two rifles lying on the floor, and tossed them behind him. He turned and waved for Angela to come to his side.

"Which button is for the top floor?" he asked as he dug out the explosive charge from a pocket in his pants.

"This one," she replied, pressing the button.

Cole activated the timer and tossed in the explosives. He watched as the elevator began its return trip to the surface.

"Hey, you, what are you doing out of your cell block?" called out a voice from farther down the tunnel.

Cole hid his pistol behind his back, turned his head, and saw a man in prison clothing walking toward him. Behind him were four Chosen soldiers with rifles in their hands.

"Who is that?" Cole asked Angela.

"He's another collaborator."

Cole waited a few seconds. He wanted the Chosen to get closer before he opened fire.

The traitor opened his mouth to say something when the elevator exploded. The sound of the explosion rocketed down the shaft, surprising the Chosen warriors, who were now less than ten meters away. Cole dropped to one knee, whipped his pistol from behind his back, and shot the closest soldier in the chest before firing on the next man.

Angela dropped to the ground, picked up one of the rifles, and pulled the trigger without aiming. She had never fired a gun in her life. Rounds flew everywhere as she sprayed the Chosen soldiers. One man fell right away, the other was killed by Cole. The only survivor was the human traitor who stood there with his mouth agape.

Cole brought his weapon around and fired off one shot. The collaborator fell back onto the ground. Cole bent down, picked up the other rifle, and tossed his pistol at Wendy. He looked into the faces of the two women and saw fear. He was scared too but would never admit it. After checking that the Kurgan rifle's safety was off, he said, "Follow me."

They began to jog the last couple of hundred meters to the Chosen duty station. A soldier with his hand on his aching head stepped out into the tunnel to see what all the ruckus was about. His curiosity cost him his life.

Cole leaped over the dead body and kicked in the door to the quarters. He brought his rifle to his shoulder, and with merciless intent, he shot down everyone he could see. He was so focused that he never heard Wendy and Angela join him. For the drunken Chosen staggering about the room, it was as if the Kurgan version of the Grim Reaper had appeared to take their souls.

In less than ten seconds, the deed was done. The guards' bodies lay sprawled about the room. Rivers of blood flowed along the ground. Cole lowered his rifle and saw Wendy still looking through her weapon's sights. He put a hand on her rifle and gently pushed it down toward the ground. "It's okay. It's over. Now, Wendy, I need you to guard the door while Angela and I look for ammo and any more explosives."

Wendy nodded and stepped back to cover the entrance.

A few minutes later, they all stood in the tunnel with their rifles in their hands and their pockets full of grenades.

Cole said, "Okay, we need to split up and disable the rest of the elevators. Angela and Wendy, you go to the left and I'll go to the right. We'll meet up back here when the job is done. Also, look for anything that could be used to block the tunnel at both ends so the Kurgs can't get to the prisoners before the Marines get here." With that, they parted and rushed off to find the nearest elevators. Cole wasn't bothered by what he had just done. It was his job. He, however, doubted that either woman would ever forget the sight of the Chosen dead until the day they died.

34

Sheridan felt the train begin to decelerate. He took a fleeting look into Tarina's eyes before leaving her with the other prisoners. He joined Sergeant Lee in the engineering compartment.

"How long until we come to a complete stop?" Sheridan asked the engineer.

"Less than a minute," replied the man without taking his eyes off the computer screen in front of him. A digitized speedometer raced down toward zero.

"The very second this train stops, I want you to input the code for the return trip. I'll be watching you, so don't try anything foolish."

"Just keep your sergeant away from me and I'll do whatever you say."

Lee chuckled when he heard the translation.

The engineer began to count down. "Ten-nine-eight."

Sheridan leaned forward to see out of the compartment's front windows. At first, he couldn't see a thing in the dark, then ever so slowly he began to see a long line of torches spread out in front of the track.

When the engineer said zero, the train came to a smooth halt. Lee jammed the barrel of his rifle against the man's temple to encourage him to type faster.

"My God," said Sheridan when he realized that he was looking at hundreds of Kurgans formed up in three ranks across the tracks. He saw an officer with his sword in his hand move in front of the formation and point at the train. A loud growl erupted from the throats of the Kurgan soldiers as they drew their swords and held them above their heads. The razor-sharp blades gleamed in the light of a hundred torches. As one, they began to chant. Sheridan's mouth turned dry when he recognized that they were repeating the words 'no prisoners' over and over.

"Get us the hell out of here, now!" yelled Sheridan at the engineer.

"I'm going as fast as I can. I've typed in the command, but I'm getting no response from the station back at the mine."

"Call them and tell them to input the return code from their end."

The engineer picked up a phone from the console and tried to reach the duty engineer back in the prison. He shook his head and looked up at Sheridan. "There's no signal. It's as if the prison has disappeared."

The sound of the chanting from outside grew louder.

Sheridan ground his teeth. There could only be one explanation: the task force had arrived and destroyed all of the comms towers around the mine. There would be no return signal coming for their train. He was glad that they had arrived, but their timing could have been better.

"What's going on, sir?" asked Lee.

"We're going to be attacked by a battalion of Kurgans in the next few seconds if we don't get this piece of crap moving again."

Lee dropped his rifle, drew a knife from behind his back and jammed it against the engineer's throat. "Do something or I'll slit your throat."

The terrified man did not need Sheridan to translate for him. The message was clear enough. He turned in his seat and pointed to a panel on the wall. "Please don't kill me. The manual override is in there."

Sheridan opened the box, saw a switch, and flipped it down. The lights inside the compartment went off and then came back on again. The engineer's fingers hurried to type in the necessary commands to get the train moving.

Outside, the chanting stopped. With a loud, lusty cry, the Kurgans surged toward the train.

With a slight shudder, the locomotive's engine kicked in. Far too slowly for Sheridan's liking, the train began to pull back from the onrushing mass of soldiers. He flipped his rifle around and smashed open the glass windows at the front of the compartment with the butt of his weapon. The Kurgans were barely ten meters away when Sheridan brought his weapon to his shoulder, flipped the selector to automatic, and opened fire. Several soldiers fell to the rocky ground while others, although hit, kept on coming.

"Give me your pistol," said Sheridan to Lee.

"What's up?" Lee asked as he handed over the gun.

"The train isn't moving fast enough. We're going to be boarded."

"I can fight."

"No. I need you to encourage our friend to get this thing out of here before we all die." Sheridan drew his own pistol and moved to the back of the engine compartment. There were doors on either side of the carriage that led to the outside. He brought up both pistols and waited. Within seconds, the door to his right was yanked open and a Kurgan jumped inside. Sheridan turned at the waist and fired off both weapons into the stunned soldier's face at point-blank range. His body fell backward knocking another Kurgan off the train. Sheridan dashed over and closed the door just as the one behind him opened. He spun about and opened fire. His first couple of shots went off to the right of the Kurgan, but the next two hit the soldier in the neck. Blood sprayed the wall of the compartment as the dying Kurgan dropped to his knees before falling face-first to the floor.

The train began to pick up speed. Sheridan saw a Kurgan reach for the outside railing by the open door but was too slow. His gloved hand couldn't grab a hold in time before the train was moving too fast for the armored warrior to catch it.

Sheridan warily edged to the door and pulled it closed. Out of a small window, he could see dozens of Kurgans give up the chase and yell impotently at the escaping locomotive. He bent over and paused to catch his breath when he heard gunfire in the next carriage.

Tarina watched in horror as one of her fellow prisoners was cut down by a Kurgan soldier. Behind the Kurgan, another one appeared. People screamed and pushed at one another to get back from the murderous-looking soldiers. Tarina had no idea where the Kurgans had come from, nor did she care. There was nowhere to run. She could fight or die. She yelled at the top of her lungs as she pushed a man out of the way and brought up her rifle to her shoulder.

The closest Kurgan saw her and hissed loudly. It went to lift up its blood-stained sword when Tarina pulled back on the trigger of her rifle. The first burst struck the Kurgan in its chest. It staggered back but was unharmed as its body armor had stopped the rounds from penetrating. The enraged warrior took a step forward only to be hit in the face by Tarina's second burst. The Kurgan died before it could take another step. Its body tumbled to the floor of the carriage.

"Look out!" hollered Crewman Jones as the second Kurgan threw its sword at Tarina. She turned to her side and watched the blade strike the wall beside her. The Kurgan fell to its knees and reached for a pistol dropped on the floor. Tarina saw the move and fired her weapon. With a hole blasted through its skull, the Kurgan leaned to one side before collapsing in a bloody heap.

With adrenaline coursing through her veins, Tarina looked over her weapon's sights and saw that there were no more targets to engage. She lowered her rifle and turned to thank Jones when another Kurgan soldier forced its way into the carriage. It hissed at Tarina and brought up its sword to strike her in the chest when a shot rang out. The Kurgan staggered forward a couple of paces before dropping to the floor, dead.

Sheridan lowered his pistol, walked past the dead Kurgans, and strode to Tarina's side. He wrapped his arms around her and hugged her. "Are you okay?"

"Yeah. How about you?"

He let go of her and nodded. "I think this is it. I don't think any more Kurgs got onboard. However, just to be safe, I think it we should search the train from the front to rear."

"I'll come with you, sir," said Jones.

"Me too," added Tarina.

Sheridan smiled. "Okay then. Keep behind me and if we see a Kurgan don't hesitate to shoot it in the face. It's the only way to bring them down using small arms." They moved warily to the next carriage and pulled open the door. They were met by a crowd of worried-looking faces, but no Kurgan warriors. It was a good sign as far as Sheridan was concerned.

Colonel Kuhr stood with his jaw clenched tight as the train filled with the prisoners he needed for the bloodletting ritual pulled away. Inside his blood boiled at Lieutenant Colonel Kulk's failure. He had told him not to waste time and to act quickly and decisively, neither of which he had done. He would have words with Kulk but not until everything had first been set right.

"Sir, I think there may be a problem at the mine," said Captain Kazar, Kuhr's adjutant.

"What is wrong?"

"I can't reach them on any frequency."

Kuhr looked over at his adjutant. "So the two gunships they dispatched are still coming to intercept the train?"

"As far as I can tell, that is correct, Colonel."

Kuhr shook his head. Things just kept going from bad to worse.

"Sir, that's not everything. The GPS and long-range communications signals are also gone. It's as if the orbiting satellites had just vanished."

"No, Captain, they haven't vanished; they were destroyed."

"Sir, I don't understand."

"Captain, there can only be one logical answer, the mine is under attack. The Terrans are here to rescue their people. Get the regiment mounted up in its transports. I'll take three battalions with me to the mine. Lieutenant Colonel Kulk with his battalion and the one hundred Old Guard inductees will pursue the train and kill every last human inside of it."

Kazar hesitated. "Sir, without the GPS signal to help guide the pilots, how will we reach the mine?"

"The old-fashioned way. They will fly in loose formations and use their eyes. They have a co-pilot who can read the map for them. No more talk, Captain, get the regiment loaded up."

"Yes, sir." Kazar hurried to pass the order.

Kuhr's despondent mood began to lift. If the humans knew where he was, they would have destroyed his camp by now. He had never seen combat before. With three airmobile battalions at his disposal, he was more than confident that he could defeat whatever force had just landed. A victory here would all but guarantee him ascension to the ranks of the Old Guard. No Kuhr had ever been accepted into the empire's elite fighting force. He intended to ensure that in a few hours from now, he would be the first.

35

Killam stared down at the image on the computer screen and swore. At the furthest reach of the task force's sensors, a small Kurgan freighter had been detected. When its calls to the mine had gone unanswered, it had to have surmised that something was wrong and jumped away.

"Her last transmission was intercepted and decoded, sir," explained Roy. "She sent a warning before jumping."

Admiral Sheridan sat down in his chair and looked over at the tactical display. Colonel White's force had just landed and was already in contact with the enemy. He had confidence that the Marines could destroy whatever opposition they came across. His greatest concern had always been the amount of time it would take to evacuate the prisoners from the mine.

Killam brought up a star chart on the main screen and studied it for a minute before turning to face the admiral. "Sir, if the Kurgans have any combat vessels in this sector, I believe that it will take them about four hours at maximum speed to get here."

Admiral Sheridan looked over at the chart. "What makes you say that, Captain?"

"Their nearest habitable star systems are four hours away from Klatt. They will undoubtedly react to this incursion into their space. What they can muster to send against us, I have no idea, sir. But something is coming our way."

The admiral nodded. "Pass the word to the task force that the enemy knows we are here and they should be prepared to jump back to our side of the disputed zone in four hours' time."

Roy brought up a timer set for four hours on the screen and activated it. It began to count down. Time was already slipping through their hands.

"Captain Killam, contact Colonel White and inform him of this new time constraint. Let him know that I won't abandon him, but the sooner he can accomplish his mission, the better it will be for everyone involved."

"Aye, sir."

The sound of small-arms fire filled the night. The Kurgans had been mercilessly pounded by incoming missile fire and the task force's fighter-bombers. All of the mine's outer buildings were on fire.

Colonel White received the information from Killam with considerable sangfroid. If it bothered him, it did not show on his face. He glanced down at his watch and shrugged. He'd always planned to be in and out in just over a couple of hours, regardless of the tactical situation. His small battle staff consisting of his communicator, an aerospace officer, and fire effects officer kept their distance so they wouldn't draw any unnecessary enemy fire.

"Sir, Viper Six reports that he has established a blocking position to the west of the mine along a rocky ridge," said Sergeant Bowen, the colonel's communications specialist.

White nodded. Viper Six was a mechanized combat team in fast attack vehicles that had skirted the mine and rushed forward to prevent any potential Kurgan counterattack from interfering with the evacuation. Built low to the ground with eight wheels, the team's vehicles could negotiate even the toughest terrain at speeds of over one hundred kilometers an hour. Armed with anti-tank weapons, machine guns, and mortars, White knew that the combat team could easily hold off a force several times its size. To augment their considerable firepower, three UAVs armed with missiles had been placed under Viper Six's command.

"Has Guardian Six sent a report?" White asked. Guardian was the name he had given to the reinforced battalion whose mission was to seize the mine and evacuate the prisoners.

Sergeant Bowen nodded. "Sir, they report that they have entered the mine but have not yet found any prisoners. Resistance so far has been light."

White stood up and cradled his standard issue M5A2 assault rifle in his right arm. A lightweight and sturdy weapon that fired 4.22mm caseless ammunition at a rate of six hundred rounds per minute. Built into the forestock was a grenade launcher capable of reaching out to three hundred meters. White looked over at his staff and said, "Okay, let's push onto the edge of the mine and see what we can see."

It did not take long for the signs of battle to become visible. Several Chosen soldiers' bodies lay facedown on the ground. White and his people paid them no heed. He did, however, stop for a minute at an aid station to check on the men and women who had been brought there for medical care. Most had non-life-threatening wounds, but two dead Marines lay off to the side on the ground. They were covered by blankets so no one could see their faces.

"Who were they?" White asked a corpsman.

"Second Lieutenant Ireland and Private Dioli, sir," replied the medic.

"I want their remains moved back to the landing ships right away."

The corpsman nodded and rushed to find a couple of people to carry out the order.

At the mine's entrance, White caught up with Major Altonen, Guardian Six's XO. "How goes the fight, Andrew?"

"Casualties have been light so far. By the looks of it, we caught the Kurgs by surprise. Many of the Chosen warriors we encountered on the first floor were drunk."

"Unbelievable. Drunk, you say?"

"Yes, sir."

"Where is Guardian Six?"

"He's just behind the lead company," replied Altonen, showing White the location of the company on his tactical tablet. "Sir, Guardian Six has just reported that resistance has stiffened on the second level. The Kurgs aren't backing down. They're giving as good as they are getting."

"Can't have everything our way, now can we? Tell him to keep up the good fight and push on. We must find and rescue those prisoners as soon as possible."

White stepped to one side as a wounded Marine was carried out of the mine with a blood-soaked field dressing on the side of his head. He shook his head and tried to mask his growing frustration. The reconnaissance team that had been dispatched to the planet had passed on precious little information regarding the prisoners. The only thing he knew was that they were somewhere in the mine. What he did not know was where they were or if they were even still alive.

36

Sheridan lowered his rifle and waved at his colleagues to do the same. They had gone from carriage to carriage all the way to the back of the train and found that no other Kurgans had managed to get onboard. They were safe for now.

"Michael, when do you plan to disable the engine?" asked Tarina.

He glanced at his watch. "In about ten minutes' time."

"Okay, I'll start getting the people ready to help move the wounded from the train the moment it stops."

Sheridan smiled at her. She was always thinking of others before herself. It was one of the many reasons why he deeply loved her. "Good idea. I'm going to head up to the engineer's compartment and check on the train's computer for the best place to stop."

In the engine room, Sheridan found an exasperated Sergeant Lee haranguing the engineer. "What's the problem, Sergeant?"

Lee pointed at the computer screen. "I can't speak a word of Kurgan but after months of working in the mine, I've learned how to read their numbers. We're barely going over one hundred kilometers an hour."

Sheridan checked. Lee was Right; they were traveling at just over one hundred and eleven kilometers an hour, far slower than the train was capable of. He looked at the engineer and asked, "Why are we not moving faster?"

"I think during all the fighting that the engine was hit," replied the engineer. "We're lucky to be going as fast as we are."

"I hope for our sake that you're not deliberately going slow to allow the Kurgans a chance to catch up with us."

The man shook his head. "Look for yourself. I have warning indicators going off all along the right side of the engine."

Sheridan saw the lights and decided to check out the engineer's story for himself. He moved back into the engine room, lifted a panel from the right side of the engine, and shone a light inside. He gritted his teeth when he saw fluid gushing from several bullet holes lower down on the engine. The engineer had been telling the truth. He swore and smashed his fist into the wall. With a sick feeling brewing in the pit of his stomach, Sheridan walked back and looked down at the frazzled engineer. "The engine is leaking like a sieve. I want to know the truth; do you think it's going to seize up?"

"It's a possibility."

"How much time do we have?"

"I have no idea. Without checking the damage myself, all I can go on are my instruments. I'd say were okay for another hour, but after that, who knows."

Sheridan did not like what he heard but doubted that the Chosen engineer was lying to him. He was about to head back and pass on the bad news when he thought he saw something out of a side window moving parallel to the train. He leaned over and looked out into the dark. At first, he thought perhaps his imagination had played a trick on him. A couple of seconds later, he swore when he recognized the darkened shape as a Kurgan gunship. With two rotors on either side of the sleek body, the craft looked more like a giant prehistoric insect than a helicopter. He looked back at the engineer. "We've got company. Try and go faster."

"What gives, sir?" asked Lee.

"There's a Kurgan gunship trailing us. Depending how badly the Kurgs want all of the prisoners alive will drive whether or not it attacks us. Either way, I'm going to warn the others to take cover behind whatever they can find."

"Right, sir,"

Sheridan moved back through the engine compartment, stopping for a few seconds to check that they were still being followed. When he saw that there were now two gunships flying near the train, his gut told him to be wary. He opened the door to the first carriage and had just stepped inside when things turned hot.

The two helicopters rose up in the air, locked their autocannons on the engine, and opened fire. Forty-millimeter shells tore through the metal walls of the compartment like a hot knife through butter. The sound of metal being torn asunder was deafening.

Sheridan watched as the engine was ripped apart. Sparks flew like fireflies into the night as the rounds chewed through everything that they hit. Sheridan cursed the enemy pilots. He knew that there was no way that Sergeant Lee could have survived the deadly barrage. Within seconds, the train began to slow. Outside, Sheridan could see flames engulfing the engine compartment. He turned and saw the gunships break off their attack. He had expected them to rake the train carriages. Instead, they rose up into the star-filled sky and banked over. A split second later he was surprised to see both craft explode in a pair of bright fireballs that lit up the sky. He hurried to open the door and stuck his head outside. Sheridan had to know what had brought down their attackers.

With a loud roar, two Terran fighter-bombers flew over the train and quickly disappeared over the horizon. He waved up into the night sky thanking their saviors before closing the door.

"Everyone, on your feet!" yelled Sheridan at the people on the floor of the car. "When this train stops, I want everyone to get off on the right side of the train and wait for me there." He took off on the double to pass the word. When the train came to a sliding halt, he opened the nearest door, jumped down, and looked about. Silhouetted against the sky was a rocky hill less than two hundred meters from the track. He turned about and helped an injured woman down onto the ground.

He spotted Tarina's friend, Crewman Jones, and reached out to grab his arm. He pulled him close and said, "Lead everyone up onto the top of that hill. I'll bring up the rear of the column. I know you're not a combat soldier but try and find a spot with plenty of cover."

"Aye, sir, you can count on me."

"Get a move on. The Kurgs will be here soon enough."

Jones brought his fingers to his mouth and let out a loud whistle. "Follow me. We're going to the top of that hill," he said pointing at the darkened shape.

Sheridan watched as the former prisoners fell into line behind Jones and began to walk away from the train. They were slowed up by the people requiring help to walk. The only thing going in their favor was that the Kurgans had not arrived—at least not yet.

"Michael," called out Tarina as she walked toward him.

He turned and slung his rifle over his back. "Are you the last one off the train?"

"Yes. I checked it myself. Aside from the dead, everyone is now off."

He didn't like the idea of leaving their dead behind, but he didn't have much choice in the matter. "We'll get their remains when this is all over."

Tarina nodded. "Shall we?" she said, looking up at the hill.

"Why not."

Together they walked in silence. It took longer than Sheridan had hoped for them to reach the top of the steep, rocky hill. He was pleased to see that Jones had selected a large depression in the ground from which to fight from. It was more than large enough for all of the survivors to take cover in.

Sheridan sat down on a rock and looked back at the way they had come.

Tarina joined him. "Now what do we do?"

"First we get organized, and then we wait to see who gets here first."

"Michael, I counted, we only have fifteen automatic weapons and a handful of Kurgan swords to defend ourselves with."

"I know. That's why we need to get ready to defend this position. Come on, let's see who is capable of fighting and who is not."

Sheridan stood up. His muscles and joints ached with every step he took. When he was in the middle of the group he said, "Okay, everyone, listen up. We have to face the facts. The Kurgs won't give up that easily. They want you for their ritual and like all good fanatics they're not going to give in until you, or they, are all dead."

"What about the fleet?" asked a man with a bandaged arm. "Those fighters that took out the Kurgan gunships. They'll be coming back for us, right?"

"Yes. Eventually. Right now, they're probably fighting the Kurgs to free your fellow prisoners. Once they've got them loaded up on the transports, then and only then, will they come looking for us. People, we're not the task force's main effort."

"So what do you want us to do, sir?" asked a familiar voice.

Sheridan couldn't believe his ears. "Sergeant Lee, is that you?"

Lee stepped from the crowd. "In the flesh, sir." He had wrapped a piece of his shirt around his head to staunch the bleeding from yet another injury.

"My God. I thought you were dead."

"I jumped from the train just before the gunships opened up on us. Not sure what happened to the engineer, nor do I really care."

Sheridan smiled. "Well, I, for one, am more than relieved that you are here. We need to redistribute the weapons to people who are good shots. From here on out it's one shot—one kill. No one is to use automatic fire. We have to conserve what ammo we have left."

"Leave it to me, sir," said Lee. "I'll get this sorry bunch sorted out in no time."

"Thanks," replied Sheridan. Lee was a good NCO, but he missed his friend. For the first time in a while, he wondered how Cole was doing.

37

The dull crump of grenades going off mixed with the sound of automatic gunfire created a cacophony of noise that told Cole the fight on the level above them was in a desperate struggle to the death. After disabling the elevators, Cole had linked back up with Wendy and Angela at the far end of the tunnel that led up to the next floor. He saw that the ground sloped up and turned at a bend before disappearing from sight. Cole was frustrated that he had been unable to find any working machinery that he could have used to block the passageway. The couple of excavators that he encountered had seen better days and sat in the dark covered in dust, slowly rusting away.

"I'm open to suggestions," said Cole. "If either of you two ladies have an idea how to barricade the tunnel entrance, I'd love to hear about it."

Wendy looked over at Angela, who shook her head. "Sorry, the only working machines I've ever seen are near the bottom of the mine. It would take you nearly an hour to get down there and drive it back up here."

"I guess the only thing we've got going for us is that, for now, the Kurgs seem intent on fighting and dying on the level above us."

Wendy nodded.

Cole scrunched up his face and peered into the nearest cave filled with prisoners. A second later, he smiled and snapped his fingers. "The bunks! We can drag them out and create a makeshift barricade. It won't hold them out forever, but it might slow them down long enough for the Marines to get to us."

"Something is better than nothing," said Wendy.

Cole strode into the cavern and ignored the confused looks on the faces of the people cowering inside. He grabbed a hold of the first bunk bed that stood at least five meters tall and pulled it with all his might. It stood motionless as if rooted to the ground. Wendy and Angela hurried over to help him topple the bunk bed. It ever so slowly began to move and then fell to the ground with a loud crash.

Cole looked around at the prisoners and yelled out, "If you value your lives, you'll give us a hand to block the corridor. My name is Master Sergeant Cole. The sound that you hear is coming from small arms fired by Marines who have come to save you. Remember who you once were and step forward to help us."

At first, no one moved. Then a slender, frail-looking woman hobbled over to the bunk bed, grabbed it, and pulled. Cole smiled and joined with her as did Wendy and Angela. More people, shaken out of their fear, placed their hands on the bunk and helped to drag it out of the cave and into the tunnel.

"We're gonna need every last one of them," announced Cole, looking at the heap of wood lying on the ground.

"Come on, let's grab the next one," said Wendy as she rushed back into the cavern.

They had all just moved into the cell block when a thunderous explosion shook the ground. Cole struggled to remain standing. For a brief moment, the lights in the cavern went off. In the dark, a woman screamed. Charges strategically positioned throughout the mine had been detonated by the Kurgans in a last-ditch attempt to prevent the Marines from taking it intact. What they did not realize was that the people were more important to the assault force than the perlinium in the depths of the pit. In the blink of an eye, tons of rocks collapsed down blocking the way in and out of each level. The lights returned just as a blinding wall of dust raced through the tunnel, making it impossible for anyone to see more than an arm's length away.

"Wendy, Angela, are you all right?" Cole called out, unable to see either woman.

"I'm okay," replied Wendy, coughing and hacking dirt out of her lungs. "Although, my head feels like it was just kicked by one really pissed off mule."

"I'm okay as well," said Angela, placing a hand on Cole. He took her by the hand and moved through the swirling dust to where he had heard Wendy's voice. His hand touched someone. "Wendy?"

"You've found me. What happened?"

"I think the Kurgs realized that they weren't going to win and decided to seal off the mine so our forces couldn't get our hands on the perlinium."

Angela asked, "What are we going to do? There has to be tons of rock between us and your Marines."

"I know. When the dust settles, we'll have to get everyone we can into the tunnel. We're going to have to start moving the rocks by hand."

Colonel White brought up a hand to wipe the dust off his combat glasses. The blast had thrown him off his feet. He sat up and tried looking around the room he had been in when the charges had gone off. Dust wafted as far as the eye could see. Pieces of paper floated down to the floor like oversized dirty snowflakes.

"Is everyone okay?" he asked his team.

Everyone called out to let him know that they were all still with him. White stood and walked to the front door of the room.

He couldn't see too far into the corridor, but he could hear people coughing. He shook his head when he heard someone moaning in pain.

"Corpsman . . . I need a corpsman up here," called out White.

"Coming," responded a woman still hidden from view in the cloud of dirt and dust.

White saw the medic coming toward him. He reached out and grabbed the woman by the arm and pointed down the corridor. "I think someone is badly hurt up there."

She nodded and carried on.

"Sir, Viper Six is calling for you," said Sergeant Bowen, the colonel's radio operator.

White took the handset and listened. "Sir, we're still sorting through the mess down here. Looks like the Kurgs set off some charges to block our way to the next level. I've sent a couple of Marines to the surface to find something that can help us move these rocks out of the way."

"What are your Casualties?"

"Three dead, sixteen wounded so far. Thankfully none of my people were near the blast when it went off, or it would have been a lot worse."

"What about Kurgs?"

"They're all dead. Not a single one surrendered. Even the Chosen warriors committed suicide rather than be taken alive."

"Okay, I'll pass this on to Trident Six and let him know that it's going to take us a while to get down to the next level." White knew that Admiral Sheridan would not be pleased to hear that they had still not secured the prisoners. With a potential enemy fleet on its way to the planet, he knew that every second counted.

White paused for a second. "Sergeant Bowen, digging our way down to the next level is going to take too long. Get a hold of my XO at headquarters and find me some combat engineers. I want to blast those damned rocks out of my way."

Cole stood speechless staring at the wall of rocks blocking the way out of the tunnel. It seemed an impossible task, yet he knew that they had to try. He bent down, picked up a jagged boulder, and tossed it behind him. He was about to reach for another rock when Wendy tapped him on the shoulder.

"Master Sergeant, Angela has a way to get some of these people up to the surface."

"Say again," said Cole, not sure that he had heard her correctly.

"It's a bit of a long story, but Angela discovered a hidden tunnel that leads to the top of the mine. It's narrow and can only be reached by climbing, but she feels that she can help lead some of the more mobile prisoners out of here."

"Yes, by all means get her going. Make sure that she takes something to help identify her as a prisoner and not an enemy combatant."

Wendy cringed. "In that case, I think I'll go first and make contact with our forces and let them know what's going on."

Cole shrugged. "Whatever works."

Wendy nodded and jogged off to help organize the prisoners.

Cole reached down and picked up another rock. Tired-looking men and women in filthy rags shuffled over and joined him. The work was slow and backbreaking but no one stopped, no one complained; they all knew what was at stake.

38

Sheridan stared out into the night as an odd humming noise grew closer. He couldn't see what was making the sound, yet it seemed to be all around them.

"Michael, look!" said Tarina, pointing at a dark shape hovering over the burning train wreckage. "What is it?"

He shook his head. "I have no idea. I've never seen anything like it before." The craft was large and triangular with a downward pointing nose at the front. It pivoted around in the air before landing. At the rear, a ramp dropped and Kurgan soldiers ran out. Within a minute, four other craft had landed and disgorged their passengers.

"Looks like they've found us," said Lee, clenching his rifle tight in his hands.

"Yeah, looks that way," replied Sheridan. "Have everyone take cover. Pass the word that no one fires until I do, then it's one shot and one shot only per Kurgan. Tell them to aim for the officers and the NCOs first. If they don't know how to tell one from another, tell them to kill anyone who is trying to lead the others forward."

"Roger, sir. Shoot the officers, it's a non-com's wet dream."

Tarina held on to Sheridan's right arm. "What do you think our chances are?"

He pulled her in close and looked into her eyes. "I don't know. They're coming here with one thought on their minds, to butcher you and your friends. I say we give them a warm welcome."

Tarina nodded. "Yes, let's."

Together they stepped back and got down behind some large rocks on the lip of the depression. Already they could hear the sound of boots scraping on the rocks as the Kurgans began to climb up the side of the hill.

Sheridan rested his rifle on the ground and looked through the weapon's thermal sight, picking a spot he was sure the Kurgans would appear. He was surprised that he was as calm as he was. He had expected to feel scared, but his many months of combat had taught him that whatever happened next was out of his hands. All he could do now was his job and trust in his comrades to do the same.

Less than a minute passed before the first wave of Kurgans hauled themselves up onto the top of the rocky hill. Sheridan spotted a Kurgan with a flag in his arms yelling at the soldiers behind him to follow. Although dark, Sheridan knew that the flag would be crimson-colored for the Kurgan religion. He laid his weapon's sight on the officer's forehead before gently taking up the pressure on his rifle's trigger. With a sound like that of a whip cracking, the bullet shot forth and struck the Kurgan right between the eyes. He keeled over, dropping the flag. Another soldier ran to pick it up. Sheridan took aim and killed him as well.

Beside him, Tarina and Lee brought down several more Kurgans as they came into view. Like a dam bursting, the Kurgans surged forward like a living wave. With their swords held high above their heads and with hate in their hearts, the Kurgans charged straight at the people taking refuge in the crater. One or two fell wounded, but the majority died before they could make it more than ten meters from the side of the hill. In under a minute, the first attack petered out and stopped. A Kurgan hissed defiantly at Sheridan and the other defenders before helping one of the severely wounded soldiers. A macabre row of dead Kurgans marked the farthest limit of their advance.

A cheer burst from the people huddled in the darkened crater.

Sheridan stood up. "Quieten down. No cheering. That was only a probe. They'll be back and from more than one direction next time." He turned and looked over at Lee. "Sergeant, check the bodies to see if any of them was carrying something other than a sword."

Lee nodded and dashed from the depression, quickly searching the remains.

"How long before they come back?" Tarina asked.

"If we're lucky, ten minutes, perhaps."

"And if we're unlucky?"

"Five or less."

She leaned over and kissed Sheridan on the cheek. "Well. Let's hope for today that you're lucky."

He smiled back at her.

Tarina shook her head. "Not that kind of lucky, mister."

On the outskirts of the mining camp, Viper Six lowered his thermal imaging binoculars and glanced down at his watch. They had been in position for close to two hours and had yet to see a single Kurgan. The fighting behind him had died down a while back, now the only sound was coming from the burning wreckage of the old mining complex. A twenty-year veteran, Viper Six's real name was Lieutenant-Colonel Joseph Okiro. He was a bull of a man with broad shoulders and a muscle-bound body.

"I guess we're not going to see any action tonight, sir," said Sergeant Day, Okiro's radio operator.

"No. I suppose not."

"That's a real shame. I was really hoping to get the chance to kick some Kurgan arse."

Okiro chuckled at his youthful sergeant's remark.

All of a sudden, Day sat straight up in his chair and looked over at Okiro. "Sir, the *Saratoga* says that they have just detected a large formation of ships heading this way."

Okiro glanced over and saw that there was nothing on his vehicle's scanners. If they were out there, they were flying nap of the earth. He stuck his head outside and helplessly watched as one by one, the drones flying in support of his team were blown from the sky.

"What the hell is going on?" remarked Okiro, unable to discern what had brought down his UAVs.

The sound of additional incoming missiles turned his blood cold. Only the warheads, not the attack ships, racing at supersonic speed at his position showed up on Day's monitor. Okiro and his sergeant died a second later when his command vehicle was blasted into thousands of pieces by a Kurgan missile. All along his defensive line, anything with a power source was hit. In less than three seconds, twenty vehicles and their crews were gone. Orange and red flames licked the night sky. Only the Marines who had dug in with their heavy weapons had survived the attack.

"Calm down, son, and tell me again what just happened," said Colonel White into a handset.

"Sir, we are under attack. Viper Six is dead and over half of the combat team has been destroyed," replied a flustered lieutenant on the burning ridgeline.

"Hang on, I'm on my way to your position." White turned and jogged out of the mine. He clenched his jaw when he saw the burning hulks of what had once been a robust fighting force illuminating the horizon. Out of the corner of his eye, he saw three Marines he didn't recognize carrying radios on their backs running as fast as they could toward the wrecked combat team.

"Just a minute, who are you people?" called out White.

A woman turned to face the colonel. "Sir, my name is First Lieutenant Toscano; my men and I were part of the recce team who were sent ahead to scout out the mine. We saw what just happened and are going to see if we can help."

"What's your MOS Toscano?"

"I'm a fire effects officer, sir."

"Okay then, get up on the ridge, make contact with the task force, and start raining down all the ordnance you can into the desert. I got a feeling that a storm is coming our way."

"Yes, sir." Toscano took off running with Sergeant Urban and Private Snow by her side.

White heard an odd humming noise and turned to look up at the star-filled sky just as a dark triangular shape, followed closely by another, flew right over the top of the mine. His stomach clenched in a knot when he realized that they had to be Kurgan attack ships of some kind. He didn't recognize them but knew that they meant to do his people harm.

His mind barely had time to process what was going on when the two Kurgan ships let loose a volley of missiles into the landing craft sitting defenseless a kilometer away from the mine. The sound of the ships exploding rocked the night. White swore as the large transports were destroyed by the nearly invisible assailants. In the blink of an eye, everything had changed. For the first time since he had stepped foot on Klatt, White began to face the possibility of failure. As it wasn't in his or the Corps ethos to give in without a fight, he quickly formed a plan in his mind.

"Sergeant Bowen, the handset, if you please." White wasn't finished—not by a long shot.

Admiral Sheridan listened to the incoming reports and tried to imagine himself on the surface of the planet fighting for his life. He shuddered at the thought of the loss of life that had just occurred among the Marines and the transport flight crews. He willed himself to block out such thoughts until they could be dealt with when the engagement was behind them.

"Sir, thank God you didn't send the rest of the landing craft down to the surface or they'd be gone too," said Killam.

"Captain, does fleet intel have anything on these new Kurgan attack craft?"

Killam shook his head. "No, sir."

"Hell of a way to find out."

"Aye, sir."

Roy joined the conversation. "Admiral, Colonel White wants us to bring as much fire as we can onto the ground in front of Viper Six's old location. He believes that a ground assault by overwhelming Kurgan forces is just minutes away."

Admiral Sheridan said, "Have the missile cruiser *Ford* support the call for fire with everything she's got, and then tell the *Saratoga* to launch two squadrons ASAP to support the beleaguered Marines."

"Aye, sir," responded Roy. She moved back to her duty station, picked up her tablet, and typed out the orders.

Killam lowered his voice. "Sir, we've now lost four of our twelve landing craft. We needed nine to evacuate everyone off the planet."

"I know. I want you to order the support ship *Arctic* to jettison everything that she does not need from her cargo holds.

She's going to be turned into our last transport. We can cross load some of the first people brought up from the planet and make this work."

Killam nodded. "Aye, that might just do the trick."

"It had better as we're rapidly running out of options to make this work."

"I'll speak with the captain of the *Arctic* myself and tell him precisely what you want him to do."

Admiral Sheridan glanced over at the timer counting down to zero. They had just over two hours to go before any Kurgan fighting ships could arrive. He was also cognizant of the fact that they had yet to find, let alone move, a single POW up from the planet. He took a deep breath to clear his mind, placed his hands behind his back, and resumed his pacing.

39

With a loud roar from one hundred throats, the second attack began. As Sheridan had anticipated, the Kurgans had maneuvered around and came at them from two different directions this time. Luckily, the paths they had to use to reach the top of the hill were narrow, canalizing the attackers into coming at them in twos and threes at a time. While Sheridan led the fight from his end of the crater, Sergeant Lee did the same at the other. The Kurgans never flinched nor wavered. Regardless of their losses, they kept on coming. Before long, their bodies covered the ground around the depression, yet they would not give in. Driven by a bloodlust, the Kurgans were hell-bent on killing their enemy so they could honor their ancestors by advancing into the ranks of the Old Guard.

With a quick glance down, Sheridan saw that his rifle had only forty rounds left in its magazine. When they were gone, he would be out of ammo. He suspected that the others around him had even less ammunition remaining as they tended to fire more shots than necessary to bring down an enemy soldier. He watched as Tarina got up on one knee, took aim, and brought down a Kurgan NCO, who had just taken possession of their battle flag from a fallen comrade.

From somewhere in the night, a horn blared. The Kurgans stopped their advance and, as if nothing had happened, turned about and walked away from the carnage.

"Hold your fire, they're retiring," called out Sheridan. The defenders' guns fell silent. The unsettling moans of several wounded Kurgans unable to crawl back for medical aid filled the air.

"Michael, I've only got twelve rounds left," said Tarina.

"Check with the others and see how many they have left as well."

Sheridan stood up and glanced over at the horizon and saw the first faint rays of the approaching dawn. He checked on the rest of his people, stressing to each person with a weapon to conserve what remained of their ammunition.

Tarina and Lee joined him. "Sir, on average we're down to fifteen rounds per rifle," explained Lee. "The few pistols we have are still fully loaded, but they're only good close in. I've handed around as many swords as I could find. But I doubt we'd last more than a couple of minutes against the Kurgs if all we had left to defend ourselves with were those weapons."

Sheridan nodded. Their future prospects were indeed bleak. There were close to eighty people taking cover in the crater. Some of them had been injured during the fight on the train and would be unable to fight back should the Kurgans break through their slender perimeter. He was desperate to think of a solution when he recalled a lesson from one of his history classes.

"Sergeant Lee, get everyone on their feet. I want you to form a square."

"A square, sir?"

"Yes. Make it tight and have a person with a sword standing next to a person with a gun. Ensure that our wounded are moved to the middle of the formation."

Lee stared back at Sheridan as if he had lost his mind.

"Hurry, Sergeant, we don't have long until they come back."

It didn't take Lee very long to push everyone into something that resembled a square formation. Sheridan walked over and looked into the worried faces of the men and women who were at a loss to understand what they were doing.

"People, we're almost out of ammo. We need to make every round count if we are to survive until help arrives. I know this next order may seem counterintuitive to those of you with a sword, but I don't want you to defend yourselves, you are to protect the person with the gun to your right. If the Kurgans get close enough to use their swords, they will lift their sword arm above their heads to deliver the killing blow. That is when they will be vulnerable. Their segmented armor is weak under the armpit. Wait until his arm is fully raised and then jam yours home."

The sound of a horn echoed over the top of the hill.

Sheridan took his place in the square and called out. "Here they come. Show them no mercy, as they will not show you any. If you must, sell your life dearly."

In the gray light of dawn, the crimson banner was raised. A lone officer stood up on the top of the hill and let out a deep cry. His call was answered by hundreds more eager to get to grips with their foe. Dozens of soldiers scrambled up onto the top of the hill and rushed to form up under their officers.

Sheridan could see that they had brought up two fresh companies of soldiers from the bottom of the hill. He doubted that the Kurgans had any warriors left in reserve. This was it. All or nothing.

The Kurgan officer moved in front of his soldiers and began to beat his sword on his chest. Within seconds, two hundred Kurgans joined in.

Lee raised his rifle. "Let me take down that son of a bitch."

"Steady on," warned Sheridan. "I want them to get a lot closer before we open up. We can't afford to miss."

The Kurgan colonel grabbed his unit's flag, raised it high in the air, and yelled the order to attack. The attackers broke ranks and ran forward. Each warrior wanted to be the first to thrust his sword into an enemy's stomach.

The sound of two hundred pairs of feet running across the rocky ground was like listening to an avalanche of rocks hurtling down the side of a mountain.

"Wait for it," cried out Sheridan. He could feel the fear and tension gripping the people around him. He waited until the first Kurgan was less than fifty paces from the square when he yelled out, "Fire!"

At that range, they couldn't miss. The first rank of Kurgans fell to the ground. Those behind them jumped over the fallen only to be hit themselves. Bodies of the dead and dying soon covered the ground.

Sheridan switched targets and pulled back on the trigger. He didn't wait to see if the soldier he had just shot was down; he was too busy selecting his next victim. Over the din of battle, Sheridan heard the guns near him begin to fall silent. He glanced over the top of his rifle and saw that the Kurgans had stopped rushing his end of the square. Like a river looking for the path of least resistance, they had veered off to the backside of the formation where the fire had slackened. He turned, grabbed a man from behind him, and handed the man his rifle. Sheridan drew his pistol and pushed his way through the square until he stood alongside Sergeant Lee.

The enemy was almost on them. Hate and anger filled their golden eyes.

"Remember what I said," hollered Sheridan. "Kill the warrior to your right." He brought up his pistol and shot the closest Kurgan to him. The soldier spun about and dropped to the ground with a gaping wound in his neck.

A second later, the Kurgans smashed headlong into the defenders. The noise was like a wave hitting the rocks during a storm. Those with ammunition left fired at point-blank range into the swarm of Kurgans. Some people did as Sheridan had ordered and struck the enemy soldier to their right. Others panicked and tried to fight the warrior facing them only to die, cut down by the fitter and more experienced Kurgan soldiers.

Sheridan felt the square buckle and begin to step backward. He glanced out of the corner of his eye and saw a Kurgan slice a man's skull open. He shot the Kurgan before he could kill anyone else.

Sergeant Lee dropped his empty weapon and picked up a discarded sword and swung at a Kurgan who had pushed his dying comrade aside and brought up his arm to strike Sheridan. The blade sunk home in the soldier's lightly protected underarm. Mortally wounded, the Kurgan hissed as he fell to its knees before toppling over.

Before long, numbers began to tell. More and more people fell under the relentless hacking and slashing of the Kurgan swords. It was as Sheridan feared, the fitter and stronger Kurgans were hacking down everything in their path. The formation started to come apart as more defenders died. Sheridan stepped back, nearly tripping over the dead body of one of his comrades, trying to keep in line with Lee. Just when it seemed that the Kurgans had won the day, Tarina burst through the line along with two other people armed with rifles. She fired her weapon at the nearest officer before turning her attention to any Kurgan with a bloodied blade. The warriors began to hesitate in the face of such a deadly fusillade. Their courage seemed to evaporate in seconds.

Sheridan saw the growing look of confusion on the Kurgans' faces. He pointed at the Kurgans and yelled, "They won't hold!"

He grabbed a Kurgan sword at his feet. With a war cry on his lips, he ran forward and swung his blade at the head of a warrior who blocked the move with his own sword.

The Kurgan saw his friends lose heart. He dropped his sword and ran for his life.

Sheridan had never seen Kurgans run before. He was about to take a step forward when he noticed the body of a Kurgan lieutenant colonel lying on the ground with a gunshot wound to the side of the head. He looked back at Tarina and realized that she must have killed their commander. With all of their other officers down, the leaderless Kurgans fled.

Sheridan smiled at Tarina. "Where on earth did you get the extra ammo?"

"One of our wounded from the train had it on her. I found it by pure luck when I went to pull her back from the fight; the magazines fell out of a bag she had with her."

"Why didn't she say anything earlier?"

"She's unconscious, that's why."

"Well, whoever she is, thank God for her."

Sheridan jammed his sword in the ground and looked around. There were piles of Kurgan bodies interspaced with dead humans. "Sergeant Lee, report."

Lee ran over. Sheridan saw that he had received yet another wound to his head.

"Sergeant, organize a detail to pull our people back from the Kurgan dead and get me a headcount. I need to know how many are still fit to fight, and have someone check the wounded for ammo."

"Yes, sir." Lee snapped his fingers at a young Marine and put him to work.

"How many do you think we've killed?" Tarina asked Sheridan as she looked over at the Kurgan corpses.

"I don't know. They came at us three times. There's maybe two hundred dead and dying Kurgs spread out over the top of the hill."

"Do you think this is over? Are we safe now?"

He let out a mournful sigh and shook his head. "They're Imperial Guard troops; once they find an officer to lead them, they'll be back."

Tarina sat down on the ground cradling her rifle in her arms. "When is this nightmare going to end, Michael? I'm so very tired and I don't want to die out here."

"No one wants to die," said Sheridan as he took a seat beside her and wrapped his arm around her. She leaned her head over and rested it on his shoulder. For a brief moment, they forgot their troubles and found solace in each other's company.

40

"It looks like it's safe enough to proceed," declared Angela as she peered out into the dark.

Wendy worked her way past Angela, lifted the wooden cover to the shaft, and took a quick look around. The world outside looked like it was on fire. The mining complex was consumed in flames. Thick black smoke rose up into the air. If a Kurgan shuttle had landed before the attack, it was long gone. The spot Angela had identified as the place where the shuttle should be located was nothing more than a smoldering crater. What troubled her were the destroyed Terran vehicles and transport craft that she could see. *Whatever had happened had not gone well for the Marines,* she thought. She felt like running back for the safety of the mine when she first heard, and then saw, missiles streak down from the sky and explode behind a long ridgeline. The massive detonations were so close to the camp that she felt the ground shudder under her feet. Wendy screwed up her courage, climbed out, and took cover behind some tall rocks. The last thing she wanted was to be mistaken for an enemy soldier and shot before she could make contact with the invasion force. Wendy raised her head up and looked down at the ground around the destroyed buildings. Her heart leaped for joy when she spotted a group of Maines making their way through the wreckage.

She stood up and energetically waved her hands above her head, yelling, "Hello, down there."

The party of Marines stopped and looked up at her.

Wendy kept waving her arms. "Please help me; I've got some escaped prisoners with me."

The Marines turned, waved back, and sprinted straight toward her.

"Do you think it's safe to come out?" asked Angela.

"Yes, yes it is," replied Wendy with tears of joy streaming down her dirty face.

Major Altonen removed his helmet and shook Wendy's hand. It was plain to see that she looked tired and in need of some medical attention. He handed her his canteen before saying, "You are to be commended, Miss?"

"Captain Wendy Sullivan," she replied, taking the flask and opening it.

"Captain, how many people did you manage to bring out with you?"

Wendy took a long sip of water. She wiped her mouth with the back of her hand and returned the water bottle. "Sir, Angela, my colleague, brought out thirty-three. She's already on her way back into the mine to fetch the next batch, but there are thousands more waiting down below to be rescued."

"We should have them out soon; we're having explosives placed on the rocks as we speak. We're going to blast our way inside."

Wendy balked at the news. "Major, there are people working at the other end to remove the rocks. You have to warn them that you're going to blow the debris away, or you may kill a whole bunch of the people you are here to save."

Altonen nodded and reached for his radio's handset. "Echo One, hold what you're doing. Do not, I say again, do not detonate the explosives until we contact the POWs on the next level."

"Sir, I can head back down below and warn them," offered Wendy.

"No, that'll take too long; besides we have other ways to pass the message."

Cole wiped the dirt from his sweat-covered brow and stood up straight. His back ached worse than it ever had in his life. Any thought of taking a break was erased when he saw that the people around him had not paused for even one minute since he had asked for their help. He reached out for a rock and almost jumped out of his skin when an insect the length of his boot crawled out from between a gap in the rocks.

It stopped moving and looked up at the people working in the tunnel.

"Damn," said Cole when he realized that he wasn't looking at a disconcertingly long centipede but a miniaturized crawler robot. He picked it up and held it in his hand.

"Master Sergeant, get everyone back behind cover," explained Wendy through a speaker on the robot, "they're going to blast the rocks out of the way."

Cole turned and called out, "Everyone, back in your caves right now and take cover."

The prisoners stared back at Cole as if not comprehending what he wanted them to do.

"Folks, I'm not kidding, move your butts or you'll become a permanent resident down here."

First Lieutenant Toscano could feel each thunderous explosion in her chest. Although she was well protected by the rocky berm, the missiles were impacting barely one hundred meters from her position. The first volley had all but obliterated a

Kurgan battalion caught out in the open trying to rush the Viper combat team survivors huddled on the ridge.

Sergeant Urban tapped her on the shoulder and handed her a handset. He had to yell to be heard. "Ma'am, it's the *Ford* calling again. They want a damage assessment."

"Tell them to wait a minute." Toscano crawled up and peered out at the open plain. The image of hundreds of mangled and torn bodies was one she would not easily forget. She brought up her binoculars and looked where the missiles had hit. If there were any Kurgans out there, they had long since gone to ground. She slid back down beside Urban and shook her head.

"*Ford*, this is Ghost One, target destroyed," reported Urban.

Colonel White and his team walked over and took a seat. The man was so calm that he looked to Toscano as if he were out for an early morning stroll. "I thought you'd like to know that they've linked up with the POWs and have begun to bring them out of the mine. The first wave of landing craft accompanied by a squadron of fighters is on the way down."

"That is good news. Sir, before I forget, we had survivors at our crash site. Could you please ask someone to rescue them as well?"

"I'm on it, sir," said Sergeant Bowen, digging out a map for Urban to pinpoint the survivor's location.

White smiled. "I swear, Sergeant Bowen could replace me and no one would ever know."

Toscano was going to point out that Bowen was black while the colonel lived up to his name and was white. She, nonetheless, understood the meaning of the colonel's compliment to the efficient non-com. "Sir, what's your plan now?"

"I brought up a company of Marines from Guardian's battalion with me. When the time is right, we'll leapfrog back by companies to our landing craft. You and I, Captain, will be the last two Marines to leave this accursed rock."

"Got it, sir."

"Glad to hear it," said White patting Toscano on the shoulder before heading down the line to check on the other Marines.

"That's one cool customer," remarked Urban.

"He and his kind were born for this war. Having said that, I'd rather have Colonel White to lead me in a frontal assault on the Kurgan home world than a thousand bureaucrats from Allied Defense Force Headquarters back home on Earth."

"Amen to that, ma'am."

41

Colonel Kuhr had never seen such deadly and accurate firepower in his military career. His lead battalion had all but ceased to exist in a wall of flame. In under a minute, his ground attack plan was in tatters. His next wave of soldiers had been forced to take cover in a long, dry riverbed and were pinned down, unable to advance or retreat. That left him with his reserve battalion still intact. He thought about moving them around to a flank but ruled it out when he spotted Terran fighters flying a combat air patrol over the mine. His attack ships may be hard to detect, but they weren't invisible. With the night fading away, he didn't want to risk his ships being spotted and destroyed.

"Sir, what do you want to do?" asked Kuhr's adjutant.

"Have everyone keep their heads down until the humans begin to withdraw. We might not be able to stop them, but we can still inflict grievous casualties on them."

"I'll pass the word."

Kuhr nodded. He had hoped to catch the Terran forces before they could recover from the blow his craft had dealt them. However, they had proven to be more resilient than he had expected, and now it was his soldiers that were being cut to pieces, not theirs. He prayed that the soldiers he had left behind had proven their worth and had dispatched all of the humans at the train wreck. He could use the reinforcements.

Sergeant Kurka, Kuhr's trusted old friend, walked over and saluted as if he were on parade. "Sir, I can't raise anyone on the communicators. The humans are jamming all of our frequencies."

"If we were in their place, we would too. Before you lost comms, did you manage to speak with the fourth battalion?"

"It was garbled. But I think that Lieutenant Colonel Kulk is dead, along with a couple of hundred of his men."

The news struck Kuhr like a thunderbolt. "That can't be. A battalion of Young Guard soldiers brought low by a handful of human prisoners. Kulk must have been overconfident and walked into an ambush; there can be no other explanation."

"Yes, sir," replied the old soldier.

Kuhr stood and looked back at the reddish glow on the horizon as if he could somehow see the disaster that had befallen his subordinate. He gnashed his pointed teeth together and cursed god for not helping him in his hour of need. He couldn't understand, he was a loyal adherent to the word of the lord. Victory, not defeat, should have been his reward this day.

Kuhr placed a hand on Sergeant Kurka's shoulder. "Sergeant, I want you to take a company from the third battalion and personally deal with those wretched humans who have dared to soil the proud history of the Young Guard."

Kurka nodded. He was a veteran soldier with years of combat experience under his belt. He would deal with the non-believers and restore honor in his regiment. Kurka saluted, turned, and ran for the landing site where the third battalion was waiting.

With his dreams of glory and admission into the Old Guard all but gone, Kuhr began to plot his way out of this mess. No matter what happened now, Lieutenant Colonel Kulk would be his scapegoat. The officer had not followed his orders correctly and had led his men into a trap. Kulk's family name, not his, would go down in history as the architect of this disaster.

42

"Here you go. You're in good hands now," said Cole to a man he had helped out of the mine. He found the fresh morning air invigorating after hours of backbreaking labor.

"We'll take him from here," said a young Marine as he placed an arm around the exhausted prisoner and guided him through the open doors of a landing craft. The ship had landed right outside of the mine to minimize the time it took to load each one. Inside, a platoon of medics rushed about looking after the emaciated and exhausted former POWs.

Cole stepped back and looked up at the ship. The larger battalion-sized vessels always reminded him of a metal tortoise's shell.

"Master Sergeant Cole," called out Wendy as she made her way through the throng of people to reach Cole. "I'm glad I found you," she sounded flustered. "I tried speaking with some of the senior Marines here, but they all brushed me aside. I told them about the people taken to the Kurg camp in the desert to be murdered, but no one wants to listen to me. They all keep saying that they are too busy to help me."

"Leave it to me, ma'am," replied Cole. His eyes narrowed when he spotted a couple of officers standing off to one side chatting. He smiled at Wendy. "Why don't you go and see if you can find your friend Angela and meet me back here in five minutes' time."

Cole strode straight at the officers. "Excuse me, gentlemen, is your commanding officer around? I'd like to speak with him."

"There's no time to talk," replied a slender second lieutenant. "Our CO is busy. You can thank her later. Just follow the line of people getting into the landing craft, and we'll have you back home in no time."

Cole's tone turned belligerent. "Okay, sir, I'm not asking, I'm telling you. Where is your CO?"

The second lieutenant pursed his lips. "I don't know who you are, but I'm an officer and won't allow you to speak to me in a disrespectful manner. I don't care if you are a former POW, show some respect to the rank."

Cole saw red flash before his eyes. He clenched his right fist and pulled back his arm when someone from behind grabbed his arm. Cole turned his head ready to punch whoever it was.

"Master Sergeant Cole, is that you?" asked a man in full combat gear.

"Yes, sir," responded Cole when he saw the lieutenant colonel's rank on the short man's collar.

"Sergeant, It's me, Lieutenant Colonel Kimura. We met on the *Colossus*. I'm from General Denisov's staff."

Cole unclenched his fist and lowered his arm. "Yeah, now that you mention it, sir. I do remember speaking to you."

Kimura looked over at the young officers. "Standing there won't help these people. If your Marines are helping the POWs, so should you two. Get to work, gents."

"Yes, sir," replied the chastised officers in unison.

"Sir, I really need your help," said Cole.

"Name it."

Captain Killam drummed his fingers on his console while he waited for his call to be returned. Kimura's message had sent Killam into a near panic to find a solution to what seemed to be an insurmountable problem. He hadn't told Admiral Sheridan of the danger his son and up to one hundred POWs were facing. He knew that there was no wiggle room for error. There was only so much troop lift available in the task force, and with four landing craft already gone, there was nothing left to send down to extract the missing prisoners.

"Anything?" whispered Commander Roy.

Killam shook his head.

Roy glanced over at the timer on the screen and bit her lip. They had just under forty minutes before the first Kurgan ships could arrive in orbit. Time itself was now their enemy as well.

"Status Report, Captain?" asked Admiral Sheridan.

Killam looked away from his computer and quickly collected his thoughts. "Sir, the first landing craft transferred its passengers to the *Arctic* and is on its way back down to the planet's surface. The *Arctic* has already spooled up her engines and will be jumping to the RV point beyond the asteroid belt in the next two minutes."

Admiral Sheridan nodded. "That is good news."

"Sir, two more landing craft are on their way up and will be in orbit shortly. Once they signal that they are ready, the *Churchill* will accompany the ships to the RV."

"What is the prognosis from down below? Are we going to get everyone off before the Kurgans arrive here in force?"

Killam hesitated, unsure of what to say next. He cleared his throat and said, "It's going to be tight. Colonel White still has to collapse his perimeter and get his forces onto the last couple of transports."

"Please remind him of the time."

Killam nodded. He felt awful for not telling the admiral the true situation on the planet's surface. He let out a deep sigh and turned to pass the message when he saw a dispatch on his computer screen. A smile crept across his face. Before jumping, the *Arctic* had just been able to fix up an old medical shuttle and send it down to the mine to link up with Master Sergeant Cole.

"Excuse me, sir, but there's been a development I need to brief you on," Killam said, rising from his desk.

From the grave look on his face, Admiral Sheridan knew that his operations officer had something important to pass on. "Very good, Captain. Let's hear it."

43

The cold gray light of dawn crept over the top of the rocky hill. For the first time since they had arrived, Sheridan was able to take in everything that had happened. He walked solemnly past the rows of dead. In some places, bodies were stacked one on top of the other. Kurgan and Terran corpses covered the ground.

"Michael, I thought you should know that two more people have just died," said Tarina as she made her way to her lover's side.

"What does that bring the total to?"

"We've got twelve uninjured and seven wounded. Corporal Wu probably won't last long if we don't get him medical attention. That last fight really tore us to ribbons."

Sheridan felt a pang of remorse in his chest. He had no idea how many they had lost until now. He took Tarina by the hand and held it tightly. "If the Kurgs knew how badly off we are right now, they'd be on us before you could blink an eye."

Sergeant Lee waved at Sheridan and jogged over. For the past hour, he had been keeping an eye on the Kurgans. "Sir, I don't get it. The Kurgans are just standing around at the bottom of the hill. It's like they have no clue what to do next. Surely, they've got non-coms who could lead them?"

"They do, but there's aren't like ours. They only have three rank levels for their conscripts: private, corporal, and sergeant. In their military, the officers make all the important decisions. Stuff we'd leave to a sergeant in our armed forces is usually done by a lieutenant in theirs. I've read of some veteran sergeants taking command in battle, but it's a rarity. I suspect that with all of their officers down, they're waiting for an officer to arrive to take charge."

"What about our people?" asked Tarina. "They must have freed the other prisoners by now. Wendy would have told them where we are."

"As would have Cole," added Sheridan. "Let's go with the assumption that help is on the way. Sergeant, pair off some of the stronger people with the wounded and be ready to leave on a moment's notice."

"Can do, sir."

Tarina raised a hand to block the rising sun. In the far distance, she could make out three craft flying low to the ground. A chill ran down her spine when she realized that they were heading in their direction. "Michael, look!"

Sheridan turned to see what Tarina was pointing at and swore when he recognized the triangular ships as being like the ones he had seen the night before. "Looks like we're going to have to hold out for a little while longer."

Tarina's voice grew concerned. "We only have about fifty rounds left. We don't stand a chance."

"Head back to the others and warn them that the Kurgans are getting reinforcements and will be coming up as soon as they sort themselves out."

"What are you going to do, Michael?"

"I'm going to buy us some time." He turned his head and looked into Tarina's eyes. If what he did next saved her life, then it would be worth it. "I love you, Tarina Pheto."

Her voice cracked. "I love you, too."

With that, Sheridan handed Tarina his rifle and picked up a sword. He turned his back on her and walked to the edge of the cliff.

She stood there with her heart aching so bad she thought it would break. Tears filled her eyes as she watched him vanish from sight.

Cole shook Lieutenant Colonel Kimura's hand before running over to the shuttlecraft. The side door was already down when he got there. He ran straight inside and made his way to the cockpit where he found a couple of eager pilots waiting for him.

"Where to, Sergeant?" asked the pilot, an Asian woman wearing a second lieutenant's bar on her collar.

"One second," Cole responded. He looked over his shoulder and saw Wendy and Angela rush inside the craft and close the door behind them. "Take off and follow the train tracks out into the desert. I think we'll know what we're looking for when we see it."

"Roger that," said the co-pilot, an equally young woman with a thick Australian accent. The shuttle pilot applied power to the engine and brought the craft up in the air. When the shuttle reached an altitude of three hundred meters, a pair of fighters from the *Saratoga* formed up on either side of it.

"Hang on," announced the pilot as the speed of the shuttle changed from floating stationary in the air over the mine to almost five hundred kilometers an hour in mere seconds.

Cole grabbed the back of the co-pilot's chair to steady himself as the craft leaped forward. He waited a moment in the cockpit to make sure that they were heading in the right direction before heading back to speak with his comrades.

"My God, they tore everything out of the back," said Wendy, looking around the empty crew compartment. "They even removed all of the benches and chairs."

"Needed to be done," Cole replied. "We still have no idea how many people we're going to have to fit in back here."

Wendy crossed her fingers. "I'm praying for one hundred."

"And one," threw in Cole.

Without warning, the shuttle banked over hard to the left and dove for the ground. Cole, Wendy, and Angela had to scramble to find something to hold onto to prevent themselves from being thrown around. Luckily, someone had thought to tie in dozens of ropes to be used as handholds for the passengers. Although he was used to flying, the sudden drop sent Cole's stomach up into his throat.

The co-pilot's voice came over the intercom. "Sorry about that. Our laser warning indicator went off up here. Someone down below was trying to lock a missile onto us. The fighter escort locked onto the signal and dropped a bomb down on their heads. We should be safe now."

Cole made his way to the door and looked out of the window and saw that they were flying no more than three meters off the ground. "Ladies, please be the best flight crew in the fleet and not a pair of fighter pilot washouts," he whispered to himself.

44

The concussion from the blast sent Colonel Kuhr tumbling to the ground. His body armor helped but didn't deaden the shooting pain that he felt throughout his body. There was a painful ringing in his ears that added to the colonel's discomfort. He hissed when he saw the severed arm of one of his soldiers land near his head. He rolled over, shook his head, and stood back up. A massive crater was all that remained of a squad of soldiers who had been armed with anti-air launchers.

A soldier ran to Kuhr's side. "Sir, our forward elements report that the Terrans are withdrawing."

"Are they sure?"

"Yes, sir. One of their scout teams managed to get themselves into a good position of observation. They are pulling back from the ridge and are heading for their landing sites at the far end of the mine."

Kuhr looked at the crest of the hill and gnashed his teeth. "Order all formations to advance. I want the humans to pay for what they have done."

The soldier ran to pass the order. Within seconds, crimson banners were lifted aloft as the Kurgans got up off the ground and surged forward.

Kuhr drew his sword and said a silent prayer for victory before joining his men in a headlong race to stop the Marines from getting away.

"Here they come," called Sergeant Urban.

Toscano had been idle while she waited for the final Kurgan push onto their position. She and Urban had placed a series of laser indicators along the length of the ridgeline to mark precisely where they were. Next, she went and planned a warm reception for the enemy. She counted down in her head allowing the Kurgans to get close before keying the mic on her handset. "Bulldog Six, this is Ghost One, I request close air support in front of my position."

"Is danger close authorized?" asked Bulldog Six, the lead pilot of the fighter squadron covering the evacuation of the landing ships from the planet.

"Affirmative, Fury Six has authorized danger close."

"Roger that. Keep your heads down."

"Good hunting. Ghost One, out." Toscano turned and buried her head in the ground. The coming storm was going to shake the world.

Lieutenant Colonel Fareed, formerly the XO of the First Special Warfare Squadron, banked his Thunderbolt fighter over and lined the nose of his craft with the front of the ridgeline. Behind him, four other fighters did the same. When they were in a tight formation, Fareed dove for the ground. Hundreds of icons, each one representing a Kurgan warrior, appeared on the targeting display of his flight console. A second later, a red line came up on his screen indicating the forward edge of the Marines' trenches. He moved his thumb over on his joystick and depressed a red button. In an instant, his craft's thirty-millimeter Vulcan cannon spewed death. Capable of firing two thousand rounds a minute, Fareed and his wingmen tore the Kurgan advance to pieces. To make sure that no one survived the maelstrom, each fighter dropped two anti-personnel cluster bombs, blanketing the front of the Marine position with mines.

In seconds it was over. Fareed brought the nose of his Thunderbolt up and headed out over the desert before seeing if they were needed for a second run. His couldn't believe his eyes when he saw dozens of Kurgan attack craft sitting on the desert floor.

"Bulldogs. We've got us a turkey shoot," said Fareed into his helmet mic. He activated the missile pod underneath his fighter and dove for the hapless Kurgan vessels trapped out in the open.

The Thunderbolt fighters' cannons firing sounded to Toscano like a chainsaw cutting through the air. It was both terrifying and exhilarating at the same time. She waited until the last craft had banked away before turning her head over and looking up at the crest of the hill. The sound of anti-personnel mines exploding told her that some Kurgans had survived the aerial assault and were still trying to close with the Marines. She grasped her rifle in her right and pulled herself up with her left. Out in the desert, a thick black pall of smoke rose from where the Kurgan attack craft had been destroyed. Toscano gasped when she saw the devastation wrought upon the Kurgans. Hundreds were dead, dying, or horribly wounded. They lay in rows so straight and tight that they looked as if they had died on parade. Some Kurgans staggered forward still trying to make it to the ridge only to die when they activated a mine or were shot down by the Marines who had come out of their trenches to see what had happened.

"I think this is as good as over," said Colonel White as he walked over to Toscano.

Toscano nodded. "Sir, I have no love for the Kurgs, but you have to respect their tenacity."

"Fanaticism fueled by religion is what drives these soldiers. Come on, Miss Toscano, round up your people and let's join with Alpha Company as it pulls back to the mine."

"Yes, sir." Toscano stepped back, whistled down to Urban and Snow, and pointed to a destroyed hulk. Urban waved back, picked up his radio, and led Snow to the RV. The raid on Klatt had been Toscano's first engagement and was one that she would never forget.

Scavenger birds had already begun to circle the Kurgan dead. A large male broke from the flock and dove down. It came to land on the ground beside and a tall Kurgan with a sword still clenched in his hand. His other hand looked to be reaching for a crimson flag lying on the ground just out of reach. The bird canted its head as if studying the dead body before hopping forward on its feet. It poked at the leathery skin on the corpse's face. When it didn't move or cry out, the scavenger knew that it was dead and dug in with its beak.

Colonel Kuhr, along with hundreds of his soldiers, had become food for the carrion feeders. His body would be found when infantry reinforcements arrived a day later. Too late to help repel the Terrans, the soldiers collected and cremated the remains.

45

Sheridan's throat was as parched as the desert he was looking down on. He had stopped halfway down the hill and hid himself behind a rocky outcropping until the Kurgans had sorted themselves out. He cursed his luck when he saw an aged sergeant with scars all over his face take charge of the mob. He would have preferred a young officer who could have been provoked into making a rash decision; the NCO, on the other hand, would be calculating. Sheridan had no idea if his plan would work, but he had to do something to waste time.

The sergeant let out a deep bellow, pointed up at the crest of the hill, and began to lead the warriors forward.

It was time. Sheridan clenched his sword tight in his hand and stood up. He brandished his curved blade over his head and cried out.

The Kurgans stopped and looked up at Sheridan. The sergeant raised a hand to stop the soldiers behind him.

Sheridan knew there was no turning back now. He lowered his sword and aimed it at the sergeant. "I, Captain Michael Sheridan, son of Admiral Robert Sheridan, challenge you to *Kavana*. The prize will be my life and the life of all the people still alive on the top of the hill."

The sergeant chortled. "You—a human—challenge me to single combat."

"Yes," replied Sheridan, trying to sound as confident as he could.

"Why should I accept your challenge? I can just as easily walk up there and cut your head off with my sword."

"Because the honor of your corps demands that you accept my challenge. Or are you afraid of losing to a human?"

"I am afraid of nothing, especially an unbeliever like you."

"Then accept my challenge."

"Very well. I, Sergeant Kurka of the House Kurka, accept on one condition."

Sheridan had not expected there to be negotiations over his death. He went along with it to kill more time. "Name it."

"I will fight you, but not down here," replied Kurka. "I want to fight you on the top of the hill in front of your people. They can watch as I slice your head from your neck, knowing that they will be next."

"I agree," Sheridan said, wishing that the sergeant hadn't proposed such a spectacle. He turned and clamored back up to the top of the hill.

"Michael!" called out Tarina the instant she saw him. She went to run to his side, only to see him raise a hand and shake his head, telling her to stay where she was.

Sheridan moved over to a flat spot on the hill that wasn't covered with too many Kurgan soldiers' bodies and striped off his shirt. For the first time in days, he wished he could have had a drink to calm his nerves. A shot of Scotch, he thought, would go down good right now. He looked back toward the mine hoping to see a squadron of ships coming to rescue them. Instead, he saw a couple of scavengers flying in a circle high above the hill as if waiting in anticipation of dining on him a few minutes from now.

The Kurgan company slowly filed up onto the crest of the hill and moved over to where Sheridan was standing. They cleared away their fallen comrades' bodies before forming up around him. They kept one side open so Tarina and the other survivors could watch the fight to the death.

Sergeant Kurka walked into the makeshift arena and did something Sheridan had not expected. He reached up and unbuckled the armor from his neck. Piece by piece he peeled it off his upper torso. The old warrior's body was covered with scars, especially his back.

"I see you looking at my reminders," said Kurka to Sheridan. "I was whipped as a young soldier for failing to salute an officer I had not noticed standing in a doorway. While recovering, I re-read the scriptures and became closer with the lord. For that, I thank him each and every day. As a nonbeliever, you can pray to whatever human god you wish to. It won't help you. I'm going to kill you and give your head to my colonel as a gift."

Sheridan shrugged his shoulders in response.

"What the hell are they doing?" Tarina asked Sergeant Lee, unsure of what was going on.

"Mister Sheridan has called out their leader by the looks of it," replied Lee. "He knows that we don't have enough ammo or people left to fight off that many Kurgs. He's probably brokered a deal with that big bastard."

"What kind of deal?"

"If he wins, we get to live."

"And if he loses?"

"Then we all die."

Tarina shook her head. She wasn't afraid to die. She had been preparing for the day she would forfeit her life ever since she had been taken prisoner. She did, however, fear losing the only man in her life that she could ever love.

Sergeant Kurka twirled his sword around in the air. He glanced over at Sheridan and said, "Do you have any last words you wish to pass on to your friends?"

Sheridan grinned. "I'll tell them after I've killed you."

"So be it. Captain Michael Sheridan, son of Admiral Robert Sheridan, prepare to die." Kurka stepped forward and brought up his sword to cleave Sheridan's head in two.

Sheridan stepped back slightly and bent at the knees ready to move in an instant. He saw the sword held high in the air and jumped to his right just as the blade swung through the air, missing him by mere millimeters. He turned and swung his sword at his opponent's outstretched arm. The sharp blade sunk home, cutting a deep groove in Kurka's thick, leathery skin.

Kurka hissed in pain and pulled his arm back. He moved back a couple of paces and clapped a hand over the wound. It was a nasty cut. Blood flowed freely through the sergeant's fingers. He chuckled. "Now I have a souvenir to remind me of this day." Behind him, some of his warriors chuckled at the remark.

Sheridan kept his eyes fixed on the Kurgan's eyes, not his sword. He knew that the sergeant's eyes would betray his next move.

Kurka brought his blood-covered hand to his mouth and licked the blood off his fingers. "For a human, you're not too bad with a sword." He brought up his weapon and stepped to one side. Sheridan could see Kurka studying him, looking for any sign of weakness. A second later, the Kurgan lunged at his prey, slashing his sword at Sheridan's neck.

With lightning-fast reflexes, Sheridan jumped back, avoiding the thrust to his throat. He spun about and shot his blade at the sergeant's exposed side. He felt it cut through skin and muscle.

Kurka bellowed in pain, turned on his heel, and grabbed Sheridan's sword arm. It was his turn to inflict some pain. His prey was too close for him to use his sword properly so he smashed the hilt of his weapon as hard as he could into Sheridan's mouth.

Stars filled Sheridan's eyes. He staggered back from the blow. The coppery taste of blood filled his mouth. He was sure that he had lost a couple of teeth as well. He tried to pull his arm free from the sergeant's grip but found that the Kurgan was much stronger than he was. The next thing he knew, he was falling to the ground after Kurka had swept his feet out from underneath him. He landed hard, knocking the wind out of his lungs. Sheridan gasped in pain.

With a deep growl from his throat, Kurka hauled off and kicked his opponent hard in the ribs. He released his hold on Sheridan's arm and stepped back. A lone soldier began to chant his name; within seconds, one hundred voices called out *Kurka*. He raised his sword above his head and turned to face his men.

The pain shooting from a couple of cracked ribs reminded Sheridan of being burnt by a red-hot poker. He moaned and rolled over. He could hear the Kurgans chanting. With gritted teeth, he painfully got up onto his knees. He had expected the sergeant to strike while he was down. Instead, the old warrior waited until he was standing on his feet before resuming the fight.

"If you stand still, I can promise you a quick death," said Kurka as he brought his blade up until it was even with Sheridan's neck.

Sheridan knew that he was losing the fight. His body couldn't take the punishment for as long as a Kurgan's could. He had to do something, or he would be dead in seconds. Out of the corner of his eye, he glimpsed Tarina standing there looking frightened with her hands over her mouth. No matter what, he couldn't let her die. In a flash, he knew he must do. He staggered back a couple of paces to give himself some space between him and his opponent.

"Stand still," snarled Kurka.

The second the Kurgan stepped forward, Sheridan dove for the ground. He rolled over on his shoulder and came up on his knee right beside the sergeant. Without hesitating, Sheridan thrust his sword home. He heard the Kurgan hiss in agony when he turned the sword over in his hand. With what little strength he had left, Sheridan yanked out the bloody sword and got to his feet.

Kurka looked over at Sheridan with a disbelieving look in his eyes. He tried to bring his sword up. Instead, his knees buckled and he fell to the ground. He was dying and he knew it. He reached for his dropped sword and wrapped his hand around it as the world around him turned dark.

Sheridan stood there with his chest heaving as he fought to fill his lungs with oxygen. He pointed at Kurka's body with his blade. "He died an honorable death. I now expect you to fulfill his promise and let my people and me live."

"No," called out a youthful-looking soldier. "His pledge died with him. You are not a Kurgan. Therefore, we do not have to abide by his agreement."

Sheridan shook his head. Somehow their unwillingness to honor their dead sergeant's commitment was not a surprise to him. He knew he was taking a huge gamble when he, a non-Kurgan, challenged the old warrior to single combat.

"I now challenge you," said the young warrior.

"Sure, why not," he replied hoping to kill some more time.

"Sergeant, I think we've found them," called out the shuttle pilot.

Cole rushed into the cockpit and looked out. He swore when he saw the Kurgans clustered around Sheridan. "Can the fighters blast the Kurgs off the hill?"

"They could, but they would take your friend with them."

Cole wasn't going to give in that easy. He tapped the pilot on the shoulder and said, "Take us down."

"What are you going to do?"

"You'll see. Just tell the flyboys to cleanse the hill the second I hit the ground."

"It's your skin."

Cole rushed back, picked up a rifle, and moved to the side door. He could feel the shuttle dropping through the air. He pressed a button and opened the side door. He looked down and saw a Kurgan soldier walking toward Sheridan with a sword raised above his head. Cole flipped the selector switch on his weapon to automatic and pulled the trigger. The Kurgan soldier fell a second later. He turned his sights on the nearest Kurgans and fired until his weapon was empty.

The Kurgans looked skyward and yelled defiantly at the shuttle as they were cut down.

When the craft was less than ten meters from the top of the hill, Cole jumped out of the door and landed on the ground near Sheridan. He rolled over and dove at his friend, hauling him to the ground. He yelled at Tarina to take cover before pulling Sheridan's battered body in close and covering it with his own.

The Kurgans roared and surged at the two men lying on the ground. Each one wanted revenge for the death of their champion. Most never made it more than a couple of meters before the two fighters hovering in the air opened fire. The shells from the cannons tore huge gaps in the Kurgans' ranks. It took less than ten seconds to sweep the Kurgans off the hill.

Cole rolled over and looked around at the piles of mangled corpses. He knew that he was alive due more to Lady Luck than anything else. He slowly stood up and waved over at the two fighter pilots in the shuttlecraft to let them know he was still alive.

"Why did you have to lay on me?" moaned Sheridan as he tried to sit up.

"You're welcome, sir," replied Cole, offering his friend his hand.

Sheridan took Cole's hand and got to his feet. "I had them. I'd already killed one; it was only one hundred against one from that point on."

"Michael, thank God, you're still alive," said Tarina as she ran over and threw her arms around him.

"Easy does it." Sheridan grimaced in pain as she hugged him tight.

"Let's get out of here," Cole said, pointing back to the shuttlecraft coming down to land near the small group of survivors.

Tarina put her arm around Sheridan's waist and helped him make his way over to the shuttle.

At the open door stood Wendy. Tears filled her eyes when she spotted Tarina. She ran out and helped Tarina carry Sheridan inside.

Cole watched as the pitifully small band of former POWs made their way inside the shuttle. The last one to climb onboard was a tough-looking man he had never met before. "After you," said the man.

"No. After you," replied Cole with a bow.

"No. I insist. After you."

Cole shook his head. "Look, mister, unless you outrank a master sergeant, I suggest that you get your ass in that shuttle before I kick it in there."

Sergeant Lee finally relented and stepped inside.

Cole moved inside and closed the door. He looked up at the cockpit and gave the pilot a thumbs-up. Right away, he could feel the craft's engines kick in. The shuttle darted away from the hellish scene below and headed for the heavens.

The co-pilot's voice came over the intercom. "Master Sergeant Cole, please report to the cockpit."

Cole took a second to check on his friend before making his way to the pilots. "What's up, ladies?"

The young Asian pilot had a look of concern on her face. "The task force is under attack. Our fighters have already left us to join the battle."

"Damn, how many Kurgan ships have arrived?"

"I don't know. All I do know is that this rust bucket is probably the slowest vessel in the fleet. We'll be an easy target for any Kurg fighter that locks on to us. In short, Sergeant, there is no way we can risk trying to make it back to the task force."

Cole looked over at the flight console. "Is this shuttle jump capable?"

"Yes, but we didn't have time to load a full complement of perlinium rods into the engine core before coming to get you."

"How far do you think you can jump?"

"Perhaps six hundred million kilometers," replied the co-pilot, not sounding too sure of her guess.

"I think I may be of service," said Wendy, sticking her head in the small cockpit. "Give me your fuel reading down to the last gram of perlinium. I will also need a star chart brought up on one of the monitors in the back of the shuttle."

The co-pilot looked over at the pilot who nodded.

Wendy grabbed a pen and began her calculations, writing them down on the back of a discarded ration box.

"Until she finishes her calculations, we're going to have to stay down here or risk being spotted and destroyed," said the pilot to Cole. "We'll use the planet's troposphere to hide in for now."

"Okay, ma'am, do your best."

"I always do," replied pilot with a wink at Cole.

He smiled back before walking back to check on the other survivors. They hadn't brought out as many people as he would have liked to, but even one person spared a horrible death at the hands of the Kurgans was good enough for him.

46

"Status?" asked Robert Sheridan. His voice was as cool as ice water.

"Sir, the *Ford* has jumped away with the last of the transports carrying the prisoners and the Marines," replied Killam. "The *Algonquin* is maneuvering to engage the closest Kurgan vessel, a light cruiser."

"What is the number of enemy ships in orbit?"

"Four, sir. Before leaving, the *Ford* crippled a Kurgan light cruiser with a salvo of missiles. The largest fighting vessel facing us is an escort carrier. The *Saratoga's* fighter squadrons are more than a match for the enemy's smaller fighter complement."

"Very well, our job here is done. There's no need to wait here until some of the larger capital ships arrive. Order the *Algonquin* and the *Saratoga* to make the jump back to the RV."

Roy looked up from her console. "Sir, the shuttle carrying your son and the freed prisoners has not joined us yet."

"I'm aware of that. However, I cannot risk any more lives waiting for them. Send them an intermediate RV location and pass that to the *Algonqui*n as well. They can link up there." Admiral Sheridan cursed the Kurgans. All he needed was five more minutes to bring the last of his people up off the planet and they had robbed him of that.

"Message passed," announced Roy.

"Captain Killam, pull our fighters back and let's get the hell out of here."

"Aye, sir."

Admiral Sheridan walked over to the tactical display and watched as the Saratoga's fighter broke off their attack and began heading back to the carrier. His eye wandered to the planet below. A small blue icon showed the location of the shuttle and his son. He reached over and placed a hand on the screen for a moment. "Good luck, Michael, I'll see you soon." With that he stepped back, put his hands behind his back, and recommenced his customary pacing.

Wendy chewed on the end of her pen for a few more seconds before standing up and making her way to the cockpit. She handed the co-pilot her calculations and stood there to make sure that they were inputted correctly. It wasn't that she distrusted the young woman, it was just that she was used to doing everything herself. That way if anything went wrong, it would be her fault and hers alone.

The co-pilot double-checked the calculations for the jump before looking up at Wendy. "Ma'am, this will bring us awfully close to K-195. That gas giant is twice the size of Jupiter and has hundreds of moons and large asteroids floating around her."

Wendy nodded. "I know. We can use one of its smaller moons to mask our electronic signature while we wait for the *Algonquin* to arrive. Is the jump engine warmed up and ready to go?"

"As ready as it will ever be," said the pilot. "Don't forget that this ship was due to be mothballed and hasn't made a jump in several months."

Wendy cringed at the thought of the engine stalling in mid-jump. The last thing she wanted was to be captured once again.

Death was preferable to the horrors they would face back in the mine with a horde of enraged Kurgans.

Tarina stuck her head in the cockpit. "Why haven't we jumped? Is there a problem that I need to know about?"

"No. We were just about to make the jump to our RV," replied the pilot.

Wendy looked into the tired eyes of her friend. "I'll stay up here. Why don't you go back and look after Michael and the other passengers? They don't need two backseat pilots bugging them."

Tarina smiled at Wendy, turned, and left the cockpit.

The co-pilot activated the jump computer. "Jumping in five-four-three-two-one."

Enclosed in a black bubble, the shuttle jumped away. Fourteen minutes would pass before they came out of their jump. Wendy sat on a hard metal bench and looked over the co-pilot's shoulder at the navigational computer. When she saw that they were traveling faster than the speed of light, she sat back and allowed herself to relax for a few minutes.

"How long until we RV with the *Algonquin*?" Sheridan asked Tarina.

"I think Wendy said about half an hour. The *Algonquin* was covering the withdrawal of the rest of the task force, so we'll get there before her."

Sheridan sat up and looked around the room. The look on everyone's faces was a mix of joy and sadness. Those that could help were looking after the injured. A couple of med kits had been tossed inside the shuttle before coming down to the planet's surface. His heart ached when he saw a couple of people kneeling beside a body covered by a blanket. To have come so far only to die when they were safe did not seem fair to Sheridan. Cole had given him an injection for the pain and had taped up his chest so it didn't hurt too badly when he tried move around.

"What do you think will happen to us when we arrive back with the fleet?" asked Tarina.

"I don't know. I suspect that after a thorough medical, you'll all have to go somewhere to decompress. The intelligence boys back home are probably salivating in anticipation of interviewing all of you."

"Do you think they'll let us go back to what we were doing before we were captured?"

Sheridan knew that Tarina loved her work with the First Special Warfare Squadron and would be crushed if she couldn't get back to her old unit. "I don't see why not. But first you need to take some time off to heal your body and your mind; you've been through a lot since you were captured. You really do need to look after yourself."

"Yeah, I guess I could use a nice vacation by the beach. I wonder if they'll let me visit my parents?"

"Who knows?"

"What are you two officers taking about?" asked Cole as he took a seat on the floor. He handed over two ration packs and a couple bottles of water.

Sheridan thanked him and turned over his pack to read the menu. "Beans! After all I've been through, you give me beans."

Cole chuckled and took back the meal. "I just wanted to see the look on your face. Here, have my ravioli. I don't mind cold beans."

Wendy checked the clock counting down until their jump ended. They had forty-five seconds to go. Nervous excitement began to build up inside of her. She had never rushed through a complicated jump calculation before. With so many objects in orbit around a gas giant, she silently prayed that they didn't come out of their jump right into an asteroid.

"Okay, coming out of our jump in three-two-one," said the co-pilot.

In the blink of an eye, the shuttle ended its faster than light journey. The cockpit windows were filled with the planet K-195. Various shades of orange ran like bands around the planet's surface.

"Any sign of the *Algonquin*?" asked Wendy.

"No, none yet," replied the co-pilot. "Wait, I've got something appearing on our port side. It's fifty thousand kilometers away."

Wendy looked over at the monitor. Her blood chilled when she saw that instead of the *Algonquin,* it was a Kurgan long-range fighter. "Crap! Get us out of here."

"We don't have enough fuel left to make another jump," explained the pilot. "The best we can do is maneuver at sublight speed for about ten minutes. After that, we'll be out of fuel."

Wendy looked out the cockpit window and made a snap call. "We can't stay out here. Take us into K-159's atmosphere."

"That's insane," protested the pilot.

"Do it!"

The pilot turned and applied full power to the sublight engines. The shuttle quickly accelerated and raced toward the gas giant. On the screen, the Kurgan vessel took up the pursuit.

An automated voice came over the ship's speakers. "Warning, you are being targeted. I say again, you are being targeted. Missile inbound. Take evasive maneuvers."

The pilot gritted her teeth and banked the shuttle over to the right. Without slowing down, she dove between a couple of large asteroids, missing one by less than ten meters. Behind them, a Kurgan anti-ship missile struck one of the asteroids, blasting it apart.

"What the hell is going on?" asked Tarina as she slid down on the bench beside Wendy.

Wendy pointed at the computer screen. "We've got company."

"Where did he come from?"

Wendy shrugged just as the ship rocked as it entered the planet's atmosphere. In the back, some of the people cried out, unaware of what was going on. Within seconds out of the cockpit's windows dark orange clouds appeared. All of a sudden, the shuttle was bucked up in the air by the winds surging up from an electrical storm below them. The pilot hurried to slow the descent of the shuttle so she could better fly the craft in the turbulent atmosphere.

The co-pilot said, "We've got winds approaching five hundred kilometers an hour coming at us from the starboard side."

"Where is the Kurg fighter?" asked Tarina.

"He's followed us down," replied the pilot. "He's about three thousand kilometers back and closing."

"Take us into the electrical storm. It'll mess with his targeting computers."

"As well as our ship's electronics as well. Besides I'm not sure how far we can descend before the pressure outside crushes our hull."

"There's only one way to find out."

"Remind me not to volunteer for anything in the future," declared the pilot to her friend as she took the shuttle down into the raging storm.

Lightning flashes lit up the ship as it dropped deeper into the depths of the planet's gaseous atmosphere.

Wendy glanced over at the screen and saw the Kurgan fighter closing in on them. Its pilot must have realized what they were attempting to do and was hoping to catch them and use his ship's cannons to blow them apart.

A loud moaning shriek echoed through the shuttle. Everyone in the back compartment turned their heads up and looked at the roof of the craft as if expecting to see some horrid creature trying to rip its way inside.

"This is not my idea of an escape," said Cole, hanging onto a strap to prevent him from being thrown about the cabin.

"Mine, neither," added Sheridan.

In the cockpit, the four women stared intently at the computer monitor as it displayed the pressure building up on the hull. No one had to say it, but they all knew that they were approaching crush depth.

Wendy turned her eyes away and glanced at the targeting monitor and saw that the Kurgan fighter was nearly on them. She didn't doubt that if he didn't get them, the pressure soon would. She closed her eyes, reached over, and took Tarina's hand. If she were going to die, she would be with her best friend and not alone.

A massive crumpling sound of metal being twisted and compressed came over the shuttle's speakers. Someone in the back cried out in fear.

Wendy opened her eyes and saw that they were still in one piece. She looked for the Kurgan on the screen and saw that he was no longer there. Joy raced through her heart. "He's gone; the Kurgan is gone. He's imploded. Get us the hell out of this storm."

The pilot turned her head and saw that the monitor was blank. In a flash, she pulled back on the shuttle's controls and brought the ship's nose up. She applied power and brought them out of the maelstrom and headed back into space.

"I think there's another vessel in orbit. It's about forty thousand kilometers away," said Tarina as she read the information on the screen.

"Friendly?" asked Wendy.

Tarina smiled. "It's the *Algonquin*."

A cheer erupted from the cockpit that raced through the rest of the ship. They had made it. It was time to go home.

In a dark corner not noticed by anyone, Angela looked around at the people in the compartment with her. They weren't her people. She was alone and for the first time in months, she was afraid.

47

Not since he was a young boy, after his sister's death, did Michael Sheridan feel so helpless. He stared down at the note in his hand. He had already read it over several times, yet he found himself reading it again trying to see if there was something more to the message.

The doors to his quarters slid open. Cole walked in with a grin a mile wide on his face. "Oy, what are you doing here? I thought you'd still be at the officers' mess. After all, it's not every day that your father gets promoted to full admiral."

"I'm not in the mood to celebrate."

Cole heard the bitterness in his friend's voice and stepped inside the room. "What's up, Captain?"

Sheridan handed over the note. "Tarina slipped me this note this afternoon."

"She can't be serious?" said Cole after reading the paper.

"She has no reason to make it up."

"Wow. I never saw that coming. So Angela is a Chosen female? Have you told your dad?"

Sheridan shook his head. "Tarina and a lot of people owe her their lives. I'm not sure how to approach my father about it. I'm worried that the counterintelligence gurus back home will want to convert her and send her back as an agent when all she wants to do is get back to her children."

"You know there'll be hell to pay if fleet finds out that Tarina and Wendy are hiding a Kurgan among the other freed prisoners; they're likely to accuse them of being Kurgan sympathizers."

"I know. The problem is I can't speak to Tarina anymore."

Cole scrunched up his face. "Why not?"

"She and the rest of the prisoners have been moved from the hospital frigate, *Nightingale*, to a cruiser for the trip back to Earth. Do know where they are going to do their decompression?"

Cole shook his head.

"Camp Gault in Western Canada, that's where."

"I did my squad leaders' course there. It's in the middle of nowhere. Great spot to house people while you spend weeks debriefing them until they die of boredom."

"If Angela wasn't spotted during the preliminary medical and psych screening on the *Nightingale*, she undoubtedly will be found out at Camp Gault."

The phone on Sheridan's nightstand rang. He picked it up and listened to the message before hanging up.

Cole noticed that the look on Sheridan's face was even more somber. "Something up?"

"It was Captain Killam. My father wants to see both of us in the briefing room right away."

"Perhaps they want to promote us," said Cole trying to lighten the mood. "They were handing out promotions and commendations like candy at the mess when I left."

"I don't think so. I've never heard the captain sounding so troubled."

"God, I hope that nothing has happened to the ladies."

Sheridan stood. He put the note in a jacket pocket before quickly checking that his uniform looked proper. "Come on, Master Sergeant, let's see what my father wants."

A couple of minutes later, they entered the briefing room and found it deserted, except for Admiral Sheridan and Captain Killam sitting at the far end of the table.

Michael Sheridan came to attention. "You wanted to see us, sir."

"Yes, Michael. Please take a seat," said his father.

Both men took seats directly across the table from the two senior officers.

"Michael, I have never doubted your word and this pains me to bring this up. However, before Captain Killam shows you why you were asked to come here. I have to know if your report regarding your actions on the ice moon during the retrieval of the Kurgan codes a few months back was one-hundred percent accurate."

Sheridan sat back. He was somewhat confused by the question. "Sir, I left nothing out. Why, is there a problem that I am not aware of?"

Killam turned in his seat and pressed a remote. On the main briefing screen, a picture of the federation president appeared. He was standing outside of Allied Defense Headquarters making an announcement. A second later, the news report began.

Sheridan sat forward in his seat, studying the screen to determine what was troubling his father so much. He did not have to wait long. There was the sound of a rifle firing followed right away by the sounds of panicked and frightened people trying to take cover. The image on the screen got blurry as the cameraman also sought safety.

"Jesus, they didn't get the president, did they?" Cole asked.

"No," replied Killam. "Unfortunately, a couple of bodyguards and an innocent bystander were killed in the shootout."

"Shootout with who?" queried Sheridan.

"Chosen deep operative agents," said the admiral. "They were all killed by our security forces, but there is something you need to see at the very end of the broadcast."

Sheridan was still in shock that the president had come so close to being assassinated back home on Earth. His eyes took in each image until the program stopped just as the camera was panning the scared-looking crowd.

Sheridan's heart skipped a beat when he saw the face of a man who should not be alive.

"Hey, he's supposed to be dead," observed Cole.

It couldn't be. Sheridan was sure that his eyes were playing tricks on him. He stood up and moved over to the screen and studied the face of the man standing there. There could be no doubt it was Harry Williams, Sheridan's closest friend who had turned out to be a sleeper agent. Sheridan had been forced to kill him with a knife to the heart, yet he was still alive and loose on Earth.

Sheridan turned to speak to his father. "I don't get it. I held him in my arms and watched him die."

"Michael, I have no doubt that you believe that you killed Harry, but it would appear that he somehow survived."

"Why don't the police just go and arrest him?" said Cole.

"How do you arrest a dead man?" said Killam. "He's probably got new fingerprints and is wearing contacts so he can pass through retinal security scanners without being detected."

"There are security cameras everywhere back home," pointed out Sheridan. "Surely the facial recognition computer software can spot him."

"A simple jammer hidden on a person's body can screw with the cameras for a few seconds, so a person can walk about practically invisible," explained Killam.

Sheridan took his seat. "Admiral, what does this have to do with Master Sergeant Cole and me?"

"Michael, Admiral Oshiro has ordered the two of you back to Earth. Fleet intelligence knew that you and Harry were close, so they believe that you have a better than average chance of finding him. Admiral Oshiro wants you to arrest Harry. If he resists, you are authorized to use all force necessary up to, and including, deadly force to stop him from committing any further acts of terrorism."

"Yes, sir," replied Sheridan. All of the pent-up feelings he had worked hard to suppress after killing his friend came rushing back into his chest. He felt like he was trapped in a vise and was being squeezed until he blacked out. His mouth craved the taste of Scotch. If he could have, he would have fled the room and found comfort in the bottom of a bottle. He closed his eyes and took a deep breath to calm himself.

"Is there something bothering you, Michael?" asked his father.

"The day can't get much worse," said Cole. "Captain, tell the admiral what Captain Pheto passed on to you."

"Is Tarina okay?" asked the admiral.

"Yes, Dad, she's fine, but I'm afraid what I know will only make things a lot harder for everyone involved."

"You have my word, Michael, that whatever you have to tell me will not leave this room."

Sheridan dug out his note and handed it over to his father who calmly read it over before passing it to Killam.

"Well, it didn't rain so much as pour on the Sheridan household today," observed the admiral. "There's not a lot I can do about this right now. You've got a mission to do. Leave this with Captain Killam and me, and I'll see what we can do for this woman."

"Thanks, sir," said Sheridan as he stood up. "I guess Master Sergeant Cole and I had best hop on board a ship heading back home."

Killam said, "The *Sydney* is departing in the morning for a scheduled overhaul. I'll arrange for passage for the two of you."

Sheridan nodded. He and Cole came to attention, turned, and walked out of the room to pack their kit.

"Jesus, sir, we've got to report this," said Killam to the admiral.

"After an assassination attempt on Earth, do you honestly think this woman will be treated as anything but an enemy agent?"

"Admiral, I sympathize with her plight. But there are a lot of people who would lose their minds if they thought high-ranking officers in the fleet were deliberately hiding information that a Kurgan could be found among the prisoners freed from Klatt."

"I know. But I believe that we owe this woman some thanks for helping keep some of our people alive, even if she is from a Chosen homeworld."

"Sir, you know me. I'm not going to go behind your back and report this, but what can we possibly do from here?"

Admiral Sheridan sat back and stared at the wall for a few seconds. He got out of his chair, walked over to a table, and picked up a tablet. He touched the screen and scrolled through a list of his staff officers before stopping over a name. He began to smile. "Commander Roy has been working hard these past few months, hasn't she?"

"Yes, sir, I do believe so."

"I think it's high time for her to take some much-needed shore leave."

Killam nodded. "Yes, sir. An excellent idea."

"Please ask the commander to come see me right away."

Killam nodded and left the room to catch Roy before she went to the gym to burn off the frustrations of the day.

With a resigned sigh, Admiral Sheridan sat down again. While he waited for Roy, he brought out another note, this one from his wife. He shook his head when he read it. It was not unexpected. She had filed for divorce. It was the worst-kept secret in the fleet that she had been sleeping with a politician with his eye on the presidency. He regretted not telling his son, but knowing his fractured relationship with his mother, he probably wouldn't have cared.

The door to the room slid open. "You wanted to see me, sir," said Roy, dressed in her workout clothes.

Robert Sheridan placed both notes away and stood up. "Commander, I need you to do something very sensitive. What I'm about to tell you is for your ears only."

Roy stepped inside the room. Behind her the door closed. She saw the grave look on her boss' face and smiled. "What's the op, sir?"

Admiral Sheridan pulled out a chair for Roy and took one facing her. He dug out Tarina's message and handed it to her to read.

"My God," murmured Roy.

"Now listen very carefully. Here's what I need you to do. . ."

Printed in Great Britain
by Amazon